PRAISE FOR RACHEL VAN DYKEN

"*The Consequence of Loving Colton* is a must-read friends-to-lovers story that's as passionate and sexy as it is hilarious!"

—Melissa Foster, *New York Times* bestselling author

"Just when you think Van Dyken can't possibly get any better, she goes and delivers *The Consequence of Loving Colton*. Full of longing and breathless moments, this is what romance is about."

—Lauren Layne, *USA Today* bestselling author

"The tension between Milo and Colton made this story impossible to put down. Quick, sexy, witty—easily one of my favorite books from Rachel Van Dyken."

—R. S. Grey, *USA Today* bestselling author

"Hot, funny . . . will leave you wishing you could get marked by one of the immortals!"

—Molly McAdams, *New York Times* bestselling author, on *The Dark Ones*

"Laugh-out-loud fun! Rachel Van Dyken is on my auto-buy list."

—Jill Shalvis, *New York Times* bestselling author, on *The Wager*

"*The Dare* is a laugh-out-loud read that I could not put down. Brilliant. Just brilliant."

—Cathryn Fox, *New York Times* bestselling author

Stealing Her

ALSO BY #1 *NEW YORK TIMES* BESTSELLING
AUTHOR
RACHEL VAN DYKEN

Red Card Series

Risky Play
Kickin' It

Liars, Inc. Series

Dirty Exes
Dangerous Exes

The Players Game Series

Fraternize
Infraction

The Consequence Series

*The Consequence of Loving
Colton*
The Consequence of Revenge
The Consequence of Seduction
The Consequence of Rejection

The Wingmen Inc. Series

The Matchmaker's Playbook

*The Matchmaker's
Replacement*

Curious Liaisons Series

Cheater
Cheater's Regret

The Bet Series

The Bet
The Wager
The Dare

The Ruin Series

Ruin
Toxic
Fearless
Shame

The Eagle Elite Series

Elite
Elect
Enamor
Entice

Elicit
Bang Bang
Enforce
Ember
Elude
Empire

The Seaside Series

Tear
Pull
Shatter
Forever
Fall
Eternal
Strung
Capture

The Renwick House Series

The Ugly Duckling Debutante
The Seduction of Sebastian St. James
An Unlikely Alliance
The Redemption of Lord Rawlings
The Devil Duke Takes a Bride

The London Fairy Tales Series

Upon a Midnight Dream

Whispered Music
The Wolf's Pursuit
When Ash Falls

The Seasons of Paleo Series

Savage Winter
Feral Spring

The Wallflower Series (with Leah Sanders)

Waltzing with the Wallflower
Beguiling Bridget
Taming Wilde

The Dark Ones Saga

The Dark Ones
Untouchable Darkness
Dark Surrender

Stand-Alones

Hurt: A Collection (with Kristin Vayden and Elyse Faber)
Rip
Compromising Kessen
Every Girl Does It
The Parting Gift (with Leah Sanders)
Divine Uprising

Stealing Her

RACHEL VAN DYKEN

SKYSCAPE

▊▎▊ SKYSCAPE

Published by Skyscape, New York

www.apub.com

ISBN-13: 9781542091787
ISBN-10: 1542091780

Cover design by Letitia Hasser

Cover photography by Regina Wamba of MaeIDesign.com

Printed in the United States of America

Jill, thank you for being a shining light and inspiration, thank you for being brave, courageous, and perfectly you.

Prologue

BRIDGE

Manhattan, July 2001

"Go to your room!" Dad yelled, disappointment evident as he stared down at my twin, Julian, and then at me. "That's your second suspension this year!"

The blood left my face as I bit down on my lower lip to keep from screaming at him. To keep from screaming that the kids at school were picking on my twin and calling him names and that I wasn't going to let it happen anymore. But I never yelled at my dad; it wouldn't be tolerated. So I cleared my throat and said, "It wasn't my fault. They were making fun of me." I didn't tell him that Julian was their real target. My younger twin only wanted our father to see the best in him.

Dad shook his head. "Then you tell the little jackasses who your dad is. You don't fight every single one of them and put one in the hospital."

Julian flinched and looked over at me with fear in his eyes. I could tell he was afraid I was going to say something about him getting picked on. This wasn't the first time, and he hated it when Dad called him weak. Of course Dad didn't notice the cut on Julian's quivering lip. No, he was too focused on both of my black eyes to realize that I'd been doing what I was supposed to do, what I always did.

Protect my brother.

At all costs.

"Go to your room!" Dad pointed. "Do you realize this will make the news? That we have another deal coming down the pipeline, and because of your actions we could lose everything?"

He was exaggerating. And I hated that he brought it back to business. I was thirteen, not stupid.

We lived in a penthouse on the Upper East Side and went to private school. My dad had a driver, we had a cook and two nannies. And my dad had already told me he was going to buy my brother and me matching Audis for our sixteenth birthday.

We were fine.

So I shrugged and ran up the stairs just as I heard my mom's soft voice. "Edward, you're too hard on him."

I could feel Julian rushing after me.

And I could hear the words my mom said to my dad, soft words, from an equally soft heart that was slowly being destroyed. But his voice got louder and louder.

Julian shut the door behind him, tears in his eyes.

I walked over to him, put my hands over his ears, and whispered, "Better?"

He didn't say anything, just stared at me until I dropped my tired hands fifteen minutes later. "I'm sorry, Jules, I was just trying to help."

"You're always trying to help." He shrugged. "Maybe if I knew how to fight or had half the muscle you did they wouldn't pick on me."

I rolled my eyes. "They pick on you because you're a smart-ass, and they're idiots. Plus, every girl in school's obsessed with your hair."

He smirked. "I do have nice hair."

"Ass." I punched him in the shoulder.

And just like that, things were back to normal. He was stealing my CDs and I was pretending I didn't see him doing it. He was like that, though. He used my stuff, but if I used anything of his he threw a fit. He took after our dad that way, but I really didn't give a shit.

The rest of the day was uneventful.

We did our homework.

We went down to dinner while my father went back to the office to work, and my mom said grace and told us we were the only reason for living.

We had the best life.

Until it all came crashing down.

One year later

"Promise, Bridge!" Julian's sweaty hands gripped mine. We were freshmen in high school, both believing we owned the world because that's what our dad told us on a daily basis.

"Jules." I pulled him in for a hug and then shoved him away with a soft punch to his shoulder. "We're brothers. Of course we're going to write to each other. There's this thing called email, check it out, you—"

"Shut up." It was his turn to punch me, and I stepped back, taking a long, hard look at my twin. We were alike but still so different. His dark brown hair fell in a mess over his forehead. His braces were gone, contacts were in, and he'd finally gained a bit of muscle since he started wrestling. He was finally coming into himself. I'd never needed braces and had always been the bigger twin, born with muscle. I was proud of his physical accomplishments, even if our dad wasn't. "I'm serious," he insisted.

"We're moving to Jersey, dude, not Siberia. It's not like I'm not gonna see you at school." I tried to keep the tremble out of my voice. Something felt so wrong, I could feel the change in the air, feel it in the way my mom packed up her Lexus SUV.

My father had cheated one too many times.

And my mother couldn't handle it anymore.

And since I was the troubled kid who liked to get into fights.

The one who took care of everything with my fists.

I went with Mom.

Because I fixed things.

Because I didn't want her to be alone.

Because in a divorce, kids are too often the ones who get ripped in two directions without any say in the situation.

And because my father said that's where I was going. Period.

"It's going to be fine," I said to my brother, not realizing I was lying to him.

"You promised." He grabbed my elbow and pulled me back. "You said you'd always protect me."

"And I always will." I didn't allow myself to cry. It would be fine. People got divorced all the time.

I grabbed my Ray-Bans and put them on so he wouldn't see the pain in my eyes.

Mom drove us away from the city, away from the glitz and glamour of my dad's high-powered deals, away from towering glass-and-steel skyscrapers, and the bright lights and nonstop bustle. As the landscape changed around us, Mom alternated between hitting the steering wheel and sobbing into the tissues I kept handing her.

Her striking Italian features, pitch-black hair, and blue eyes made me think she was the prettiest woman in the world. With his light skin and medium-brown hair, my dad was the light to her dark on the surface, but on the inside he was just . . . arrogant.

They had been a beautiful couple.

But outward beauty doesn't keep a family together, doesn't keep all the cracks and breaks at bay. Dad's cruelty broke our family. And Julian and I were caught in the middle.

"Mom." I handed her another tissue. "Are you okay?"

"Yeah," she croaked. "It's going to be fine, Bridge, I promise. I'll take care of us."

"I know, Mom." But I didn't; she'd never worked a day in her life.

And it settled like a stone in my stomach. I knew Dad gave her a settlement after the divorce, but I also sadly knew there was a prenuptial agreement.

I was afraid to ask what that meant for us.

I decided not to think about it until an hour later when my mom pulled up to a small apartment complex that looked like it had been built in the fifties. The red brick wasn't exactly crumbling, but to say it had seen better days was an understatement. White stains ran from the corners of the single-paned windows, and the brown railing on the staircase to the upper units sagged in the middle. Located below the steps were two apartment doors that were disturbingly close to one another, separated only by a pair of ragged lawn chairs. The window air conditioner in one of the upper apartments dripped steadily, just missing a thirsty patch of wilting grass but managing to erode the concrete at the base of the steps.

"Uhhh, Mom?" I frowned as people stared at us and our car. "What's going on? Are we dropping something off for donations or—"

"Our apartment"—she jerked her head to the old brick building—"is the first floor on the right. It's all they had."

Relief and understanding hit me all at once. "Ohhh, until we can find a place?"

She turned off the car, bracing the steering wheel with both hands. "Do you know what a prenuptial agreement is?"

"I go to private school. I could probably write a legal document," I said with heavy sarcasm. "Why?"

"I signed one that says I get no spousal support, only child support. We have enough to get by, Bridge. We'll sell the car and use everything he gives us to invest, and I'll get a job. We aren't destitute. We just can't afford things like—"

"Private school," I finished for her, suddenly wondering why my dad didn't care enough to make sure I had the life we were used to living if he was worth so much money. "Okay." My mind worked fast, slow, then fast again as I thought about me going to Mom, and Julian going to Dad. "Mom . . ."

She didn't look at me.

She kept her eyes on the steering wheel.

"Mom." I injected a bit of urgency as I said it again. "When do we get to see Julian?"

Silence.

"MOM!" I didn't mean to raise my voice, I didn't mean for her to flinch.

And I didn't mean to cause more tears.

"I didn't realize what I was signing." She shook her head. "I loved him. I thought we were forever, Bridge, you have to know that, and I had no money to fight him, nothing . . ." She sobbed into her tissue. "No partial custody, Bridge. I get you, he gets Julian."

"But—" My body swayed as my heart leaped to my throat, making it hard to breathe. "But I promised him! I promised him, Mom!"

"You can email him, and hopefully in the future, when things settle, you can visit."

"Mom, you don't understand." I reached for her arm and held on, needing the comfort of her skin. "Mom, they'll eat Julian alive at school! If I'm not there, they'll beat him up. Dad will—" I didn't want to say it, but couldn't stop myself. "Dad will ruin him. You know Julian would do anything for his approval, hell, the only reason he hasn't been ruined already was because I kept Dad in check!"

She squeezed her eyes as two tears fell onto my arm, the one holding on to her for comfort, for help, for support. "There's nothing we can do. Email him every day, video chat, we'll try as hard as we can, okay? I promise."

But I knew, on that sad day in July.

It wouldn't be enough.

I forced a smile and said, "Why don't I grab the bags?"

And for the first time in my young life, I understood the meaning of your heart breaking in two.

Chapter One

ISOBEL

June 2019

I didn't recognize my college sweetheart any more than I think he recognized himself when he looked in the mirror. Julian Tennyson, easygoing, full of life and laughter, *that* Julian Tennyson, was gone. It was strange watching someone you love slowly lose pieces of himself until there's nothing left.

The last six months had been absolute hell, and yet I kept telling myself it would get better, he was just under a lot of stress.

After my parents died when I was in college, the Tennysons took me in because I had no other family. They'd provided for me and made me feel like family. I needed to be a part of something, and they gave that to me.

But the gifts weren't free.

It didn't matter at first. I had Julian, wonder-boy graduate, voted one of the sexiest men alive under thirty, and corporate heartthrob.

Year one, we moved in together and were ridiculously happy. I did charity work, and he hit the ground running at Tennyson Financial.

Year two, he started coming home later and later, and sometimes not at all.

Year three, the cheating started.

Six months ago, he broke my heart.

He drank the Tennyson poison, and now I was going to end it.

Except nothing was calming my racing heart, not the Xanax I'd popped before I scheduled this meeting, not the bottle of wine I knew was waiting for me at home, not even the relief I knew I'd feel once I said the words and walked out of his life.

Out of the cult that was the Tennyson family, with all of their dark secrets, greed, and textbook narcissism. I shuddered. I couldn't do it anymore.

I couldn't live in a constant state of walking on eggshells.

I would never be what my fiancé or his father wanted.

I was good.

Just not good enough.

That morning I was waiting to see Julian in the reception area outside his office.

There were two receptionists in their midtwenties with blonde hair and model-perfect makeup, neither of whom bothered to look up from their desk. Employees knew you never made eye contact with the Tennysons, and since I was engaged to the vice president and soon-to-be CEO, that meant I was looped into the crazy.

It wasn't supposed to be like this.

I wasn't supposed to have to schedule a meeting just to talk to my fiancé. That's not what normal people did.

And yet that was the expectation. I was here waiting for my "appointment," already delayed. Time, after all, was extremely valuable, and the Tennysons never seemed to have quite enough of it, especially when it came to personal matters. Julian always had time to party on yachts with celebrities and heiresses, but when it came to time alone at the penthouse with me? Never enough.

Pain stabbed me in the chest.

Pain over his careless treatment.

Pain over our drawn-out engagement.

Pain over the loss of our friendship.

"Isobel?" Kelsey, one of the perfect receptionists, stood. I'd fought with Julian when he hired her; she was too pretty, and he was easily distracted by shiny things. After all, the apple didn't fall far from the tree. "Julian will see you now."

"Perfect." I stood and primed myself with a confident smile as I made my way through the sleek, modern double doors.

The first time I walked through those doors years ago it felt like I held the keys to a new kingdom.

I didn't realize then that the kingdom was actually a dungeon and some things are covered in gold to distract from what's underneath.

"Isobel." Julian moved toward me, but his smile was for the receptionist who would report back to his father. "It's the middle of a workday."

He looked more tired than normal . . . and stressed. I was tempted to reach for him, to tell him to lean on me like he used to. But he looked almost angry when my hand started to do just that.

"It is." I ground my teeth. How had it come to this? Memories of us in college resurfaced as they always did when I was trying to match the man I fell in love with to the stranger standing in front of me.

He checked his Rolex, irritation pulsing from his large frame in waves that I could almost see in the air between us. "Walk with me. I have a meeting."

I put my hands up, ready to block his chest, to stop him from walking around me, speaking down to me. Take your pick. "Julian, it's private. I need your attention. Please." God, I hated begging a man who used to look at me with love in his eyes, a man who used to tell me we were going to live a fairy tale.

The hearts that used to be in his eyes had changed to dollar signs the minute his father promoted him right out of grad school. And with the promise of an even bigger promotion in a few short weeks . . .

He chose money.

Over me.

Because according to him, love never really did last. Not for his dad and definitely not for him, since they were both cut from the same cloth.

It hadn't always been that way.

Goodbye, Julian.

Goodbye, family I used to call mine.

Goodbye, life we created together.

I felt the loss so deeply at that moment that I couldn't breathe. This wasn't what I'd imagined three years ago when he'd proposed.

"I'm breaking off the engagement." I blurted out the words so quickly that I covered my mouth with my hands as embarrassment took over, embarrassment because he didn't even flinch, nor did he look up from his watch.

He stared at it like he hadn't heard a word I said and exhaled. Could that be relief I saw? Or was he actually hurt? He attempted to walk around me, but his steps faltered a bit. "Let's discuss this when I'm not running late."

"Julian." I moved in front of him. "This isn't a business proposal or a buyout, I'm finished, there is no discussion. I just, I thought you should know." I moved to pull off my four-karat engagement ring while he sighed as if I was inconveniencing him. I held it out. "Here, take it back."

"No." Strong hands held my shoulders as he looked down at me with a confident albeit exhausted smile. "I've been busy, too busy, I see that now. How about I cancel my meeting later tonight, and we can get dinner?" He was already shoving the ring back on my finger, lifting my hand to his lips, kissing it softly like he used to.

"No." I trembled.

"You sure?" I wished I could hate him. I wanted to hate the easy smile that reminded me of easier times. He suddenly pulled me close and looked at me like I was everything he needed, oxygen included. "Because I could really get on board with one of those steak dinners at Elliot's."

Elliot's.

The place he'd proposed.

Our favorite restaurant.

Damn him! I clenched my fist so tight the ring made an impression against my palm.

"Julian, no." I couldn't think with him this close. He had this magnetism to him that was dangerous, it sucked you into the Tennyson void and refused to let go. I refused to get manipulated again. He was too good at making me believe that we were forever, that what we had was unlike anything else in this world. And he knew exactly what to say to get me to back down. I didn't want to be weak, not anymore.

"I think I need—" he began.

"Julian!" The door opened, Amy, the other receptionist, poked her head in and pointed at her own watch, averting her eyes as she said in hushed tones, "The car's been waiting five minutes. You need to head down. Your father's not happy, and the board is waiting."

His face hardened before he adjusted his tie. "I'll call you later."

"But Julian—"

He was already gone.

I clutched my hands together, feeling the imprint of my engagement ring against my skin. Emotion clogged my throat until I felt like I was choking.

The only noise in that giant office was the sound of my heels as I walked over to the floor-to-ceiling windows overlooking Manhattan.

His kingdom.

Theirs.

Ours.

Not anymore.

Because I wouldn't sacrifice my heart for money.

Not anymore.

There was a picture of us on his desk. Our fresh happy faces were smiling, we were just out of college. I had finished my master's degree in nursing and he his MBA. I was staring at him, and he was staring at the camera.

He'd always been looking ahead.

Never at me.

Did I sound selfish? Petty?

A woman was allowed those moments when she lost the love of her life to something equally selfish and petty.

Greed.

I don't know how long I stared at that picture. Long enough for my back to tense under the poor posture brought on by my stilettos, and long enough for the sun to start to set.

Sighing, I twisted the ring around my finger and slowly walked out of his office, clicking the door shut behind me, just as Kelsey answered the phone.

Her sharp gasp drew my attention. Her face had paled, and her eyes locked with mine. "There's been an accident."

Chapter Two

BRIDGE

"Another late night?" Mom asked when I dropped my workout bag on the couch and went in search of a beer.

She knew the answer.

Yet she always had to ask the question, didn't she?

I smiled a bit as I dipped my head into the small worn fridge and pulled out an IPA. "Not too late."

Her smile was frail as she got up and tried to stand. I moved so fast the beer almost toppled over the counter. She was only in her late fifties, but you'd think she was in her seventies the way she moved these days.

Gastroparesis did that to a person. She'd gone from being healthy to weighing only ninety-five pounds. Her stomach couldn't properly digest anything, even water, which forced her to use a tube that fed her through her stomach. When she was diagnosed five years ago, we figured that we would just fight it any way we could. It's not a well-known condition and it's super hard to get a proper diagnosis, so when people ask her what's wrong and hear it's not cancer, they fucking sigh in relief like she's not facing a death sentence every single day her feeding tube malfunctions.

Pain lanced my heart, my throat, every cell in my body as I steadied her. "Where you off to so fast?"

She rolled her eyes and patted me on the right shoulder. "If that's fast . . ."

"So fast I'm gonna start calling you Flash." I winked.

Water collected in her eyes. Tears meant she was either in pain or she was sad, and I couldn't handle either of those things.

And I would do anything, cross any ocean, to make sure that the most important light of my life didn't get snuffed out by something that in my mind should be such an easy thing to fix. But I wasn't a kid anymore, I couldn't fix this with my fists and I couldn't fix it with my intellect. So I loved her as best I could. And prayed it was enough.

Her doctors kept trying new things.

Which meant I kept working more shifts so I could afford all the new treatments they claimed would give me more time with her.

We'd sold the SUV years ago in exchange for a Jeep that broke down more than it worked, and every single time the man who'd fathered me showed up on TV in a new car I wanted to scream.

But after two years of unanswered phone calls, I realized he wasn't going to come riding in on a white horse and rescue us from medical bills.

And neither was the brother who ended up turning out exactly like the guy everyone called a saint. Edward Tennyson? A saint? My ass. Just because he donated money to foundations that interested him didn't make him a saint, it made him a shrewd businessman who understood the power of public opinion.

"I was going to make us some dinner." She always said "us" even though she didn't eat solid food. She said she lived vicariously through me, so I drank her favorite milkshakes. I spent every damn day of my life dedicated to eating what she wanted to eat, and then punished my physical body afterward so that I could continue to do it.

My mom had a clear sweet tooth, and I'd be twice my size if I didn't put in two hours a day at the gym after I was done training. The sacrifices we make for those we love.

"Why don't you sit down?" I finally said, keeping the emotions I was feeling out of my voice. "And I'll whip up some of your favorite baked chicken while I tell you about my day."

Something about the way she looked at me made me sad, like she knew one day I would need someone else to talk to, someone else to share my life with, when honestly all I wanted was my mom.

All I needed was my mom.

I let myself believe that lie every single time my chest felt like it was going to crack over the loss of a part of my soul, or at least that's what it felt like. I remembered a scared Julian, one who confronted me for abandoning him a year after we moved, when in my mind I was just going across town to get us settled before seeing him at school the next day.

How wrong I'd been.

Emails between us were fewer and fewer until one day in college, they stopped altogether. I kept up to date with his escapades by reading the entertainment section of the paper, and then was so disgusted with what I saw, with the man he had become—I just stopped.

I'd like to think a healthy appetite for women helped distract me, but when they saw me, they wrongly assumed I was my estranged brother, which meant they also wrongly assumed I was rolling in it. In reality, I worked part time as a personal trainer and part time as a bartender while I tried to pick up shifts with UPS.

And being associated with my brother just pissed me off all the more.

He might as well be in a castle built out of gold.

And I went to bed at night thinking, *Damn, I'm so lucky to be here with Mom, instead of in that golden prison with Dad.*

Last year Julian sent us a check for fifty thousand dollars and I'd ripped it in half, not because we didn't need it, but because I'd been so damn angry and let my pride get ahead of me. There was no note, nothing, just a check, as if that would make everything better.

He was my father through and through.

Throw a little money at it and call it good.

"Alright, honey," Mom said as I helped her sit back down on the couch and tucked her feet under her favorite Huskies afghan. She had at least ten romance novels on the coffee table. I pointed to them with a smirk only to have her pick one up and glare. "Don't you dare make fun of me."

"Wouldn't dream of it, Mom." I kissed her cheek and made my way into the kitchen. My feet hurt from standing all day, my back hurt from deadlifts, and I had a shift at five a.m. with UPS.

At least the pay was good. I almost had enough saved to pay bills for the next two months, unless something happened with Mom, and then we'd be screwed. And that's the thing about her disease; one day she's fine, the next we're in the ER, then she's admitted to the hospital for a week.

"So your day?" Mom grinned at me, then flipped on the TV, setting it to mute. She knew me well. I liked having the news on, and I liked being able to turn up the volume if I wanted to subject myself to the chaos that was our world.

"Well, training was good. I had two new clients today, a husband and wife. They both put on baby weight and want to get healthy again, so I put them on a pretty easy partner workout regimen that I think will really help. Plus, those who suffer together . . ."

"Stay together." Mom laughed. "Though I don't believe you, I still love you for the lies you tell."

"Hah!" I pulled some chicken thighs from the freezer and popped them on a dish to defrost.

"What else?" Even sick she was beautiful and put most women to shame. Her eager expression tugged at my heart as she wrapped the afghan tighter around herself and started to shiver. Always cold. I ignored the way her collarbones jutted out from her skin along with the blue tint of the veins in her hands.

"Well, bartending is—" I stopped short when my brother's face flashed across the TV.

And then my dad was speaking.

"Turn it up." I clenched my teeth as my mom scrambled for the remote and turned up the volume.

"Early reports state that Julian Tennyson, vice president and soon-to-be CEO of Tennyson Financial, was in a head-on collision this evening. He's currently in critical condition at Manhattan Grace."

"Oh no." Mom covered her face with her hands as tears dripped off her chin. He was still her son.

My brother.

I dropped the chicken onto the counter as my heart hammered against my chest. *I'll always protect you.*

I'd promised him.

I'd failed.

It didn't matter that I hated what he'd become. I was supposed to be his other half, and he was in a hospital right now.

I reached for my keys about the same time my mom started sobbing.

"Oh, my boy." She rocked back and forth, and I was quickly moving to the living room to grab her when the doorbell rang.

We both froze, sensing that nothing good would be on the other side of that door.

Nobody visited us but the mailman.

I stood on shaky legs as I made my way to the front door and jerked it open.

I failed.

I failed.

I failed.

I smelled him first, the familiar scents of expensive scotch and cigar smoke mixed with the humid heat of Jersey during June.

And my dad, around thirty pounds heavier since I last saw him, wearing a three-piece suit and sunglasses more expensive than my rent, leaned his body against the doorframe and rasped, "He needs you. And so do I."

"Is he okay?" A dense fog of emotion threatened to smother my body as I waited for him to answer.

"I have the best doctors tending to him," he finally said, looking over my shoulder at my mom. His expression didn't change, but his posture stiffened as he looked from her back to me and whispered, "I think I have an offer you won't be able to refuse."

And in that moment, I could have sworn I heard the sound of golden handcuffs being clipped onto my wrists as I muttered, "Come in."

Chapter Three

ISOBEL

Numb, I was numb.

And I was angry.

And I was sad.

And so many other tumultuous emotions that I couldn't define or even begin to swallow, because above all else . . . I, Isobel Cunningham, felt relieved.

Relieved!

Tears stung the back of my throat as I paced the hospital hallway. Nobody would let me see Julian, and only family was allowed in, which I technically wasn't since I hadn't said *I do*.

I was a nobody, with no family other than the man I'd just broken up with who was currently fighting for his life. I realized then how heavily I'd relied on him for everything in my life.

He didn't want me to work, so I volunteered at this very hospital, in the children's cancer wing. He paid for our home, my clothes. My life revolved around him.

And despite facing his possible death.

I still felt . . . relief.

Was I a monster?

Did I deserve to burn in hell? Because all I kept thinking was that it was over. I was torn between mourning for a man I didn't recognize anymore and berating myself for feeling this weight lifting off my chest.

I refused to think about all my reasons for needing the approval of both Julian and his father, but the minute they accepted me, I had somehow started to accept myself, until I realized that their acceptance was just another fancy word for control.

We accept you, but you need to wear that designer for us.

We love you, but love takes place on the Tennyson family watch.

We'll fight for you, unless it makes us look weak, and then you're on your own and you get punished with silence, or worse, cheating.

Maybe I'd been around the Tennysons too long, maybe the worst had happened and I'd accepted that my life was going to be fake smiles in public, silent tears in private.

In college, things had been so simple, so easy. Julian's father was too busy to see him during the school year, and visits during the holidays had been like something out of a Hallmark movie. It was like living in this Hollywood dream . . . and then we graduated.

And Julian's exact words were "Time to grow up."

As if we'd been faking it all that time.

That's when the rules started.

No job. My only job was to be ready to be a Tennyson wife, learn how to plan a dinner menu, get my nails done on a weekly basis, wear my hair a certain way, wear certain designers and colors, and make sure I shopped enough to keep up appearances in the media.

At first, I did these things because I loved him and he teased me about how silly they all were, but he also said it was what his dad expected; ergo, we played by his father's rules.

Besides, what did I know about being part of a powerful family constantly in the limelight? The rules made sense. Then they started to get tedious, and when I tried to discuss my feelings with Julian, he waved me off. The distance between us grew just like his long hours at the office, then six months ago, everything finally came crashing down around us. I'd assumed once we were engaged things would return to normal; instead, I came home to a fiancé who smelled like someone else's perfume and wouldn't look me in the eyes, and when he finally did said, "It's nothing, just business."

He brushed me off, he brushed us off.

The very same week he was working late at the office and I went to surprise him only to find his stepmom standing too close, touching his back and laughing.

I caused a scene.

I yelled.

Julian told me I was seeing things.

The very next day he said we should set a date for the wedding.

And I once again believed that things would get better, that he was just under stress, that maybe I really was seeing things.

Stupid. How could I let myself be controlled so perfectly by this family? By this name?

"It doesn't matter where you come from," Julian whispered against my neck as we danced beneath the stars during our senior year of college at Duke. "Just that you'll be with me, by my side, forever. I need someone strong like you, someone who gets the sacrifice."

Tears stung my eyes.

He was perfect.

Everything a girl could dream of.

Until the dream came crashing down around me by way of greed, pride, selfishness, and too many secrets to count. He was the perfect combination of compliments and manipulations. He gave me just enough to keep me and then made me feel guilty for not being thankful for every single morsel of attention.

Soon after I saw him with his stepmom, he came home drunk, with lipstick on his cheek.

It was the final straw. We were just passing ships in the night unless his ship needed mine to do something for him. And any trust I had in him was broken, despite what he said about his actions.

I clenched my fists as my heels clicked loudly against the cheap blue-and-white hospital floor. Back and forth I paced, and somehow I managed to chew off my thumbnail as I waited.

I'd overheard the doctor telling Edward that the only possible outcome didn't look good.

I didn't ask what that was.

I finally slumped down into a chair and hung my head in my hands. My pink nail polish was chipped beyond repair. I couldn't contain my nerves.

Panic rose up in my chest as I listened to the low hum of the lights above me, the sounds of nurses talking, people walking by and laughing.

And all I wanted to do was run.

Yes. I was a horrible person. And hell didn't scare me, only the thought of seeing him in the afterlife suffering alongside me made me want to repent.

Julian's stepmom, Marla, had been on and off the phone talking in hushed tones the minute he went back into surgery. I was only three years younger than her, and at thirty-three she was already the perfect trophy wife. Marla often acted like I was her competition, and of course I always fell short of whatever was expected of me.

It had been six hours.

And still I waited.

The fluorescent lights flickered again, creating a throbbing pain at my temples as I searched through my white Birkin bag for aspirin, realizing that the bag was just another thing he had given me when I would have taken a hug instead.

Hands shaking, I finally located a stray pill bottle and clutched it between my fingertips just as the doors to Surgery 1 opened.

I stood, clutching the pills in my sweaty palm as the doctor removed his mask, his expression unreadable. Sweat collected on his brow. He looked too young to be the sort of guy who would put people's bodies back together again. His face was grim as he looked past me and straight at Marla. "I need to speak to Edward Tennyson."

"I'm his wife." She turned up her nose. And then the crazy woman looked over at me and sniffed like I was offending her by standing too close. "She's not family. Not yet, anyway." She tried to say it sadly, but my ears were attuned to the competitiveness in her voice. I had the younger version of what she was married to. Mine didn't need Viagra to get it up. Edward was a good-looking man, but he was in his early seventies and he enjoyed fine dining and whiskey too much.

"Do I have your permission, then, to speak in front of—"

"Absolutely not," Marla scoffed. "Anything that needs to be said can be said to me in private. Besides, this place is crawling with reporters."

He gave me a brief glance before turning to her. "I understand."

"You should go." Marla's leopard heels clicked against the linoleum floor as she pulled me in for a hug and very discreetly whispered in my ear, "We'll be in touch. Julian needs his family now more than ever."

I wanted to scratch her eyes out.

"We're engaged." I swallowed thick tears building in my throat. "I have a right to know he's okay!" I never raised my voice at her. I must have shocked her silent, my chest heaving as I pleaded with the surgeon. "Please, is he okay? Is he alive?"

Marla gripped me by the shoulders and tugged me against her. "Poor thing's distraught." She clung to me longer than I could tolerate.

"Ma'am, I'm sorry, but I can only release Mr. Tennyson's medical information to family," the surgeon said softly.

Right.

Family. Only.

"Marla, please keep me updated."

She inclined her head with a fake smile that basically conveyed she'd rather die than send me a text and take the chance of breaking a nail, then turned back toward the doctor. "Let's go find a private room."

I almost snorted at that.

I knew her games all too well.

That poor surgeon had no idea what he was in for. He was about to be rewarded very nicely for either saving Julian's life or for letting him die on the table, making one less claim on the Tennyson fortune.

Tears streamed down my swollen cheeks as I watched them go, uncertain about my fate and about the man on the other side of those thick doors.

I numbly walked to my waiting black BMW 7 series, just like I numbly buckled my seat belt and drove slowly toward the penthouse I'd been sharing with Julian.

I walked into an apartment that felt empty already.

The TV was off, and the maid had left something that looked like a casserole in the fridge with instructions. I kicked off my heels and pulled my hair into a ponytail as I made my way into the master bedroom.

To find my bed occupied.

By that same maid, naked.

In a pair of my silver heels.

And nothing else.

"Shit!" She pulled my down comforter to her bare chest. "Where's Julian?"

I couldn't speak.

I couldn't form words or sentences.

He'd never been so brazen.

Ever.

Not in my home.

Our home.

Tears streamed down my face, increasing the more I stared at her, the more she stared back at me, as the static tension of the room crackled with the need for something to fill its silence.

"Get. Out," I rasped.

Minutes went by.

The door slammed.

I stared at the bed I was supposed to somehow sleep in, next to the empty space for a man who might or might not be returning to it.

And I felt like a fool.

For all I knew, Julian was dead.

And he'd taken every shred of dignity I had left.

I closed my eyes and wept.

Chapter Four

BRIDGE

I hated hospitals.

I hated the way they smelled.

I hated the futile promises doctors made. And most of all I hated how much it cost for my mom to get the help she needed. Hospitals sucked the souls out of the sick, they gave them false hope, and they smiled while doing it.

So being at that hospital, with a father I wanted nothing to do with, wasn't my first choice for a Tuesday.

I was still in my workout clothes and Nikes, looking every inch lower class next to my dad, who was in his three-piece suit wearing fucking sunglasses inside like the sun was shining too hard on his perfect face.

We walked in silence down the hall to the ICU.

Julian was in a private room; that's all I knew, that's all my dad would tell me. But we were twins. I knew in my soul he was in pain, I knew in my heart something was very wrong, because for the first time in my life I didn't feel him.

And that thought was terrifying.

He could be the worst person on this planet and I would still hate that feeling, the feeling of losing something that was mine, losing my brother.

We stopped in front of the room.

I swallowed and stared at the metal door.

"Go inside, I'll wait." My dad crossed his arms.

I'd told him I had conditions.

And this was one of them.

I wanted to see him for myself.

I wanted to see that he wasn't dead.

I wanted to tell him I was sorry.

I wanted to ask for his forgiveness.

I wanted to mend all the broken bridges between us.

Most of all I wanted him to know I was doing this for him, for his legacy, for the one thing he wanted the most in this world, the one thing I loathed.

The company.

And even if he woke up hating me, I would walk away knowing I did everything in my power to help him in every way I could.

I took a deep breath and opened the door.

The room smelled like antiseptic.

The lights were low.

And he was hooked up to so many machines my eyes blurred with tears. One machine breathed for him; every second or so it made a noise that had my stomach clenching.

He was alive.

Barely.

His face was covered in bandages, and one of his legs was broken, I knew he had several broken ribs and a collapsed lung going into surgery.

"Hey, Jules." My voice sounded so loud in that room. "You look like shit."

I figured if he could hear me, he would at least smile at that.

"You're also all over the news, which should make you really happy since you love the attention, but that's not why I'm here. Dad came to visit and he said . . . some things." Shit, how was I even supposed to do this? I cursed and spun around, putting my hands on my head.

"I know how important this job and following in his footsteps is to you, and I guess I just somehow needed you to know that I'm going to work my ass off so that when you wake up, you have everything you've always wanted. I just need you to know that it's not for me, it's for you. I swore I would protect you and I failed. I can't fail in this. I won't," I rasped. "But I really need you to wake up soon because I have no idea what I'm doing, and I have no idea how to do this other than to make it look like you're okay, so that you can have everything you've always wanted." I sighed and then looked at him one last time. "I never stopped loving you. I want you to know that."

I squeezed my eyes shut and hung my head, then turned around and walked back into the hall.

My dad was talking to one of the nurses. She looked at me and I just shook my head. My dad went to great lengths to make everyone think he only had one son, so I was used to that look of confusion. I never told anyone who my father was and didn't even use the Tennyson name. It disgusted me. It represented what my father did to my mom, what he did to Julian, our family.

I took my mom's maiden name and pretended I wasn't a Tennyson.

And my dad let me because he had one son he could control and knew that wasn't me.

Until now.

He looked between me and the nurse and whispered something else, then walked back to me, his swagger so confident I wanted to punch him in the face.

His "only" son was in the ICU fighting for his life, and he was smiling. How the hell was he smiling?

30

"She won't talk." He adjusted his white silk tie. "The entire ICU's been paid off, and I made a large donation to the hospital this morning. No reporters will be allowed in, nobody knows who you are, remember?"

"I wonder how many people you had to pay off to make that happen," I shot back.

He glared. "I'm offering you a fresh start."

"Right." *Like the fresh start you gave me when you sent me away.* I could feel a headache coming on. "The only reason I'm doing this is for Mom and Julian."

He snorted out a laugh. "You realize your brother hates you."

"And I hate you, so it looks like we're all in good company."

He ignored the comment and started walking, and I knew the expectation was to walk with him so I did.

"All her medical bills," I demanded. "Nobody but the board will know my true identity, and the minute Julian wakes up, he takes over again."

"If he wakes up."

"He'll fucking wake up," I said through clenched teeth.

My dad hesitated like he needed someone to tell him that Julian would fight, and then he agreed, "He's strong. He's a Tennyson."

Chapter Five

BRIDGE

"I knew you'd say yes." My bastard of a father just wouldn't stop talking. I grunted in response and continued to read portfolio after portfolio. It's not like I didn't have a business degree, but even then I knew I was rusty enough that I'd need to put in a few sleepless nights to catch up. Next were the social media pages, a laptop that looked like it cost more than a spaceship, and the keys to an apartment I would rather burn than sleep in. It wasn't my apartment. It was his. I didn't earn it. And I hated that I would be living his dream even if I was keeping it alive for him. "You need a drink."

"What I need," I seethed, "is for you to stop acting like you're doing me a favor. I'm doing this for Mom and Julian, not for you."

"She looked healthy." He shrugged like it wasn't a big deal or worth his notice.

"She's dying, you arrogant fuck," I spat. I wanted to wrap my hands around his neck and squeeze. I wanted to watch his head pop off and roll down the street while it got run over by a fleet of taxis before finally landing in a sewer where it rotted apart from his corpse so he roamed the earth searching for his head for the rest of eternity. A bit much?

I wasn't really a believer in life after death. However, what I did know was that there was a special place in hell for the man sitting next to me sipping brandy like my brother wasn't in a coma fighting for his life while I was about to take over the only thing he'd ever lived for.

Regardless of how much I hated Julian for wanting Dad's approval. I would always hate my dad more for making my mom cry.

"Mama? You sad?"

"Oh, baby, no. Mama just stubbed her toe." She wiped the tears from her face. I was only four, but I knew that wasn't right. I frowned down at her toes. She was wearing sneakers.

I stared harder as she sniffed a bit louder and sat on the couch.

I crawled into her lap and wrapped my tiny arms around her neck then kissed each cheek before doing butterfly kisses. "You're all better now."

Her glassy eyes focused on me with such intensity, such love, that my belly fluttered a bit as she clung to me tightly and whispered against my chubby cheek. "You always make everything better."

"I keep you safe, Mama, I always keep you safe."

For some reason that made her cry harder. But she laughed through the tears, so maybe what I said was a good thing; it was making her happy again.

"Baby, you are my world."

"I must be a big boy then."

"The biggest," she agreed with a smile before pinching my nose. "Alright, let's go order pizza and forget about being sad."

I didn't think stubbing a toe could make you sad.

She plopped me back on the couch and walked out of the room. I could hear her talking on the phone and ordering my favorite.

The news was on TV, I couldn't read, but I saw my daddy's face. He looked so big and strong. Maybe that's why Mama was crying? She missed him? He wasn't home as much as I wanted him to be. But he was important, Mama said so.

And he was in a fancy suit next to a woman dressed in white.

He looked happy.

And the only reason I could think my mom was sad was because he was at work again, which made me sad too.

"You're such a good boy." Mama came back in. "Love you forever, Bridge."

"Forever and always," I agreed with a smile.

"We're here," Edward instructed. I refused to call him Father. That sort of honor didn't belong to him now, did it?

I wasn't nervous about what I was about to do. If anything, after seeing Julian, I had a singular focus: get Mom the care she needed, using the money Edward was signing over to us, and make sure that she never cried again over the fact that we couldn't pay her medical bills.

All I had to do was pretend to be Julian, give him time to heal, give him time to get back to normal, and then my life would be normal again.

I would sell myself in order to keep my mom alive. The only cost was my soul, and in return I would get two million dollars cash and the rest of her home health care paid for. I would sign paperwork naming me temporary CEO as Bridge but publicly pretend to be Julian until he woke up and took over and then I'd disappear into the mist like movie magic. The board of directors would know the truth because it was one thing to pretend to be Julian in public, but signing his name on legal documents crossed a line that could put the company in jeopardy. Besides, Edward knew they wouldn't risk any damage to the value of their stocks by complaining.

Right. I signed over twelve months of my life to a man I hated, in order to protect both Tennyson Financial and IFC from drastic drops in the stocks. Even though he was a shrewd businessman, he was still keeping every single IFC employee and managing to double his portfolio, thus making Tennyson Financial the largest finance company in the world. Thousands of people would get bonuses, promotions, I just had to remember I was helping them, not making my own father wealthier.

I may have been a personal trainer and bartender, but I knew I could do this. I was born with this company in my blood, loath as I was to admit it.

Julian and Mom, you're doing this for them. Not your dad.

"Now, it's very important"—Dad adjusted his tie—"that you stick to the script, you're focusing on family and the business, no interviews until you fully heal."

"Heal." I scowled. "Right, and how exactly do I heal up from a coma? Yoga?"

He ignored me.

"It's necessary, you know." He put his hand on my shoulder like he had a right to and then pulled back when something like a growl escaped my lips. "Wish I had known you'd be the bigger of the two, I might have picked better." He winked.

I was seconds away from getting charged with homicide.

"Oh, I think you got exactly what you deserved," I said, enjoying the way his face turned purple and then red as he put on his sunglasses and jerked his head toward the dark building.

"Your brother's a fighter." He fiddled with his tie. "He'll make it through. We just need to give him time. Meanwhile I need this buyout of IFC to happen without any surprises. The board is getting antsy, especially with its soon-to-be CEO injured, so you'll need to make some appearances in a few weeks. The doctors will call it a miracle."

The more he talked, the sicker I became, and then someone opened the door, letting all the cold air out of the limo.

The apartment building looked like it had seen better days. Mortar crumbled between dirty red bricks. The metal security door looked like a case of tetanus waiting to happen. It was just the first stop on a day of hell that would end up making me hate myself. I tried to cling to the hope my choice brought, not the anger or numbness that came with doing the devil a favor.

Two hefty bodyguards flanked us. I was dressed in my street clothes from earlier, sneakers, joggers, and a hoodie.

The larger bodyguard's head was fully tattooed, and he buzzed one of the rooms.

"Who is it?" The voice was gruff and sounded far away. Lucky bastard.

"T," he barked. "Let us up, we got the guy."

Today "the guy," tomorrow . . . I shook my head. I couldn't think about it; if I thought about it, I might just back out. Already I was tempted. The memory of the look on my mother's face was enough to make me want to run in the opposite direction, like she thought that she would never see me again once a Tennyson had me in his clutches.

Fat chance.

The door buzzed, and up we went about seven flights of concrete stairs. With each step, I clenched my fists harder until I couldn't feel the skin on my palms. All too soon, we arrived on the designated floor and began walking down the hall. Green wallpaper was peeling off the walls, the hardwood floor was worn and warped, and I knew without even looking that the place would have enough cockroaches to fill a stadium. Room 66 was at the very end of the hall. Hah, add one more six and I would just nod expectantly; this was exactly what I'd chosen.

I'd traded heaven for hell.

For them.

And I would do it every damn time.

It was like history repeating itself. I had protected Julian from the monsters when we were in school, and now I was doing it all over again. Only the monster was our dad; Julian just didn't see it, he never had and probably never would.

The door swung open before anyone knocked. Three men filled the small apartment, each of them wearing all black and leather gloves. They looked like old-school mafia. The one directly in front of me grinned like it was Christmas morning.

I had a suspicion he was happier than ham in that moment.

"Make it quick," Edward barked. "We have a lot to do."

"Pity." The guy shoved a toothpick between his teeth and grinned. "I would have liked to savor this."

I stared him down. Yeah, I bet he would.

"Not today," Edward said in a stern voice as my body was shoved through the doorway.

I sighed. "Is the plastic tarp really necessary?"

"He sounds just like him." Toothpick guy twirled the damn stick. "Pull off your hood, kid."

I gritted my teeth and pulled my hood back and stared straight into his evil eyes. "See something you like?"

His grin fell. "Yeah, you're a Tennyson, ain't ya?"

"Unfortunately." I crossed my arms. "Expecting me to bleed a lot?"

"We like to cover our tracks." He rubbed his hands together while the door shut with a resounding boom.

The three of them circled me.

I let out a sigh. "I'm not running. I'm in this, you don't need to circle me like I'm your next meal, just get it over with."

"Taunting is part of the fun," one of the short ones piped up.

"This isn't fun, this is business." I clenched my teeth and cracked my neck. "And lucky for you, this business transaction states I can't fight back, so do your fucking worst."

"You really shouldn't have said that." Toothpick guy grinned. "And yes, the tarp is very much necessary, boy."

His fist came flying across my right cheek, and the punch hurt like hell. I rubbed the skin just as the short one elbowed me in the stomach. I actually felt my ribs crack.

And I knew what was next.

After all, people could get on board with a miraculous recovery.

But no scratches after a concussion, multiple head wounds, and three broken ribs along with a broken leg? Not so much.

At the sight of toothpick guy holding a baseball bat over his head, I said a little prayer. I heard my bone crack but only briefly experienced a sharp pain before everything went blessedly black.

Chapter Six

ISOBEL

Turns out, sleeping in your ex-fiancé's bed knowing that he'd had the maid there really isn't a good recipe for rest. I ended up in one of the four guest rooms and woke up with a start at around ten a.m.

Panicked, I quickly grabbed my phone and searched through my texts. Nothing from Edward, nothing from Marla. I had a few texts from friends at the hospital, mainly Annie, offering their support and prayers. And instantly wanted to crush my phone in my hand. Annie didn't know my secret pain. I was afraid to share too much information and afraid that she would judge me for staying with a cheater, for going through the motions, even though I knew she was one of the best people in the world. Maybe it was my pride that kept me from saying anything. I sent her a thank-you text then pleaded with Edward for more information. He surprised me with a swift response.

Edward: Rest. That's what's most important. We need the entire family to stick together. Besides, things are looking up.

I stared at my phone for a solid three minutes before the tears came. Were they tears of relief? Fear?

The sting of tears returning full force, I typed out another response.

Me: When can I see Julian?

Edward: Soon.

Did that mean he was getting better? Coming home? I started to pace as my mind replayed a montage of all the times we'd been together and all the lies he told. I'd sacrificed everything for Julian. He told me right after graduation that a Tennyson wife didn't work, she planned and volunteered. I laughed because I thought he was kidding.

He wasn't.

It was our first big fight.

Julian didn't understand why I wouldn't just let it go even though he knew I'd worked my ass off to graduate. And then he threw in my face that his dad helped pay for my education so I owed it to the family to fall in line.

It was then that I started realizing he wasn't the same. He listed the things I owned and then asked me point-blank if I paid for them.

I couldn't say yes.

And he smiled, smiled at me like it was some sick game. He smiled and said it would be okay, that he would always take care of me. And I believed him because I loved him, because we never fought like that, because he was just under pressure from his father, right? Because his father treated me like one of his own kids.

I realized very quickly that Edward loved you when he could control you, and he punished you when you acted out.

I shot him a middle finger emoji, then deleted it, and sent him a thumbs-up.

I hated him so much for giving me everything, including his love, and then using it as a weapon when he needed to manipulate me.

I threw the pillow across the room and closed my eyes. What could I control? Right now, I could control getting out of bed, feeding myself, and calling in sick to the children's cancer wing where I volunteered, the one thing that Julian had approved of while he went off to work, but I could only go twice a week.

More than twice looked bad, though I'd done it a few times just to irritate him.

He made it seem like there was this weird manual for being rich and since he was all I had.

I followed it to a T.

I quickly dialed the hospital number. Annie, of course, answered.

"Hey, Annie." My heart was in my throat. "I haven't heard any news other than he seems to be getting better. I just . . . have you maybe heard anything?"

Her sigh was all I needed. "All I know is the place is crawling with security and he's been moved to a private wing."

My eyebrows shot up my forehead. "Tennysons don't do things halfway, I guess . . ."

She laughed. "Yeah, well, I'll call if I hear anything. The good news is, according to my sources, he made it through the night."

For some reason that sentence stuck out to me, *He made it through the night.*

Would he make it through the next?

Was he suffering?

Was I a horrible person for sticking to my guns and breaking things off?

"Thanks, Annie, I won't be in today obviously but I'll keep you updated too."

"Love you, friend."

"Love you too." More tears welled in my eyes as I finally made my way to the bathroom for a shower and then followed it with a cup of coffee.

I felt better once I had my second cup and eyed the chic flat-screen in the living room as I took another sip, followed by another. Did I even dare turn on the news?

I knew the minute I hit the power button it would click on to CNBC. After all, business was life, and information was power.

I snorted in disgust and chose coffee instead. I would go crazy if I stayed in that apartment, with memories of him, of us, of better times, worse times, a maid in my bed. Yeah, I needed to get out.

I grabbed my AirPods and decided to go for a run while I waited for the news, good or bad. I wasn't going to change it by sitting in the apartment thinking.

And I knew if I went to any of our usual restaurants or stores, people would just ask questions.

I made a quick call to security to make sure no reporters were outside, and I was on my way.

I got my stride quickly as I weaved in and out of crowds and breathed a sigh of relief as my heart thudded against my chest.

Whatever happened, I was going to be okay.

It would be okay.

I'd survived this long.

I could do anything.

Anything.

With a smile curling my lips, I did a few more laps and decided to grab another coffee before walking the rest of the way back to the apartment. It was strange, not having appointments scheduled by the family, appearances, or even occasional texts from Julian just to say hello, which were often sent by one of the receptionists since he didn't have the time.

Or my favorite, the random flowers and love notes that would get delivered to the hospital along with monetary donations for the children's cancer wing that made me the envy of every single human who worked there.

"You're so lucky!" Nurses fanned themselves. "He's just so giving!"

"Yes, he is." Always my perfect polished answer as I smiled and pasted a dreamy look in my eyes, when really I was thinking about how overnice he was to every female that looked at him twice, especially lately.

Julian Tennyson, so freaking nice.

I dumped my remaining coffee in the trash can outside my building and waved at Harold on my way in.

"It's a good afternoon, Miss Cunningham."

I smiled back. It wasn't his fault he was just as delusional about my relationship with Julian as the rest of the world. "Yes, it will be, at least. Hopefully."

He gave me a sympathetic look before shaking his head and offering a polite smile. "You enjoy your day off."

Right. He knew my schedule well. The pity in his eyes made my stomach sink. Like he knew that I was trapped in a life I would do anything to escape, a life I'd finally tried to escape only to have the universe pull a trump card in the end. Enjoy my day off? Doing what? Sitting alone and waiting to find out about my fate?

"Right." I nodded slowly and hit the penthouse floor. With each floor the elevator shot up, anxiety doubled, tripled, quadrupled, until my body felt heavy with it.

I exited the elevator and stared at our gorgeous marble entryway, with its modern lines and edgy pops of orange.

I'd fallen in love with it based on the entryway alone.

He'd surprised me with it that night.

A year later I discovered he'd already scoped out the building. He knew I'd like it because one of the women who worked at the company had invited him over for a drink.

We got in a huge fight about him having a private drink with a coworker, alone. He was drunk, apologized profusely, and bought me a new Maserati.

Idiot. Fool.

I was so stupid.

I'd just wanted to believe in him, in us.

He was all I had.

With a deep breath, I opened the door and dropped my phone and keys on the counter. I needed another shower and made a pact with myself to go down to the hospital. Let them escort me out if they needed to, I just had to know.

I needed to know.

Decision made, I quickly showered, pulled my hair into a sleek ponytail. I slipped into white linen pants and a loose white blouse, pairing them with a new pair of gold Louis Vuittons and gold hoop earrings.

I wasn't allowed to be caught in anything but heels when I was with Julian, and if he was . . . alive, I—God, listen to me! What? I didn't want to offend the lying, cheating bastard I'd broken up with?

I kicked off the heels, put on blue flats I knew would piss him off, and grabbed my purse just as a key turned in the lock.

My lock.

To my door.

To our apartment.

I waited, expecting to see the maid, ready to tear into her for even coming back. Anxiety spiked. What if it was another mistress? God, how sick was he?

The door opened.

And Julian locked eyes with me.

One eye to be exact, the left one was swollen shut. His jaw had a purple-and-yellow bruise marring his perfect chin, but beneath the bruises and cuts, his face was still sculpted, still perfect.

"J-Julian." I hated that I didn't feel relief. I hated that I wanted to shove him out the window. I hated the person he made me, damn him. "Thank God you're okay."

A toddler could hear the lack of sympathy in my words, but I needed to say them, because I refused to let him take away something so simple as my manners too.

He didn't speak for a full minute.

I hated this game.

I hated that he was still playing it even when he'd almost died, should have, could have.

I moved from one foot to the other. "I was just going to visit you in the hospital. They, um, wouldn't let me in yesterday."

He kept staring and then looked down at my shoes. "A bit over-dressed for the hospital, don't you think?"

His voice wasn't right.

He swayed a bit on his feet.

And then collapsed against the bar top, letting out a loud curse.

Stunned, I watched for a few brief seconds before rushing over and helping him. Instinct kicked in. I used my nursing training.

His injuries were extensive.

The doctor had looked so grim!

But he was alive!

And currently holding his weight against me, his forehead touching mine. "Sorry."

Did the man just apologize for not having the strength to stand? He really must have hit his head hard. I felt the tears then, tears brought on by one word.

Sorry.

He said sorry.

It wasn't often that he apologized. It was stupid that I wanted to cry because he did.

"How did they let you leave the hospital like this?" I asked, getting more concerned by the minute. He looked disoriented and miserable.

"Easy." He bit down on his full bottom lip. "I wanted to be home with my fiancée and my dad"—he spat *dad* like he hated the word—"threw money at them. Besides, it's better to heal at home with those you love, right?"

I almost corrected him.

In fact, I stared at him a solid minute, unable to form a coherent thought. Did he think we were still together? Did he forget about the conversation yesterday? I wasn't sure if it was a mind game or if he really meant it, because for the first time in years he actually sounded sincere about loving me, about wanting to spend time with me. It was like watering an almost dead flower, that's how desperate I was for the words, for them to have meaning behind them.

He stumbled toward our bedroom, and I rolled my eyes a bit. He'd always been so stubborn; he was going to be one of those patients, wasn't he? It wouldn't surprise me at all if he left against doctor's orders.

I let out a sigh, waited for him to trip on a piece of furniture, then finally moved after him to help carry his weight in the right direction, only the guy looked confused on which way to go, left or right.

"I, uh . . ." He winced. "My head hurts really bad, the concussion is making my memory fuzzy, I may need . . . help until I can remember everything before the accident."

"You?" I repeated. "Help?"

"Me. Help." He smirked, or it looked like he smirked. "Is that so hard to believe? I nearly died, Izzy."

"You haven't called me Izzy since we were in college," I croaked, hating how much the endearment made my heart ache. It wasn't just the way he said it, it was the way he looked at me when he said it.

"Huh." He grunted like he couldn't remember. Typical, I knew his games well. He needed help and was trying to get some empathy.

I was torn between wanting to trip him and having some human decency. I chose decency and helped him into the master bedroom and then into bed. "Sleep."

"Wait." He grabbed my wrist and held tight. Panic overtook as I waited for him to hurt me, not physically, just emotionally. "I said I needed help."

"You have a staff to help you," I said slowly. "Trust me, they're very . . . helpful."

His good eye narrowed in on me. "I'm not asking them. I'm asking you."

"As demanding as ever," I said dryly.

"Please?"

It was the *please* that did it, and I sighed reluctantly. "Fine, what do you need?"

"A bath."

I should have let him face-plant into the glass table. "Sure . . . fine." I hated myself in that moment, hated that I was weak, that all it took was for him to say please and I was jumping in headfirst with that stupid little word floating around in my brain.

Hope.

Chapter Seven

BRIDGE

She was stunning.

Absolutely breathtaking in a way that made no sense to me. Because how in the hell had my brother landed a woman like that? Rationally, I knew my brother was good-looking. I was given that reminder every day of my life when I looked in the mirror and debated whether I should take a knife to half of my face just so people stopped asking if I was him.

The differences between me and Julian were few. I had a scar below my left ear from middle school when my friend tried to shoot a bow and arrow in my direction. He had good—seriously good—aim.

Beyond that, I had a few tattoos scattered on my forearms and on my back plus one on my thumb, but lucky me, they had movie makeup for that, and it was waterproof. I just wanted to be clean. It's not like I needed the woman to wash me. Besides, the way she looked at me—or him—made me wonder if she hated him as much as she loved him.

My father hadn't been very forthcoming with details of their relationship, only that they'd dated since college and had been engaged for the last three years. He said they were madly in love and the natural heirs to the Tennyson dynasty. Which either meant he could control them, or they were just as bad as he was.

Both options . . . not great.

She was on the taller side. Her blue flats probably cost more than a month of rent and two weeks of food for me and my mom. I tried not to be bitter, but everything about this glamorous, narcissistic lifestyle made me want to set the building on fire. The fact that I'd spent half my life in it not realizing what the rest of the world lived like just made the turmoil worse. I had been so selfish then, so spoiled. I wondered how I would have turned out had I stayed with my dad, had Julian gone with my mom.

In hindsight it made sense that it happened the way it did. My dad probably knew we would butt heads and I'd end up strangling him, while Julian hung on his every word, memorized his movements, prayed at night for Dad to tell him he was good enough.

I tried not to curse as I moved.

With each step my ribs felt like they were going to poke through my skin, the pain was aggravating. I ran a hand through my freshly cut hair and tried to remember the details of Julian's relationship with Izzy.

I refused to call her Isobel, that rule could go to hell for all I cared. Isobel sounded like someone who ate kale and liked political dinners and vacations in the Hamptons.

Izzy sounded fun.

And I'd rather believe the lie, that she was fun, than believe the truth, that she was as selfish as my brother.

A true social climber.

According to my dad, the Tennysons had given her everything, cars, shopping trips, a roof over her head. They were the only family she had now, which meant she would probably do whatever it took to stay in their good graces.

Just like Julian.

I scowled.

"Something wrong?" Her voice was soft, cultured. I didn't want to like it, but it was impossible not to sense the warmth of it clinging to my body, wrapping around it over and over again.

"Just painful," I said in a gruff voice as we finally made it to the master bathroom. "Drugs aren't really helping."

At least my brother had good taste.

It was just modern enough to look trendy but not so cold that you felt like you couldn't put up family pictures, not that he would ever do such a thing.

This was Julian we were talking about. He was more likely to put up pictures of himself than of someone else, him and that damn thick mop of hair on his head. Girls had loved him for keeping it long, but it was short now, just like mine.

The pictures lining the walls were expensive and impersonal. They gave me absolutely no background into Julian's life these past few years or Izzy's position in it.

"Sorry," she finally said in a tone that sounded anything but. For some reason, that amused me, that she had some spark to her and wasn't this little Tennyson doormat.

"Are you?" I just had to ask as I sat on the edge of the tub and watched her lean over and turn the silver knobs to let out the hot water. She plugged the drain, the action giving me a view of her cleavage beneath the thin blouse. Perfect everywhere, wasn't she? I almost asked if I'd bought them, her breasts, but I figured if she had any sense in her, she'd take that opportunity to drown me, and I needed to stay very much alive.

So he could get better and let me go back to Mom where I belonged, at her bedside cooking food she couldn't eat and making sure she had a smile on her face at all times.

Getting distracted by two perky surgical breasts? Not in the cards.

"Of course I am," she finally said, meeting my gaze with a smile that didn't reach her sparkling green eyes. Her brows had the perfect dark arch. Her hair was pulled back tight into a low honey-blonde ponytail.

My gaze traveled lower as I drank her in. My brother had done one thing right in his life, it seemed. He'd landed a woman who looked like an angel, the literal kind and the Victoria's Secret kind.

"That wasn't very convincing," I joked with a smirk.

Her eyes widened in fear as she flinched.

I fucking made her flinch.

What the hell?

Did he hit her?

Was she afraid of me? Him?

"You can go now," I said in a softer tone. "Really, it's okay. I'll try not to drown on my own, alright?"

Her lips pressed together like she was holding something in, maybe a scream? What sort of world had I just stepped into?

"No, no, it's . . . it's fine." She sounded like she was trying to convince herself more than me. "I don't want you to be inconvenienced."

The hell?

I sat in stunned silence as the water trickled into the bathtub, higher and higher. "You don't live to please me, Izzy."

"And you must be high on whatever they gave you, because that's exactly what I do, and you know it." Fire lashed out of her eyes, out of her words, as she stood and pressed her hands down her pants and straightened her shoulders. "I'll bring you in two fingers of whiskey and the newspaper. Will there be anything else?"

"Yeah." I reached for her hand and grasped it. "Stop acting like my maid."

"Maid. Fiancée." She shrugged. "I guess you must get the two confused often."

"What the hell are you talking about?"

Her nostrils flared. "You told me never again."

Shit, what the hell did he do? I wasn't sure how to respond. My brother was an ass who answered to no one, but I couldn't find it within myself to be anything but kind. "Excuse me?"

"She was in our bed, Julian."

I flinched, not because of what she said but because she called me by his name. *Damn it, brother, what did you do?* I wanted to defend myself by telling her exactly what I thought of a man who would bring another woman into their bed. What the hell?

"She," I repeated, because I wasn't sure what else to say and my head was pounding.

Izzy bit on her bottom lip, turning it white. "She, as in, the maid. I know you seem to get all of your affairs confused, and the head wound probably isn't helping, but our maid. In our bed. You promised. I wish—" Tears filled her eyes as she shook her head at me. "I wish—"

"Say it." My voice was calm as I locked eyes on her. "What do you wish?"

"That's not a luxury I've been given, and you know it," she finally said after I watched one of the saddest things I'd ever seen happen right before my eyes. She took a deep breath, straightened her shoulders, and just disappeared, not into thin air, but into herself. I could almost see the cocoon of money and control wrap around her while she answered me with a fake voice, fake smile, fake posture.

I gripped the edges of the tub and moved to my knees, even though it hurt like hell, then crooked my finger at her.

She moved toward me obediently.

And in that moment, I must have lost every good part I had in me, because I wanted to put a pillow over my brother's face until he woke up and explained to me what had possessed him to do to his fiancée exactly what our father had done to our mom.

He used to cry himself to sleep at night when they fought.

And now? Now he was sleeping with the maid?

I had no leg to stand on. I wasn't allowed to be Bridge anymore, was I? I had to explain Julian's behavior the way Julian would, which wasn't at all helpful since we hadn't talked in years.

"Tell me something you want," I finally said, reaching for her hand.

She let me take it. Her skin was so smooth I had a hard time focusing, and a really hard time not rubbing my thumb across its surface, so I gave in, because this was the part I was supposed to play.

But also because I suspected the last time she'd been given any sort of attention that wasn't manipulative was when she'd been lucky enough not to know a Tennyson.

Her breath caught as she stared down at our joined hands. I told myself it was me, that I was causing that reaction, not Julian.

And I made a vow to her, even though she didn't know it. I would give her the best few weeks of her life, days that would be filled with smiles, not control.

And then do the cruelest thing a man could do.

Turn her back over to the real Julian the minute he woke up. I told myself he'd listen to reason, I told myself that I could convince him to either let her go if she was that unhappy or love her the way she clearly deserved for sticking by his side so long.

"You can't fix this with things, Julian." She looked away.

"You have enough things," I said simply. "Why don't I give you something that you truly wish for, even if that means I don't get to be a part of it."

"How many drugs do they even have you on? You know you react badly to painkillers," she said under her breath, a small smile touching her face. God, she was pretty.

I almost laughed. No drugs. Because my dad was a bastard, and also because I wanted to feel the pain, to let it remind me why I was doing this.

"Enough." I winked. "I did almost die."

"Yeah, almost." She looked ashamed.

Interesting.

I was torn between apologizing profusely and doing what my brother would do. I had to find middle ground. I didn't know the first thing about gifts for women who were scorned, but I did know my way around a kitchen.

She was still staring at me, like she was trying to figure me out, and I knew that Julian wouldn't be with her if she wasn't smart. Shit, already I felt like an imposter, and she looked at me like I was.

"Dinner," I finally said. "Why don't I cook you dinner?"

Her frown was instant, so I knew I must have said the wrong thing, and then she smiled. It wasn't the one I wanted, it didn't light up the room. It was a smile of caution and constant disappointment. "You haven't done that since college."

"I think I can do better than Top Ramen," I teased.

She pressed her lips together in a small smile. "I can't believe you remember my love for Top Ramen. Sometimes I swear I still crave it at midnight."

Midnight? Did he make it for her during study sessions? And why was I so frantic to find out the missing pieces of his life? Maybe it was because I was curious too.

Because I'd missed him too.

"Izzy, you may need to help me with some memories. The doctors said the hit was extremely hard, but I remember the important things." I lied through my teeth, feeling sicker and sicker as my words caused her smile to grow.

"Maybe you need to hit your head more often." She shrugged.

"Let's not get too aggressive. The last thing I need is you hitting me with a two-by-four every morning."

Her eyes widened, and then she laughed, quickly covering her mouth and shaking her head. "Tempting, though I hardly doubt it would do any damage to that thick skull."

I found myself grinning up at her like an idiot in over his head. And that's exactly what I was, because as she released my hand and made her way out of the bathroom, I realized that by treating her like a human.

I was dooming her to the devil.

I was Dr. Jekyll.

And the minute my brother woke up.

She would get Mr. Hyde.

Chapter Eight

My hands were shaking by the time I made it back into the living room. I wasn't sure what just happened, but it wasn't normal, Julian hadn't looked at me like that in months. I swallowed the knot in my throat as my stomach did flips.

How pathetic could I actually be?

Was I that starved for physical attention and touch that one thumb was all it took for me to jump back into his arms? The same guy who gave our maid leeway to borrow my silver stilettos during sex?

I hated the person I saw in the mirror, the person I'd become. And the sick part was that I knew better, I'd had great parents who raised me to respect myself, to respect others, and yet there I was in an emotionally abusive relationship, on a merry-go-round that refused to let me get off.

I'd loved him so much. He'd helped me through their funeral; he'd paid for it, for crying out loud! He moved me into his apartment without even asking my permission, and he listened, sometimes until two a.m., while I talked about them, while I cried in his arms. Sure, he had a wandering eye, what college student didn't, and he was a flirt, but everyone knew that. And yes, sometimes he seemed moody when things didn't go his way, but again, we were young.

And I was stupid enough to believe that he would grow out of it, and the stupid just piled on when he finally proposed and I thought, *This is it, the moment I've been waiting for, the moment that's going to solve everything.*

He was my rock.

I just wasn't quick enough to understand the dynamics of his relationship with his father, that he would do anything, become anyone, to please him, to the point of it poisoning our relationship. I truly woke up six months ago and asked myself, How did it get this far?

How did we let it get this bad?

And how could I have stopped it from happening?

I slammed my hands against the countertop, seething at myself, at him, at the maid, at the shoes all over again. I didn't want to be weak, but I didn't know what else to do, especially since his memory wasn't what it was.

Was I crazy to think that we could start over? Would it be ridiculous to even propose it? To ask him for a fresh start while he healed?

Who was I kidding? This was Julian, he'd be working from his damn laptop the minute he got out of that bathtub.

This is what Julian made me. Crazy. I was acting crazy, and still I couldn't calm my heart, not after pouring a glass of wine and downing half of it, not after pacing the living room wondering what version of him I was going to get next. Was he going to smile like he just did? Touch my hand and squeeze it lightly? Would he berate me and apologize later, telling me he loved me while kissing his way down my body?

Did it even matter anymore?

I chewed my lower lip as the consequences of my actions seemed to squeeze my throat until I felt like I was choking. We had joint bank accounts. My cars were in his name. I had nothing but the ring on my finger and the memories of our time together when we were in college.

A simpler time when all he cared about was sneaking into my dorm room.

A time when his father didn't have his claws elbow deep into Julian's psyche. A time when he was his own person and had one goal in life. A family.

Tears dripped down my cheeks as I thought of all the instances he cheated and all the stupid times I took him back.

Without a second thought, I marched into the master bedroom, grabbed the silver stilettos, and went back into the kitchen in search of a sharp knife or scissors—something, anything to ruin them, to get my aggression out, to prove to him that one tiny conversation where he pretended to find me attractive in blue flats wasn't going to erase years of emotional duress and pain.

My eyes flashed to the kitchen shears. I grabbed them with my right hand and started cutting at the heel. It didn't come off, but it did create huge slashes and slices. Frustrated, I dropped the scissors and banged the heels against the edge of the granite counter.

One of the heels broke off, dangling in my right hand while I held the other heel high in the air ready to do the same.

"Is this new?" came Julian's calm voice.

Of course he would be calm, he was always calm, never raised his voice, never hurt me, but sometimes I wished he would, so I had proof, so I could show someone, *Look, this is the cut he gave me from when I didn't wear the right outfit, that bruise on my cheek is from the day I forgot to bring his dry cleaning and wear the new pair of heels he'd just purchased from the buyer we were meeting at Saks.*

Julian's warfare was in his silence. His inaction.

And it felt like knives slicing me open every single time I got one of his disappointed stares or squeezes.

No, he didn't hurt me.

He emotionally abused me.

And I always justified coming back for more.

My left hand was still lifted high when I felt him behind me. A chill washed over me when his hand touched my skin where my thumb met the shoe, his other hand moved to my right hip, holding me there. I squeezed my eyes shut, waiting for the worst, waiting for him to tell me I was overreacting or being ridiculous. Waiting for him to be disappointed in my outlandish behavior.

The words never came.

Instead, he very slowly pulled the shoe from my hand and rested his chin on the top of my head, pulling me back against his strong chest.

It didn't feel familiar.

Maybe because it had been so long.

It was almost as if a stranger was holding me, rocking me back and forth. Everything about him felt bigger. I had to keep telling myself it was bandages and swollen muscles, really swollen muscles.

I tried to keep my tears in and was successful, until he very quietly asked me one question that I didn't realize would be my breaking point.

"Are you okay?"

"I haven't been okay," I hiccupped, "in a really long time, which you would know if you ever even paid attention to me. I have to make an appointment to even see you at your office. And these shoes?" I was really losing it, losing it. I pointed at them with shaky hands. "Were on our maid. She was naked in the bed I share with you. Naked waiting for you with her legs high in the air like you were getting ready to play some sort of sexual Hunger Games!"

He stiffened and bit out a curse.

Good. Let him be upset. I was screwed already. Why not keep going? The entire Tennyson kingdom was going to come crashing down on my head. I was dead already, wasn't I?

Never good enough.

Not for them.

A complete imposter.

They would enjoy my fall.

I should get them popcorn for the big show.

These were all the things going through my head when Julian turned me in his arms and let out a long sigh.

There it was, the disappointment. I felt it like a blow to the chest.

The words didn't come, though.

He just sighed again and held me against his chest.

He smelled like his favorite body wash, the one I used to use when he was traveling. The one I once smelled on his stepmother, thinking I was imagining things.

"I think," Julian said slowly, "that you need to rest."

I rolled my eyes and pulled away. "I'm not a toddler. I don't need a nap."

"You're mutilating expensive"—he waved his fingers at the shoes like he didn't know the brand—"heels." Great, now he was pretending not to care about designers. The effects of narcotics and head wounds, folks.

"They're tarnished," I said through clenched teeth all the while wondering why he was staring at the shoes like he'd never seen them before when he's the one who bought them.

He stared me down, his green-eyed gaze intense, like his only focus was me, which only meant he was probably daydreaming about dollar signs and giant fake breasts. "Alright, I guess if they're tarnished you should probably do it right."

"Do what right?"

He grabbed the shoe that was still intact and broke off the heel like a cracker, then placed it on the counter, pulled a knife I wasn't even aware he was carrying out of his pocket, and started cutting the fabric until all that was left was a sole and a few sparkles. "Better?"

I stared at the shreds of shoes littering the white granite table and then stared up at him, something wasn't right. "Did they do something to your hair at the hospital?"

He hesitated briefly then smirked. "Yes, they have a masseuse there as well. Figured I'd get the royal treatment since I almost died." His lips pursed and then he let out a low laugh. "Now, any other ridiculous questions?" He crossed his arms like he was up for a challenge and tilted his head like I amused him.

I let out a defeated sigh as I felt my shoulders roll forward like they tended to do when I wasn't reminding myself to keep my perfect posture. "No."

"I'm still making you dinner. Go do something that helps you relax a bit and we can eat in a few hours."

"You never cook, Julian."

"Things change." He said it while looking at me, not through me. I felt my heart cracking a bit. "Let me take care of you, the way you take care of me."

And there it was.

I gaped at him in stunned disbelief as tears filled my eyes. "Are you sure you aren't on morphine?"

"Why do you keep assuming I'm on hard drugs?" His easy smile was back. "Izzy, go lie down, I'm serious, I know how stressed you are, I can feel it." He braced me with his hands and leaned over, touching his forehead to mine. "You're soft, you know that?" He cleared his throat and shook his head.

Strange.

I watched him stumble a bit toward the middle of the kitchen, and despite my conflicting feelings about him, couldn't help but be concerned. He'd clearly cleaned up, wearing a white button-down and trousers that hugged his body tighter than usual. They stretched across his chest and ass, not that I was staring. He stumbled again against the counter and winced.

Okay, I was definitely staring. He'd always been beautiful, perfect.

"Shit," he hissed under his breath. "I think I'm missing ribs or cartilage or something necessary for life."

"Here, sit down." I hurried over and grabbed a chair. I might be rusty, but I knew how to make sure all his ribs were at least in place and not poking lungs.

"What?" He frowned. "Why?"

"Wow, the concussion must have really done a number on you. Nursing major, remember? Let me just . . ." I gulped as I reached for him then pulled back. Why did this feel so different? "If you could just lift your shirt, I'll make sure that you're not dying."

"I could be dying."

"If they let you out of the hospital, you're not dying," I pointed out.

"What if I escaped?" The corners of his mouth lifted up into a teasing smile that completely disarmed me. "You know, grabbed my clothes, ripped out my IV, and made a run for it with my bare ass flashing every nurse on the floor."

"That sounds like college Julian, or drunk Julian, not grown-up Julian with his expensive suits and preference for brunettes." It slipped.

He flinched.

"Sorry."

"Don't be, not if it's true." He slowly pulled his shirt back. I let out a little gasp. "Knew it, I'm dead and this is heaven."

I laughed a little, I couldn't help it. "No, it's just . . . you must have a lot of swelling, I mean you look, then again you've been working late nights so I haven't really been paying attention to what's under . . . you know what?" I stood abruptly. "You're hurt, you shouldn't be cooking."

"I'm fine," he insisted softly. "Let's not start insulting my manhood. I've already endured a catheter, alright?"

"Ah, found one small enough, did they?" I teased. I couldn't help it. He was making it easy. He was making me feel young again, as stupid as that sounded.

Julian burst out laughing. "Right, I deserved that."

My own smile fell. This wasn't real. It was a fantasy, wasn't it? Soon he'd go back to work. Things would go back to normal, and I'd be crushed. I asked the question I didn't want the answer to. I needed to prepare my heart, because already he was crawling back into it like he'd never left. "When can I expect the drugs to wear off and for all of this"—I waved him up and down—"to disappear?"

His expression sobered as he whispered roughly, "If I had my way . . . never."

Julian turned his back to me.

He was done with the conversation.

And instead of napping, all I kept wondering was why he made it sound like he had no control over his own mind.

Chapter Nine

BRIDGE

I found out quickly that they had absolutely no food in the apartment, but I did locate a list of takeout numbers, which only made me turn up my nose. Takeout? Home-cooked meals were the way to go, and after going through the prices of Chinese, I figured I'd be better off trying to get groceries delivered. We were in the heart of the Upper East Side; if you couldn't get groceries delivered in an hour, what was the point?

I grabbed the new cell phone out of my pocket.

The one with every number preprogrammed for me, for the new Julian. I'd felt like a prostitute when my father gave it to me, with a gleam in his eye like he had me exactly where he wanted me.

Which was bullshit. I'd be leaving the minute Julian woke up. I refused to let my dad think he had the upper hand. He needed me more than I needed him, and that was a fact. Besides, it was temporary. I knew he would have the best doctors fixing up Julian to the point where he would probably walk out of that hospital looking better than the day before the accident.

I just hoped it was sooner rather than later, because every time Izzy looked at me, I felt guilty. Every time she touched me and her expression went from hurt to soft, I wanted to pummel my twin—and probably would, once he woke up.

I couldn't keep up this ruse forever. We might look alike, but we were clearly two very different people with different morals and different interests.

He might prefer brunettes, but I was starting to prefer blondes.

Shit, I should have thought this through more. The last thing I needed was one more regret between me and my brother, one more thing separating us from each other.

It was like being stuck in the Twilight Zone, and I hated that there were innocent people involved, people like Izzy.

I swallowed the dryness in my throat.

One thing was at least clear.

She hated Julian.

And she mourned the loss of what they used to have.

She also needed him. He was all she had left, and that was enough for her to stay. I knew how charismatic my brother could be. Hell, he talked himself out of a C in chemistry in eighth grade; it had taken him twenty minutes.

He won student of the week.

He set his eyes on something, he got it. Period.

My father had done a good job grooming him into his Edward Tennyson mini-me. If she was still here, my bet was that he gave her just enough to keep her by his side and made her pay for it when she didn't fall at his feet in thankfulness.

With a sigh, I typed in the address for grocery delivery. Amazon could deliver within the hour.

Perfect.

I grabbed his wallet—not mine, his. I stared at his picture on his license. I held his heavy black card in my hand and felt like I was in over my head.

I tapped the black card against my fingertips and started typing out the numbers that would be my secret prison over the next few weeks.

I shoved the wallet back into my expensive slacks and wondered if the guy had anything other than clothes that belonged in a boardroom.

The groceries wouldn't be there for an hour.

The least I could do was change into something comfortable and watch some TV, or even study the several digital portfolios my father had sent to me via Julian's email.

I had his briefcase as well, with details of the buyout highlighted for me to read.

I didn't get to just pretend to live his life.

I had to become him.

I could only hope that I wouldn't fall victim to the manipulations too. As long as I remembered who the real monster was, I wouldn't succumb to my greed like Julian had, I wouldn't let it control me. I would keep my focus.

And I would keep my promise.

I stumbled into the bedroom, careful to keep quiet. Izzy was on her side, her delicate hands tucked beneath her chin, her breathing heavy. Good, she needed to sleep, she deserved sleep, my brother was probably the type of guy that would wake up a perfectly happy woman and ask for a blow job. I wouldn't put it past him.

I ignored the pull to her, the need to grab the purple afghan and drape it over her small body. I also ignored the way I wanted to stare at her curves.

I was being incredibly creepy.

She wasn't mine to stare at or to want.

And yet a tiny voice in my head said she was.

That she was more mine than she was his.

Because at least when I looked at her, I saw her.

"Do whatever it takes. Izzy won't say a word against you, but you have to make her believe it, she'll have questions . . . if you need to make her

feel like she's going insane, so be it." Father chuckled as anger boiled to the surface of my psyche. I could kill him and feel no guilt. How did a person get to that place?

I shook my head and walked into the large closet. It had a chandelier hanging in the middle, a couch with a minibar right next to it, and a flat-screen. It was a mix between a living room and a closet.

Tags still clung to half the clothes dangling on her side. And on my side, suits, jackets, coats, furs. A case of Rolex watches with another case of sunglasses above it, at least forty pairs, mainly Ray-Bans, stared back at me.

Shoes of every color and type were to the left by the minibar. He had a few pairs of Pumas and Nikes that looked like they'd never seen the sun. I grabbed a pair of high-tops and located an Under Armour hoodie and a pair of black joggers that wouldn't look like shit.

I sat on the chair and peeled off my pants, the pain too intense to take anymore. God, I wish he had given me medication. All I had was Advil and memories of guys beating me senseless so I would look like I'd been run over by a truck—literally.

It took me at least fifteen minutes to put on my pants, and by then I was ready to give up. I couldn't bend over to even get them past my feet, so it took about a dozen tries. I had started sweating by the time I tried to peel my shirt over my head. It had been easier before, maybe because my adrenaline had been pumping. Now I was just in pain, agony, actually.

A throat cleared.

Izzy stood in the doorway, the purple afghan wrapped around her. "I don't think I've ever heard so many creative ways to curse."

"Yeah, well, you get in a head-on collision and get back to me. My skin hurts," I said honestly, not remembering even saying anything except *shit*, so yeah, maybe I wasn't exactly silent. And now I was ready to curse even louder. She was seeing me without a shirt for the second time. What the hell was I supposed to tell her? I was taking human growth hormones overnight?

"Taking your pain out on your clothing, that's new." She tentatively walked into the room and dropped the afghan. The air moved, causing her blouse to billow up enough for me to see two creamy breasts.

Damn it, I needed to get my lust under control and stop staring. That's what happens when you live with your mother and ignore women who hit on you; you start losing your mind and lusting after your induced-coma twin's fiancée.

"Let me help." She got down on her knees in front of me.

I hated it instantly.

She served no one. Least of all me.

"Get up," I barked, not meaning it to sound as aggressive as it did.

She shot up so fast she almost toppled over me. "Sorry, I was just trying to—"

"Help, I know, and while I'm extremely thankful for that help, I couldn't—" I gulped. "I didn't like seeing you putting on my shoes. Women like you don't put on men's shoes like servants."

"Even if I wanted to?"

"Even if you wanted to. Women like you never belong on their knees." I swallowed thickly as her lips parted. "Or their backs."

Pain flashed across her face as she looked down at the shoes she was holding. "Here."

She handed me a tennis shoe and then helped me lean forward to put it on. I held the scream in while putting on both shoes. Sweat drenched my back, so much for that bath.

I still had the hoodie to put on.

I just wanted to be comfortable, in something that made sense, something that felt like me, not like I was stepping into someone else's skin like a body snatcher.

I tried pulling my shirt up.

Failed.

Tried again.

Gave her a wince and watched as she exhaled and moved her perfectly manicured hands to the bottom of my shirt, once again standing in front of me. I didn't know what possessed me to put my hands on her hips. Maybe the pain was driving me insane, maybe I just needed to make sure she was real, not something I conjured up in my wildest fantasies, because that's what she looked like standing there with her long honey hair freed from the tight ponytail and hanging past her breasts, swollen pink lips, and concentration in her eyes like she cared—about me, not him, about this moment between us—when I knew in all reality she didn't, she didn't even know me.

"Go slow," I rasped.

Her eyes flickered to my lips and stayed there for a few brief, charged seconds before she started slowly spreading the shirt off my shoulders. I wanted to kiss her.

I was going crazy.

What would Julian do? Would he mock her? Kiss her? Would he pull her into his arms?

"Is this okay?" she asked, her movements slowing.

More than okay.

I nodded, not trusting my voice.

She was tender, even when she probably had no reason to be. To her I was a cheater, a liar, a manipulator.

"Damn, you would have been a really good nurse, Izzy." The words were out before I could stop them.

I prayed to God the makeup covering my tattoos hadn't somehow washed off. I had been told it was good with soap and water for over thirty-six hours.

Her head whipped to mine. "What?"

"You were a nursing major." Shit, shit, shit. "All I'm saying is you would have been a really good nurse, fantastic, actually."

Her eyes filled with unshed tears, she bit on her lower lip and nodded. "I think I would have been too, it's unfortunate that the Tennyson women don't work, right?"

The hell?

"Uh, right." Mom hadn't worked. Had Julian told Isobel she wasn't allowed to?

I tried to school my expression as her breath hitched and her palms touched my shoulders, tugging the sleeves down.

And I knew in that moment.

She knew something wasn't right.

Maybe my brother hadn't kept up his vigorous running routine.

Maybe we'd made an error in judgment.

According to Dad, she had no idea Julian was a twin.

Maybe she would assume she was exhausted, hallucinating. I had to make this work. I had to lie and say whatever it took to convince her. I hadn't thought of the opposite. That she would be thankful I looked different from what she remembered, that her eyes would dilate the minute they met mine, that she would look at me and her breathing would hitch.

I was doing that to her.

And I was ready to do a lot more.

Ready to tell her everything.

To take her away from the nightmare. After knowing her for only a few hours I was ready to step up as the white knight.

And that's why I needed to keep my distance.

Because I already had a damsel to save.

And she was dying.

Not to mention a twin who was in a coma fighting for his life.

This wasn't about me.

It never would be.

My thoughts sobered as Izzy finally got the shirt free and pulled it down, dropping it to the floor.

Her eyes raked over me like the stranger I was.

"You're staring," I whispered.

"I'm not stupid."

"Nobody said you were," I countered, waiting for the worst.

Her hands moved to my biceps like she wanted to make sure they were real. They slid from my biceps back to my shoulders and then to my face as she cupped it between her hands and turned my head slowly from side to side like she was examining me or looking for clues.

I grabbed her by the wrists and smiled as genuinely as I could. "You're starting to scare me a bit."

"Me? Scare you?" Her eyes narrowed. "I went to sleep thinking you were dead."

At least she didn't say *hoping you were dead*. That was progress, right?

"And this afternoon you show up on my doorstep like nothing was wrong, like you didn't just have life-saving surgery. I haven't seen any sutures large enough to look like they cut you open. All I see is a lot of bruising and obvious . . . swelling." She gulped.

"That happens in surgery," I said casually. "The swelling."

"Bullshit," she fired back. "Otherwise every scrawny guy would get in a car accident in hopes of looking this . . . swollen."

I grinned at that. "I've always worked out. I've been lifting more, and you know I've been busy with the buyout. I have no reason to lie to you."

Her face fell. I hated that I was lying just as much as I hated the disappointment in her eyes that I was, in her mind, the same man she couldn't trust.

"You don't need to remind me of all the time you haven't been spending with me, and you're right, I guess I just missed it." She started to pull away. I hated it.

"It's been months, Izzy." I tilted her chin toward me and pressed a soft kiss on the corner of her mouth. "And I'm sorry for that. Once this buyout is finished we'll go to the Hamptons or something." I loathed saying that entire sentence. "Maybe even Hawaii?"

"You haven't taken a vacation in over a year, least of all with me."

"Then I'm clearly an idiot for turning down any opportunity of seeing you in a bikini."

She laughed at that. "Ah, honesty at last, you just want sex."

"Who said anything about sex? I just want to stare at you and show you off."

Her entire demeanor changed. She pulled away. Mentally. Physically. Emotionally. "Well, you may have started working out more, but you're still the same on the inside, aren't you?"

"In some ways," I said tightly. "But in others, completely changed."

"I think you're right, about needing rest." She walked away from me. "Do you think you can manage putting on the fresh pullover?"

"I'll make sure to wake you with my cursing if I struggle again." I winked.

I could have sworn I heard her whisper under her breath, "Must be some drugs."

I put on the shirt despite protests from every muscle in my body.

I made dinner.

And when it was time for bed, I crawled in next to her and stared at her back while she slept, wondering how the hell I was going to stay away when all I wanted to do was pull her into my arms and tell her that for now at least, she was safe from my father and that until Julian woke up, I would protect her the way I'd failed to protect Julian.

I would keep her safe.

Even if it meant from the other Tennyson.

The eldest brother meant to rule the empire.

The prodigal who'd never wanted to return but had no choice.

I would keep her from the sweet-tasting poison if it was the last thing I did. Damn, I just *had* to be in the story where not one but two women needed saving, and I had a brother who hated me. I could only hope to God the dragon didn't wake up.

Chapter Ten

Isobel

One week later

He slept a lot.

Not saying it was weird. The guy was healing, and every time I walked into the living room to have the talk about our broken engagement, he'd do something sweet like ask me how my day was going.

I'd officially told the hospital that I wasn't going to be volunteering for a few weeks while Julian healed.

Which left me a lot of free time to go on runs and come home and make sure that everything was as it should be.

Because that's what I'd always done for him.

And because that's what was expected.

I wanted to talk to him about us.

And yet I didn't.

Because he looked at me differently.

It was the worst excuse I could come up with, but there it was, he didn't seem to remember that I was in the process of breaking up with him that day, and even though he said he would need my help with his memory, it just seemed like a really big thing to forget.

"Hey." He was sitting on the couch, the bruising starting to look a little better, and at least his eyes were fully open now, no swelling.

He was the same.

But altered.

In a way that I couldn't explain because he looked exactly the same except for the giant muscles bulging all over his body, which further proved my point that I'd been blind to so much, hadn't I? He'd been cheating and doing God knows what, and apparently lifting weights like it was his new hobby.

"Hi." I tucked my hair behind my ear and made my way to the fridge. "I was going to start dinner. Did you want—"

"Let me help." He was already on his feet, limping over to me. Making me feel slightly guilty for feeling angry at him when he was in such a weakened state. It was difficult to be mad when he was so vulnerable.

Ever since my freak-out with the shoes, he'd been patient, calm, and acted like everything I said was interesting. The old Julian would have been holed up in his office working from home.

The new Julian was offering to help me cook.

I sighed. "Julian, you almost died. Maybe you should just keep taking it easy. It's only been a week, and you know your father will want you back at the offices as soon as you're able."

My stomach clenched.

Why was I upset about him working?

It wasn't like we were spending much time together at the apartment. We were like passing ships in the night.

And yet I could swear there was this electric charge every single time he walked by me, like he was a stranger, but with Julian's face and mannerisms.

"I'm fine." He gave me a sweet smile and then grabbed a pot while I pulled out some pasta. "Besides, you've done nothing but take care of me for the past few days. Let me help you. I've been doing nothing but sitting on my ass."

"Because it's bruised," I said under my breath.

Julian let out a little chuckle. "I think my ass is the only thing that's not bruised, but good to know you're concerned about it." He winked. "It is a really nice ass."

Heat flooded my face. "I didn't say that."

"No, you were thinking it." He tapped the side of his head. "Mind reader."

I smiled and rolled my eyes. "Maybe you should have used those magical forces before the car hit you."

"Right, but then I wouldn't have a stunningly sexy woman nursing me back to health."

My whole body began to tremble with want. He rarely complimented me anymore. Did he just call me sexy? I narrowed my eyes at him. "What game are you playing?"

"Game?" He crossed his arms. "Calling my fiancée sexy shouldn't be a game. It's just a truth, like the sky is blue, turtles are green."

"Some are yellow."

"Really?" He took a step toward me. "Are you trying to argue against your own sexiness? Because I could easily list all the things about you that are sexy, starting with the smatter of freckles on your nose. I counted seven, I love them."

Who was this man?

My heart thundered in my chest, with hope, with stupid, painful hope.

"Y-you counted my freckles?"

He nodded, getting closer. The simple gray T-shirt hugged his chest so much that I thought he was going to rip it in half, and his jeans hung low on his hips as his smile spread. "And your eyes."

"What about my eyes?"

"They're pretty, but they look sad more often than they should, and I don't like it. I fucking hate it, Izzy."

"Maybe next time you cheat, you'll remember my eyes then." Anger boiled inside me. How dare he tease me and compliment me when I knew—I *knew*—it wouldn't last. It was the cruelest thing he could do, and yet I didn't want him to stop.

"Won't be a next time." His jaw clenched.

"Don't make promises—"

"Hey . . ." He pulled me into his arms. I felt so safe, so secure. I always thought Julian had the best arms, but now? Now they felt bigger, they felt protective. I wanted desperately to lay my head against his chest while he told me everything was going to be okay, that we would have a future that wasn't overshadowed by his greedy father and his need to control everything down to the clothes I wore and the colors in my closet. "I swear to you that the man standing here, in front of you, will never cheat on you. Ever."

I looked up into his eyes, for the first time noticing that his lashes looked slightly longer. My body screamed it was right, my mind told me that I was hallucinating, because people's eyelashes didn't just change, did they?

I sighed and stepped out of his arms. "Cheat on me one more time, Julian, and we're done."

I felt weak saying that.

I'd said it numerous times to him in the past, and he always apologized profusely and we'd be happy for a while only to go through the same cycle when he'd inevitably cheat again. I stayed because he always seemed so sorry and things would be so good that I'd convince myself he would never do it again. I wanted to believe the best of him, of us, but eventually I realized that I was so tied up in Julian Tennyson and his world and my place in it that I'd lost what made me me. I lost my identity and swapped it out for the one he gave me.

I expected him to say *Done!* like he always did.

Instead, he grabbed my hand and kissed the back of it. "Only a fool would cheat on you."

"So you're a fool now?"

"Jackass, idiot, fool, all of the above." His smile was lazy as his eyes narrowed. "You know, my memory's still a bit cloudy . . . tell me one thing from college that you miss."

I smiled sadly. "Holding your hand."

"Done." He picked up my hand again and squeezed it. "But I'm feeling greedy, what else?"

Oh God, he was staring at me like he used to. I didn't know how to define that look, how to categorize it, how to defend against it, so I let him in and prayed it wouldn't kill me.

"Junk food," I said in a serious voice. "I miss ice cream. No, I don't just miss ice cream, I miss chocolate, I miss SpaghettiOs, and all the junk food we used to keep in the apartment before your trust fund."

"SpaghettiOs." He nodded. "With or without meatballs?"

"Julian, don't insult me, there's only one way, and that's with meat!"

He burst out laughing and pulled me against him. "I could get on board with that."

"Really?" My eyebrows rose to my hairline. "The last time you caught me eating junk food, in the closet, mind you, you warned me that I was going to get fat."

He pulled away from me, grabbed a knife, and handed it over. "You should probably stab me for that, just make sure you don't hit anything vital. You were supposed to be a nurse, so . . ." He squeezed his eyes shut. "I'll wait."

I gave him a silly look. "I'm not going to stab you. It was a year ago, and it was only peanut butter M&Ms."

He let out a gasp. "The king of M&M's. That's a crime; I think I owe you a five-pound bag."

"And if I gain five pounds?" I countered, knowing what he would say.

"Then . . ." He lowered his eyes and checked out my backside. "I'll pray it's in your ass."

I gently shoved him. "You always said you were a boob guy."

"Nah." He checked me out again, my own fiancé, and I liked it; no, I loved it. "I think you just converted me . . ."

"Eyes up here," I teased.

"I can't help it . . ." he whispered. "You're breathtaking."

And for the first time in three years.

I believed him.

Chapter Eleven

BRIDGE

Two weeks later

I was going stir-crazy. My dad was texting on a daily basis. The board was getting antsy and since news of my miraculous recovery was all anyone talked about or printed in the paper, he wanted me to come into the office and make an appearance.

My first of many.

The board would know it was Bridge walking through those doors.

The rest of the world would assume all was right within Tennyson Financial, and Julian would rest while I quietly did what he couldn't, run a multibillion-dollar company.

Right. What could possibly go wrong?

I still felt exhausted and beat up, so I asked him for one more day.

And it wasn't just because I was still healing, it was because I was intrigued by her, because everything Izzy did had purpose, and because every single time she smiled at me, it was either sad as hell or faraway.

And I hated it.

I let that hate fester in my soul.

My hatred toward my father.

And a growing resentment toward my brother, toward a man I was trying to help. Then again, I hadn't expected to walk into this role and see a whole different side of him through her eyes.

A side that was often cruel.

And selfish.

A side I knew had existed when we were kids but was repressed because we had each other and we had Mom.

Living with Izzy was like living with a horse whose spirit had been broken. I almost wondered what the woman was living for. It sure as hell wasn't Julian.

The only family she now had was mine.

Depressing as fuck, if you asked me.

One more day with her.

And I was still clueless why someone so obviously unhappy would stay in this relationship.

She would be back from her morning run in a few minutes, because her schedule was the same every day. The woman woke up at seven, ran at seven thirty, came home, made a smoothie, stared at the bacon in the fridge like it was going to make itself, sighed, and took a shower.

She'd start making lunch because apparently Julian was such an asshole that he didn't eat sandwiches. When I asked her, she said she knew I would want something hot for my meal.

She was acting like my maid.

I loved the attention, hated the reasons for it.

And she seemed almost insulted when I helped her do anything.

Thank God the flinching finally stopped.

I eyed the door, the knob twisted, and in she came, wearing black running pants, a pink tank top, sweatshirt, and a beanie that looked adorable on her head.

She looked up at me, her gaze narrowed. "Why are you grinning like that?"

"I think it's the hat." I leaned forward, resting my forearms on my thighs. "You look cute in hats."

"Cute?"

"Yeah." I patted the spot next to me on the couch. "In fact, you should probably come over here, with that hat, so I can get a closer look."

"Are you . . ." She swallowed and then put her hands on her hips. "High?"

"High," I deadpanned.

"High," she repeated. "You know, from the drugs you have to keep taking."

"I'm popping Advil," I pointed out. "And no, I'm not high. Can't a man find his fiancée attractive?"

"Oh, he can." She slowly made her way toward me. I was loving those tight leggings and the way they hugged her ass. "But my fiancé hasn't called me cute, ever."

"Then he's a total dick." I meant it too.

She stared at me, and then burst out laughing. "Did the untouchable Julian Tennyson just call himself a dick?"

"I think he did." I shrugged. "Trust me, it was a low blow."

She smirked.

"Very hard," I added.

Soft laughter.

God, I felt like I was winning the Olympics.

Finally!

"Extremely—"

"Disappointing?" she offered.

I dropped my jaw. "Are you calling my dick disappointing?"

She lifted a shoulder like she was challenging me. "Maybe, maybe not."

"I see the gauntlet's been thrown." I stood.

"Oh no you don't." She grabbed my hands. I loved it. I wanted her to hold my hands more. I wanted to tell her I wasn't my asshole brother, that I knew how to use my own equipment so well she'd never want to leave that damn bed and would beg me to cuff her to it. "You're still healing."

"I go back to work tomorrow." My chest felt heavy.

"Yeah." She looked away but didn't drop my hands.

"Which means . . ." I squeezed her fingertips. "You should shower and then come out here and have a movie day with me. It's our last day of freedom before we have to adult again."

"You don't sit and watch movies with me, Julian." Her voice was strong, soft, defiant.

"Ah, but remember I'm turning over a new leaf and I did almost die, so I do, in fact, want to watch movies with you, as soon as possible, and I'll even let you hold the remote because I'm a gentleman," I teased.

She tilted her head to the side. "You're acting funny."

"Again, I almost died. How would you act if you had one day with the most beautiful woman in the world?"

"Now I know you're high," she grumbled.

"Izzy? Please?"

She licked her lips and then finally nodded. "Yeah, I'll watch movies with you, Julian."

She turned around and made her way into the living room, so she didn't see the face I made after she called me by his name.

Or the helpless feeling in my soul when I realized that I was making headway for a man who hated me, and I was falling for a woman who was and would always be his.

Chapter Twelve

ISOBEL

I woke up to texts.

Several texts from Edward asking about how Julian was feeling and if he was coming into work. Was the man insane?

Edward: Where is he? He should be here by now. We have a company to run.

Edward: He isn't answering me, his phone might be off. Tell him he needs to get his ass in the office now.

Edward: This isn't a joke.

Edward: WHERE IS HE!

Finally, I responded.

Isobel: I just woke up, it's only seven in the morning. He nearly died, cut him some slack. Besides, he's never even taken a vacation! He's in a lot of pain, and last night I heard him moaning in his sleep.

Okay, so he was actually doing a lot better and it had been three weeks, but I felt protective. For the first time in months, I didn't want to see Julian walk out that door, I wanted to stay and hold hands with him on the couch, I wanted to feel that thrill in my stomach when he smiled at me or teased me.

God, it had been so long since he'd done any of that.

Edward: I don't care if he's missing his arms and legs, a promise is a promise, please relay this message to him, I'll expect him and you within the hour.

Isobel: Me? Why me?

Edward: I don't explain myself to you. Wear white.

With shaking hands, I dropped my phone back onto the bed and went in search of Julian. I saw him the minute I walked out of the master suite, or I saw skin, a lot of tanned skin, because he wasn't wearing a shirt.

Light bruises marred his back and arms.

I felt my stomach lurch when I saw all the scars covering him; they'd healed fast even if they still looked angry and red. I'd been harsh these past few weeks. Somehow, after a fitful sleep and relaxing with him on the couch I realized I was the one acting crazy for once, not him, yet I had good reason to wait for the other shoe to drop. He'd been everything like the old Julian, the one I had fallen in love with—better actually.

He moved effortlessly around the kitchen, and my stomach grumbled as the smell of bacon filled the air. He looked over his shoulder and called, "Want a cup of coffee?"

See? Normal. Julian always had coffee ready for me in the morning come hell or high water.

Everything was starting off the same, like a typical work morning.

So why was I so disappointed?

He was going back to work.

I was going back to volunteer at the hospital he didn't want me working at.

The last three weeks hadn't happened.

I was on the verge of tears when I answered. "Sure. Yeah." I pulled my hair back into a low ponytail and walked into the kitchen.

Without me even asking, he handed over a black coffee cup with a soft-blue bear in the middle, one of my favorites because it reminded me of simpler times when we used to live on campus and order cheap Chinese. It was one of his first presents to me before his trust fund, before his father gave him a job, before everything.

It was all he could afford.

A black Starbucks mug.

"Cream or sugar?" he asked, his green eyes locking on mine, cream in one hand, two packets of sugar in the other.

I took both packets and nodded to his left hand. "Just a little cream."

He poured it in and turned around again. "I figured you'd be hungry so I made us some breakfast."

"I swear your new love language these past few weeks is feeding me."

He froze, and then flashed me a huge grin. "Are you complaining about your bacon? Because if you are . . ." He started pulling the plate away like he was going to put it back in the cupboard.

I swatted his hand. "Don't you dare."

And then he grabbed mine and kissed my fingertips. "So much better than your morning smoothies, right?"

"Right," I agreed, happy that he was smiling so much, that things might be back to normal routinewise, but that his attitude was still the same. Relaxed.

"Did you get summoned too?" he said after a few more seconds.

"Yeah. It's time." I was silent after that.

He started piling food onto two plates then handed me a fork. "He can wait, life can wait. I almost died and I want breakfast, preferably while sitting next to you. If he can't handle that then he can go to hell." He grinned and then chomped down on a piece of bacon.

And my heart, the one I thought would never heal again, thudded wildly against my chest.

Because for the first time in months, maybe in the last year.

He'd chosen us.

Over his father.

It was a meaningless breakfast, a few stolen moments. But it was enough to lighten the pressure on my chest, enough to make me smile.

I sighed in relief and then covered his left hand with mine. "Good plan."

He just shrugged like he wasn't sure why I looked ready to cry, but he did squeeze my hand back.

It wasn't until later that morning when I was sitting across from Edward and Marla that I realized why his touch had felt foreign.

His hands had calluses.

Chapter Thirteen

BRIDGE

I thought I hated my father more than anyone on this planet. I was wrong. Marla was coming in hot to take his place, and I do mean hot. In the last hour she'd grabbed my ass twice, attempted to stroke my dick once, and was in the process of tugging up her skirt each time she crossed and uncrossed her legs.

I gripped Izzy's hand because I didn't know what else to do, or how else to get the point across.

I wasn't a cheater.

And I would rather get hit by a bus than let her within ten feet of me without a hazmat suit available.

"Julian, son." My father gave me a sly smile. "I know you have a lot going on, but I wanted to bring both of you in here for something important."

Why did I feel like I was getting manipulated?

Why did this feel like another game?

"Of course," I said with clenched teeth. I wanted to tell him to go to hell, but he was holding all the cards, and Mom had a full-time nurse now. She'd texted earlier to check on me and sent a selfie.

She was smiling.

Reading.

She had all her favorite books around her.

And her nurse was grinning in the picture with her.

Safe. Cared for. With enough money to stay living.

So I smiled at my father like he was my partner in crime when in reality I wanted to strangle him until his legs stopped kicking.

I had no updates on Julian, which only made things worse. I was stuck, and he knew it. Julian was still sleeping away the trauma done to his body, and I was the imposter taking his place.

"Once the buyout is complete, we'd like to announce the wedding." My father smiled wide.

I stared at him like he was insane. Because he was. This was never part of the deal. What the hell was his angle now? Our agreement involved a job, not a wedding. Did he really think I'd stoop so low as to marry my brother's fiancée?! How would that help Julian? As much as I hated the way my brother had treated Izzy, I couldn't do that to him. Even though my reasons were honorable, I still felt like I was stealing his life while he fought for it day after day.

"Um." I cleared my throat. "Shouldn't we be focusing on the business deal with IFC first?"

"IFC is almost a done deal, son. We just need the paperwork signed next week. We'll shake hands at the banquet this Friday, take pictures, and announce your wedding date!"

I suddenly felt hot in my impeccably cut, too-tight suit.

I tugged at my tie and stole a glance at Isobel. She'd gone completely still in her chair, her nails dug into my hand.

I didn't blame her.

At all.

"Edward . . ." I hated the tone Izzy used, like she was trying to sound happy and in control when I knew she felt nothing but chaos inside. I could tell by the way she held on to me. Trapped between two Tennysons and a psycho soon-to-be mother-in-law.

Welcome to hell, folks.

"I thought we agreed on next spring."

"We did," my father said softly like he cared, even leaning forward to pat her knee. He disgusted me. "But that was before Julian almost died. We have to think about what would have happened to you. You aren't in his will, you couldn't even see him at the hospital, Marla had to take care of everything because you couldn't. You've been a part of this family for years now. It's time to finally make it legal." He shared a look with Marla. "Should we tell them?"

Shit. Tell us what?

"Of course, darling." She leaned in and kissed his cheek.

The woman could be his daughter.

I waited for the second shoe to drop.

Or for Julian to waltz in and say it was a prank, all of it.

"We were able to secure the club for next week," my father announced. "Not only will you be a part of our family, Isobel, but it's going to be the wedding of the year. Several designers have already contacted our publicity team, and you know how the press has been dying to get more details. It will be a welcome distraction from the accident. After all, we lost a lot of money that day. The only way to recoup losses is to get the contracts signed and to give the public, the media, the shareholders something else to focus on. You two."

I was going to be sick.

No wonder he didn't want Izzy to know it was me, not Julian. He'd had a plan all along, hadn't he? Get us married and give the world a huge distraction. I knew how much he would probably gain financially from a single wedding, how much free press his company would get after one of the biggest buyouts in history. And not just free press. He would direct the media's attention to the Tennyson good fortune. A buyout, a miraculous healing, and the wedding of the year? All within a few weeks? It was too good to be true, like a Hollywood drama with requisite happy ending. There would be countless interviews, media coverage to salivate over, not to mention endorsement deals. And he'd be laughing all the way to the bank while waving at the adoring public.

He wasn't just using Julian's accident as an excuse, he was using it as a way to make money.

Sick bastard.

Dad gave me a blank stare and then smiled like he knew I was ready to jump across the coffee table but couldn't.

One week.

I was getting married in one week.

Without my mother.

To someone who didn't belong to me.

I wasn't stupid.

I'd signed a contract that said I would take on everything about Julian from his mannerisms to his belongings.

According to that contract . . . I *was* Julian Tennyson.

And Julian Tennyson was engaged.

I needed air.

I stood, noticed my father's thunderous expression, and quickly sat back down and lazily wrapped an arm around Izzy. "Dad, you know that's not very fair to Izzy. She wanted to plan her own wedding and now everything's getting done without her input. She doesn't even get to shop for a dress."

She might already have a dress, but I had no idea and could blame the accident for my bad memory.

"She'll wear what's chosen for her by the team. They have a few designers lined up for the rehearsal dinner, ceremony, and of course the reception," Marla said with glee. "They'll be outfitting the entire family."

"Great," I said through clenched teeth. "What do you say, Izzy?"

Please let this be the time where she decides to stand up to my father or starts crying, reacting, doing anything that saves us from this fate. Because pretending, kissing her hand, flirting was one thing.

A wedding was something else entirely, wasn't it?

Julian would hate me.

No, he wouldn't just hate me.

He would never speak to me again. What progress I might have made with him by filling in while he healed would be demolished. Because I knew if I was in his position and I woke up to find that my twin had not only touched what was mine but had sex with her or even saw her naked—blind rage filled my line of vision.

And I hated myself, because that's exactly what I would be doing. What groom doesn't have sex with his bride? Could I even excuse myself out of that with a headache?

Shit.

Tears filled her eyes. She quickly wiped under her right eye and smiled a forced smile that made me want to strangle everyone in that room. "It sounds like you've thought of everything."

"We really have," my father responded swiftly. It was a double meaning; he really had thought of everything, hadn't he?

I stood quickly. "Can I discuss something with you, Dad? In private?"

"Of course!" Damn, he was a good actor. I knew better than most how much he loathed me. Probably because I was everything Julian wasn't. Good, let him hate me for being taller, thicker, for not needing his approval or wanting it.

"Isobel, you and Marla probably have a lot to talk about. Why don't you step into the conference room and go over a few details? I'll have some champagne sent in."

Damn it, at least she got champagne out of this, while I was getting nothing but hives and severe pain in my right side where my ribs had snapped.

The women left.

The doors closed.

I turned on him. "You sick son of a bitch!"

"Is that any way to talk to your father, Julian?" He grinned menacingly and moved to sit behind his massive desk, which was placed in front of giant windows that overlooked the financial district.

The Tennyson family was focused on one thing and one thing alone: money.

And I was helping him rule.

I looked into his eyes, thinking for a second that for sure they would roll back while horns popped through the skin on his forehead. Instead, his eyes were green just like mine, his obviously dyed jet-black hair was slicked back, and what wrinkles he had lining his face were in obvious defiance against the Botox he probably stuck into them on a biweekly basis. His all-black suit was pulled tight around his gut, and his heavily ringed fingers clasped behind his back like he didn't have a care in the world.

Why would he?

He controlled it.

"I'm not Julian," I hissed, lunging toward his desk.

He held up his right hand. "Actually, I have a contract that says you are. Utter one more sentence like that again, and I'll have your mother institutionalized. Are we clear?"

"She's sick, not crazy."

"People believe what I tell them." He smiled. "Remember who holds the keys to this massive kingdom and we'll be just fine. You will marry her, you will say your vows with adoration and love in your voice, you will give her your body and your soul, and when Julian wakes up, we talk. What he doesn't know won't kill him." He sighed, and for the first time I saw the stress in his eyes as he jabbed his finger into a stack of papers. "Not that you care, but there's been talk these last three weeks. Talk about you not being mentally able to continue working for me, talk that you and Isobel are headed for a split . . ."

My stomach dropped. "Well, maybe if someone could keep it in his pants."

My dad's eyes flashed. "It's part of the game, son, part of the lifestyle. Julian knows how to play the game well. He knows the sacrifices that need to be made. Do you?"

"I'm only in this for Julian and Mom."

"Exactly," my dad snapped. "You were always so stubborn, so defiant. At the time I saw it as a weakness, now I see it as your greatest strength. Prove the media wrong and get the deal inked." He opened a leather folder and turned it around, showing it to me.

"Thirty percent equity," I read out loud, "of Tennyson Financial." My stomach dropped. "Bridge Anderson, dated—" My entire body swayed as I continued reading the stipulations. All the zeroes. And the little yellow brick road that took me into marriage with Izzy and a big fat check I would cash once we said "I do." "Are you telling me that I've had a trust fund this entire time?"

Dad gave me a smug look. "I figured you'd come to your senses, that you'd finally realize the grass was greener. You think I don't know you work two jobs? Sometimes three? That you can barely put food on the table with her medical bills?"

"So?" I threw my hands up in the air. "I've had money this entire time? And what? You want me to finally claim it?" Blood money, that's what it was.

"Son, it's your inheritance. Besides, Julian was the one that kept pressuring me to contact you after you graduated from school, but months turned into years, and well, if I'm being honest, I didn't want to give that woman you call your mother a cent."

I flinched. "You cheated on her."

"She left me," my father fired back. "Me!"

"Ah." I crossed my arms. "Pride still bruised?"

He narrowed his eyes. "Take the portfolio. If you have questions, I left a card from one of the company lawyers in front. It's your choice.

Once Julian is awake, you'll walk away a very rich man." If I married Izzy. If I did what he said. If I kept my mouth shut. And then what? I'd just pass her off to my brother? After all of that? She would be left to believe that he'd been here the whole time, and I'd be taking money for it.

"What happens if he doesn't?" I was afraid to ask, but it needed to be out there in the universe. It felt like the sentence hung between us, unsure of its own answer as much as I was.

Dad sobered and then stared me down. "I refuse to believe that any of my sons would be so weak as to give in to death."

I shook my head. "You're insane."

"Maybe." He shrugged. "Maybe not. But everything I have is because I've fought for it. We sign contracts Monday, we celebrate this weekend at the banquet with IFC. Try not to look so pissed. You're about to have sex with one of *People*'s most beautiful women alive, son. Just think about it, while your brother's dreaming of unicorns, you'll be between her thighs. Tell me, which do you prefer?"

At the sharp pain in my jaw, I realized I had clenched it tight. "Talk about her like that again and I'm going to—"

"I don't have time for any more petty threats. We both know you signed an ironclad contract. Take Isobel home, convince her any way you know how. You have one day before the announcement. I suggest you attempt to look better than you do now so the board sees you as fit to run Tennyson Financial. Try not to be an embarrassment. I know it's your default, but you're a Tennyson above all else, and people will be watching."

I fisted my hands, beyond prepared to use them on my father. "I'm twice the man you are. Watch me."

And before I gave him my back, I saw it, the flicker of excitement and challenge in his eyes.

My father loved control.

He loved a challenge more.

And I'd just jumped into the arena and asked him to fight.

One way or another there would be blood.

Chapter Fourteen

Isobel

Julian rescued me about thirty minutes later. At about that time Marla was arguing with me over flowers and cake, and I had a fleeting memory of my birthday last year when things were still good between us, when Julian bought me the biggest cake I'd ever seen and told me it tasted like strawberries, just like me.

I'd blushed.

He'd kissed me soundly in front of everyone.

And I'd thought, *This is perfect.*

What we have is perfect.

"Sweetheart." Julian's voice made me jump as he poked his head in the conference room. His body looked massive in the doorway, his suit too small, and his confidence was like a tsunami headed straight toward the table. "Time to go."

Marla sighed next to me, and I almost strangled her. It wasn't a sigh of anger, it was a sigh of jealousy.

A sigh that said she wanted to touch him.

That her Tennyson was too old and she thought she deserved mine.

I wasn't getting out of this wedding. I could see the veiled threat beneath Edward's gaze, the way he looked at me with a forced smile. He would get his way. That much I knew. And I hated to admit that a part of me, after these last three weeks, was thrilled at the thought that maybe, just maybe this was going to be the game changer for us. Julian was getting back to being the man I fell in love with in college. Maybe the pressure of becoming CEO had been too much. He was always so worried about his dad being proud of him, and well, now it seemed like he'd rather strangle his own father than wait for him to say he was proud.

He was becoming his own man.

I flashed him a smile and gripped my purse, trying to sidestep him since we were in the office and he was always adamant that there be no PDA. Instead, he grabbed me by the shoulders and kissed me softly on the mouth, earning a curse from Marla and a few shocked gasps from people passing by.

I swayed on my feet a bit and almost touched my lips. *What just happened?*

"I can't wait to marry you," he said so genuinely that I felt tears well in my eyes. "Why don't we go to lunch and we can talk about all the ways we can piss my father off. I'm thinking Twinkies instead of a cake, you?"

Marla gasped in her seat. "The cake has already been—"

"Marla, you must be under the impression I was talking to you." Frost laced his voice as he added, "I wasn't."

I gawked at Julian. He didn't even look at her.

I could feel her anger behind me. If she could dig her nails into my back and hold tight she would. I had no doubts about it.

"Lunch sounds good." I found my voice; it sounded off, like I couldn't quite catch my breath. It could be the butterflies in my stomach, or it could be the way my heart was hammering in my chest.

Because it was the first time in forever that he'd kissed me in front of people at his office, and in front of her.

And it was the first time in six months that he'd made me feel owned.

Like I really was his.

This was what danger felt like.

But I couldn't find it in my heart to do anything but cling to him as we walked through the offices and entered the elevators.

"Thank you," I said once the doors closed behind us. "For that, with Marla, back there, I . . ." Damn it, I couldn't get emotional now. He'd use it against me. "I can't stand her."

"She probably can't even stand herself." He grinned.

"Funny, since you seem to be alone with her a lot."

Julian stiffened.

Why couldn't I just keep my mouth shut and stop attacking him? It did nothing but make me angry over his lies and him angry over my inability to believe them!

I felt like I was in this constant state of push-pull; I wanted his promises, I wanted that kiss, but what I wanted wasn't real. I would always be disappointed in the end, and I knew any more disappointments where Julian was concerned would prove devastating. The heart was only so strong.

I pulled away from him.

I couldn't handle the feeling he had given me in the last three weeks, the feeling of my heart beating faster, my fingers yearning for his touch, my mouth telling me his lips would feel different this time. My treacherous body was so on board with the way he was making me feel—nurtured, cared for—that I wanted to slap myself. It was almost more cruel than the cheating, than the words, than the stupid maid.

Movement caught my eye as he hit the red button on the elevator, stopping it in its place and jolting both of us against the wall.

"Look at me." His voice was commanding but soft.

We locked eyes.

I waited for the demeaning words, for the threats, for the *Don't you love me and want to make me happy?*

Julian got down on one knee and grabbed my hand. "Forgive me."

"Wh-what?"

"Forgive me." His eyes pleaded. "For being a jackass, for not seeing what was in front of me all along, for getting in over my head, but most of all for not seeing you. Forgive me for forgetting the most important thing in my life. I haven't been good to you. At all. I want to fix that. I need to fix that."

"Stop, just stop." I tried to pull free, but he held me there with his hands, with the pleading in his eyes. "You can't just ask for forgiveness and make everything okay! I know how this works, Julian, I'm not stupid. Maybe things will be great for now, but sooner or later, there will be another maid, another model, actress, receptionist. I want to believe you, but I don't. I'm sorry."

He stood abruptly. "Then I'll prove it to you. I swear. I'll be different."

It was on the tip of my tongue to say he already had been.

"What happens when you can't do it, Julian?"

"If I mess up . . ." He cupped my face with his hands. "If I go back on my promise, kick me in the balls and ask for a divorce."

"And the prenup?"

"Fuck the prenup," he said swiftly. "At the very least you should be given money for emotional suffering if I do anything to hurt you again."

I still wasn't convinced.

I wanted to be, but I knew how good a manipulator he was.

I could walk away.

I could leave this.

I still had time.

"Izzy." He cupped my chin with the barest touch and locked eyes with me. "Let me prove myself to you. Please, just one more chance to show you that the most important thing in my life is not just your heart but your future—our future. Give me until the wedding, let me show you how it should be, and if you're still not satisfied, I'll call it off myself."

It was everything I'd always wanted to hear.

It couldn't be real.

I looked at him, really looked at him. "Don't you think it's too late to ask for that, Julian? I'll admit you've been acting different, really different. But something feels off. Maybe it's the sudden attitude change, or maybe it's the fact that you almost died. I just . . . I'm terrified of putting myself out there again. Besides that, it feels like I'm still missing something."

"I am. Different, that is."

"What are you talking about?" I just had to point it out even though I felt stupid stating the obvious. He tensed and then relaxed against me.

"I'm whoever you need me to be right now, Izzy, even if that means I need to be the white knight that rescues you from the castle you're trapped in, or the guy that feeds you junk food so you smile for a while. Trust when I say that I'm me, and that's all that matters."

What did I expect him to say? That he was a reincarnated version of himself only he kept the better parts that seemed to get sucked away by his own father year after year?

His eyes zeroed in on my mouth.

I wanted him to press me against the elevator wall, to kiss me senseless. I wanted so many things, like the passion we used to feel between each other when we always felt like we didn't have enough time to be together.

"I missed you," I whispered, more to myself, and then shook my head. I still didn't trust him, not completely. "I'm tired, let's . . . let's do lunch another day, alright?" I put distance between us and hit the stop button again. The elevator made a groaning noise as it descended once again toward the lobby.

"Why?" he asked once we were walking side by side through the glass doors out into the bustle of suits walking like a sea of fish in front of us.

I put on my Prada sunglasses, looked up at the skyscrapers, and inhaled deeply. "Because you'll be on your phone the entire time while I make excuses to the waiter over you sending back your blackened salmon, and I'm not in the mood."

"Pizza." He let out a low chuckle. "That way I'm not tempted."

I whipped my head around and stared at him. "Pizza? You?"

"You've seen my six-pack. I think I can take it."

"Yeah, your swollen six-pack." I rolled my eyes. "Something isn't right, Julian. I know that, you know that. Are we just going to pretend there isn't some elephant hiding in the room ready to pop out at any point and ruin everything?"

He was silent for a minute and then, "I don't think we really have a choice, do you, Izzy?"

I sighed in defeat. "When it comes to Edward Tennyson, no, you rarely have a choice."

Chapter Fifteen

Pizza.

You'd think I'd just offered her an animal sacrifice with the way she looked at me when I said that word. I was doing everything wrong when it came to her, but I couldn't stand one more minute of her flinching or pulling away or thinking that I was the monster in this story even when all signs still pointed to me being exactly that.

Mom was getting treatment.

Julian was healing.

If I focused on those two things, I could justify everything else.

A few cameras homed in on us while we sat there and ate. I looked up and froze as I eyed the flat-screen in the corner. It showed Julian's face and was talking about the miraculous recovery, him becoming CEO, finance's golden boy. To the world, Julian Tennyson was perfect.

And breathing on his own.

One thing was for certain, the accident was still front-page news, which irritated me even more because that meant Dad was right.

The media needed something else to talk about.

I stared across the table at Izzy, then reached for her hand and squeezed it.

All I wanted to do was tell her the whole sordid story. I was the other half, the part my father didn't want. I was the one that got in fights at school trying to protect Julian, I was the brother who didn't care about his grades and flirted my way through my eighth grade year knowing the world was mine because of who my dad was, even though we didn't have a good relationship. I was arrogant, rash, and didn't care about anything but my brother and my mom.

And Julian? Julian was the one I always wanted to protect, the brother who I'd find crying himself to sleep after he showed our dad his A only to have that father ask him why it wasn't an A-plus. I always told Julian that grades were bullshit, but it was never enough. All he wanted—all he *ever* wanted—was that moment you see in the movies were the dad hugs the son and says, "Well done."

Julian would be waiting an eternity.

"So . . ." I bit off a large piece of pepperoni pizza and let out a moan that earned me at least two stares from people sitting across the room and a slack-jawed expression from Izzy. "Sorry, that's incredible. I was starving." I took another bite and wiped my face with my napkin, then said to hell with it and polished off the entire piece.

Izzy cut her pizza with her knife and fork, hands shaking, and lifted a piece to her perfect pout.

"No." I shook my fork at her. "That not how you eat pizza."

"I'm wearing all white."

That was another thing. "*Why* are you wearing all white?" I just had to ask, not that she wasn't beautiful with her pink lips and cascading hair.

She frowned like I should know the answer then shrugged. "Your father says white's a powerful color. It's hard to clean, expensive to put together, and always stands out in a room full of suits. The man likes all his women in white."

I scowled. "Once we're married I give you permission to burn all the white clothes and start wearing sweats. It's the least I can do. Besides, white seems too innocent."

She choked on her sip of water and croaked out, "Are you saying I'm not innocent?"

Was she flirting or pissed?

I went with flirting and leaned forward. "You tell me."

Her cheeks flushed. "We're in public."

"So that's a no for sex next to the pizza?"

Her eyes widened a fraction before she tugged in her lower lip and sucked it. "Remember that time senior year at the Mexican restaurant?" No. And I didn't want to know how my brother had his mouth on her, or how she screamed his name, would scream his name, not mine.

"I'd love to hear you tell me." I had no other choice.

"Hmmm, not appropriate, just like it wasn't appropriate for you to lock us in the only bathroom and hike my dress up past my hips when you found out I wasn't wearing any underwear."

I choked down a bite of pizza and tried not to let my mind go there, even though it completely did. Her, no underwear, me hiking up her skirt.

I smiled at that. "What did you expect would happen?"

"Hah, that's exactly what I wanted to happen, and you know it. I was always trying to make you push your boundaries. You know how you were, so worried about your brand, your family's image, what your dad would say if he found out you were having sex in the bathroom . . ." Her voice trailed off, her smile slipped. "Sorry, what was the question?"

"Oh, that." I tossed down my napkin. "Public nudity. Yea or nay?" I started to stand. Her arm jerked out and she grabbed my hand, her eyes wide with horror.

With a smug laugh, I leaned across the table and pressed a chaste kiss to her lips. "I'm too jealous to let everyone see your body. Let's just say that's the reason I'm not shoving the pizza aside and tossing parmesan on your belly button so I can see how long it will take me to lick it off."

"Wow," she rasped with a giggle. "You think that's what's gonna make me happy? A little parmesan?"

"First of all." I sat back down. "Cheese."

"Hah!" She sipped her Diet Coke. "You've got me there. And second?"

"I think feeling free will make you happy."

She dropped her fork, splattering tiny dots of red sauce all over the front of her white silk tank and a few on her white tuxedo jacket.

"Here." I stood and helped her out of her jacket then grabbed a napkin and dipped it into the water. "We probably need to get it dry cleaned but it's not enough to ruin it, unless that was your intention, and then my suggestion would be to just take two slices and put them facedown on your chest. More dramatic that way." I winked.

She gawked and then burst out laughing. "Who are you?"

"Just me." I smiled at her. "You still look beautiful despite the stains, you know."

She shifted her gaze away.

"I hate that I've done that, forced you to look away when I give you a compliment," I said softly, returning to my seat. "You really are beautiful, though. I'm sorry for not saying it enough." Or possibly at all.

She searched my eyes. I wondered if she saw me there, not Julian, but me, Bridge. I wondered if she saw the purity of the words, the sincerity behind them, the man standing in front of her, pretending to be better than the one she would be stuck with the rest of her life.

I wondered if she saw the lie.

Izzy's lips parted. She licked the bottom one and exhaled softly. "You're going to break my heart, aren't you?"

And because I didn't want to be him, because I couldn't stand to hear the lie fall from my lips.

I kissed her cheek and whispered a weak "Yes."

Chapter Sixteen

ISOBEL

That night, I lay in bed with tears streaming down my cheeks, tears of misunderstanding, mistrust, confusion, and finally, lust.

Lust and love for a man who was acting like the man I'd fallen head over heels in love with in college.

He'd been healing in the guest room since after that first night back and said since he was getting up so much to take Advil it was best we sleep apart. I thought it was just another ruse so that I wouldn't notice when he left to go meet with the maid or with whomever he was cheating.

But true to his word, he'd been different.

"Hey . . ." Julian walked into the room. He was walking better, actually, and his face was damn near perfect again, intense, sharper, and perfect. He flashed me a smile and then pulled his shirt over his head, keeping his low-slung pajama pants on. He crawled into bed and pulled me into his arms. "I heard you crying and then talking to yourself. I just wanted to make sure you were okay and also double-check that you weren't sticking a voodoo doll with pins since my ribs still feel like death."

"I'd just kick you, not resort to magic," I said through a sniffle. "And I didn't realize I was being so loud."

"Izzy," he sighed and held me tighter. It felt so good.

The way he held me was perfect.

The way he spoke to me, straightforward, honest.

God, how I'd missed honesty with another human being. I hadn't realized how much I needed to hear truth.

He'd said he was going to break my heart.

And I believed him.

And I also didn't care, because for now, he was healing it. Better let my heart get broken by this version of Julian than get suffocated by the older version I knew would return one day.

I wracked my brain for reasons behind his behavior and his physical appearance, but the only thing I came up with was he'd finally realized that his father's approval wasn't worth it, that our love was stronger than all the things in the world he thought he needed, money, power, position.

For the first time in our relationship, I didn't have a sick feeling about what was coming, or what Edward would do next.

Because Julian was strong now.

And we had each other.

He kept claiming that being near death changed a person. If that was the case, when did that feeling wear off? I almost googled it because I felt like I was losing my mind.

Julian kissed me on my cheek and turned on his side. He didn't touch me, which was strange, now that he was back in our bed. We knew each other inside and out, and he knew that I always wanted to at least touch him as I fell asleep. We used to fall asleep holding hands. It helped me feel safe, wanted, and then six months ago it turned into this touch of possession and I'd hated it, like he was fighting to keep me by his side when he knew I was already pulling away.

I had almost forgotten what it was like to find peace in your sleep.

Except now I needed comfort and I didn't know how to ask for it. I turned to face him.

He was on his side and the bruises were barely visible.

And every muscle seemed to flex even in his sleep.

A thrill shot through me as I watched him.

I ignored common sense, I ignored rational thinking, and I just accepted what was lying in front of me, the man I would soon marry.

Julian sighed again. I knew he was exhausted. After the pizza, he had lain on the couch and gone over document after document that I knew he'd already memorized. He reminded me that his memory was fuzzy.

So I'd gone to bed and stayed there.

I reached to touch his face and was surprised when his hand shot out and grabbed my wrist. He brought that same hand to his lips and pressed a kiss to my fingertips. "Change your mind about the voodoo doll?"

I smiled as his eyes opened. They crinkled sexily at the sides, and his smirk was playful like he was getting ready to pounce on me and kiss me senseless. Butterflies took flight in my stomach as I watched his green eyes smolder, lock onto my mouth, and then onto my eyes. "Well?"

"I was just thinking."

"Thinking's completely overrated," he said quickly. "Thinking is what gets us into messes we can't get out of. The best decisions in life are made from the heart, from the soul, from the place that most people refuse to listen to anymore."

I gaped. "This coming from the man who overthinks and analyzes everything."

"Yeah, well . . ." He licked his full lips. "Some things change. Maybe nearly dying's caused me to rethink a few things."

"Ah-hah, you said *think*," I teased.

He kissed my fingertips again then pulled my arm around his shoulders. He gripped me by the ass and tugged my body flush against his. "Guess what I'm thinking now."

I gulped and tried to insult him. "You're thinking about mergers, portfolios, money."

"Who in their right mind would be thinking about money right now?" He chuckled low in his throat. "I have a beautiful woman staring at me while I try to sleep. I'm not thinking about anything except you. That's the truth."

"Me over money. I have to say it's been a while."

"Pathetic that it should even be an issue, right?"

"Right."

"Izzy?"

"Yeah?"

"Don't overthink this moment, alright? Don't overthink anything, just exist today. Hell, wait to use your brain for at least another year, just be present, with me."

I stared him down. Who was this man? Had Julian come back to me? Had he realized that life was too short to constantly worry about what people thought? About money? Image?

"I think"—he leaned in and kissed my chin—"that you're doing it again."

"Sorry, I just . . ." I dug my hand into his thick, dark hair and started playing with it, remembering how he used to let me touch him while we lay in bed, and all the years that followed where he wasn't even in bed with me anymore. "You're different, I'm trying to adjust, I feel like I'm walking on eggshells, like any minute I'm going to do something wrong and you're going to snap, and this is going to be gone and—" Oh God, I was going to start crying again. "I just can't . . . I don't know what to do, just tell me what to do."

"Damn it." He wrapped his arms around me and turned me onto my back as his body covered mine. "That's not what I wanted to do. I don't want you to doubt. Like I said, we still have a wedding to get through, a life to live."

"What happens after the wedding, Julian?"

His expression shuttered and he looked away, face filling with rage. "We'll figure it out, together."

"Promise?"

"I swear, this man that I am now won't abandon you."

I exhaled in relief. "And you're not going to get mad if I wear flats?"

His laugh did funny things to me as he ran his fingers through my hair. "Wear whatever you want, just make sure you have clothes on, because the last thing we need is for me to end up in prison over you walking the streets naked."

I laughed. "Do you know me at all? That's the last thing I would ever do. Remember, I haven't even been skinny-dipping."

His look was playful, his eyes twinkled. Damn, the man was beautiful to look at, too beautiful, too tempting. I should have looked away, but I found I couldn't, I was living for the next words out of his mouth, the deep voice that said my name. I was falling for him again, falling into the same old trap. I played along. I played into it, fully knowing that I would never come back from whatever this was.

I only had a few pieces of my heart left.

And I knew he would demand them all.

"Tell me something you wish you could do but are too afraid to pull off."

My eyebrows shot up. "Hmmm, I thought you knew everything about me."

"Humor me," he said, resting his forehead against mine, waiting patiently for my answer.

It was hard to focus with him staring at me so intently, with his warm muscled body covering mine protectively like he would do anything to keep me safe. "I always wanted to be a part of a flash mob."

"Tame." He nodded. "But I'll take it." He tilted his head. "A flash mob, huh? Why's that?"

"It just seems so . . ." I shrugged. "Magical, like all those romantic comedies you see where everyone knows the same song and dance, everyone's happy and part of the same wonderful thing." I sighed. "I know it sounds childish, but—"

"Not." He covered my mouth with two fingers. "Not at all."

"Alright, what about you?"

"Ahhh, so we're both playing?"

"It's only fair."

"It's two a.m."

"Is it?"

"Hah." He grinned. "You're cute, you know that?"

"You're full of compliments, and you're also deflecting," I pointed out.

He sighed. "Fine, I've always wanted to go to culinary school."

"What?" I almost shot up out of bed. He'd never shared that with me before, not in all the years we'd known each other. "But you majored in business, and you were always going to take over for your father."

"Exactly." He sounded disgusted. "It may look nice, knowing that you never have to worry about money, but what you don't take into account is passion. I love cooking. I love food. I love the looks on people's faces when they try something you just made up. It's a pipe dream, one I will never follow, but that's the thing about dreams. Even if we don't accomplish them, they still exist, floating around in our psyche reminding us that there are things we need to do before we leave this earth, and making us feel resentful that we'll probably never be able to do them."

I was quiet for a minute. "Do you think your father would—"

"Yeah, I'm gonna stop you right there. We both know how he is."

"I have a confession."

"Wow, two in one night? How'd I get so lucky?" he teased, tucking my hair behind my ear and patiently waiting for my next words, like he was just happy to be in that moment with me, talking, when I knew we both had a busy few days ahead of us. He always woke up before the crack of dawn to work out. Time was a precious commodity he didn't have enough of, and yet there we were, using it up to talk about things that would never come true.

How wonderful and heartbreaking.

I wasn't sure how he would respond to what I was going to say, but at least it would be proof that he really was trying to change. "I always thought that's what you wanted, to be exactly like your father."

Julian made a disgusted face then quickly recovered as if he hadn't done it. He shook his head and looked away. "Nobody wants to be Edward Tennyson, not even Edward Tennyson."

I was so shocked I couldn't speak. "Are you actually admitting that you don't want that life?"

"What I want"—his words toppled over each other—"is a life of my own, on my own terms, with you."

My heart melted as he ducked his head and pressed a feather-soft kiss to my lips.

It wasn't his normal kiss.

I defined Julian's kisses and separated them into boxes. There was the kiss he gave me in public, hardly any tongue, but he held my embrace long enough to prove ownership. There was the kiss in the privacy of his office as opposed to home, often on the cheek, sometimes on the corner of my mouth because in his mind there was no room for PDA at work. There was the kiss he gave me when he wanted sex, usually sloppy, aggressive, dominating. And then there was the kiss he gave me when he wanted me to do something I didn't want to do.

That kiss was always, sadly, perfect.

This kiss didn't fit into any of those boxes; it had no definitions, no restrictions, no hidden meanings.

This kiss was raw.

Powerful.

This was the sort of kiss that made a person forget their own name and pray never to remember it again.

His lips felt swollen as they slid against mine, his hands gripped the sides of my face like he was holding something precious. The weight of his body was delicious and hot.

Julian rocked his hips slowly against me like he was asking permission when I was already mentally stripping myself bare for him.

His tongue pressed and twisted as he switched angles, deepening the kiss, making me whimper when he pulled away, chest heaving, to stare at me.

I wasn't sure how long we stayed in each other's arms like that, breathless, wanting more.

Finally, I broke the silence by saying, "You've never kissed me like that before."

Something flared in his eyes as he whispered, "Good."

He looked away like he was ashamed. I wanted to ask why, but then he shifted his gaze back to me and kissed my forehead. "Sleep."

I would have to be blind not to see the evidence of his arousal or the way every muscle in his body was strung tight, ready for attack.

He was holding back.

And for once, I didn't want him to.

I wanted all of him.

But a part of me was scared that the minute I opened myself up to whatever this new version of him was—I would be crushed.

And as I gave him a watery smile and tucked myself against his chest and closed my eyes, I remembered his warning.

He would break my heart.

A part of me wondered if he already had.

Chapter Seventeen

BRIDGE

I slept like complete shit.

Felt like a monster.

Woke up and went to the home gym and started lifting like a madman. Julian had a nice setup, though I needed heavier dumbbells and weights, but this would have to do for now.

Three hours after kissing her, I got up and started pumping iron. It was the only way I could keep myself from taking her, from doing the worst sort of thing a man in my position could do.

Take advantage of someone who thought I was someone else, a man she used to love, when I was a complete stranger.

The more I thought about it, the sicker I became.

Is that what being a Tennyson did to someone? Did it make you justify everything to get what you want?

Last night I justified the kiss because I told myself that's what he would have done, and then I mentally berated myself because I was being a complete dick and I had nobody to call me out on it.

I couldn't seduce her when she thought I was him.

I couldn't fall for her while he reaped the credit for my good behavior when he was a complete jackass who happened to be in a coma.

I couldn't do any of those things.

I dropped my dumbbell on the ground, wiped the sweat from my brow with my towel, and looked up.

There she was, an angel of torture in spandex and a tank top. Her arms were crossed, making her breasts look like they needed to be released because they were bound too tight, and since I was the only person available . . .

I needed to get the fuck out of that apartment.

She tossed me a clean towel and winked. "Thought we could work out together."

My jaw dropped when she bent over to tie her shoe, giving me a wonderful view of her ass. "You want to work out . . . with me?"

Come on, dumbass, you're a personal trainer!

"Why not?" She grinned. "You said you've been lifting more and . . ." Her face fell at my expression. "Actually, it's okay, I can just go get on the elliptical—"

"If you value your life, you will not finish that sentence," I grumbled. "The elliptical isn't even a real machine. A workout usually produces sweat, you shouldn't be able to have a full conversation with your best friend while reading *Cosmo* and call it working out."

Her eyebrows shot up with amusement. "Oh? And Mr. I-go-for-runs-and-use-my-Bluetooth-the-whole-time comes from a place of knowledge on this?"

No wonder she was shocked at my body. My brother was an idiot for not noticing her more, for not giving her everything in the fucking world. For not seeing that she just wanted to be loved.

"Like I said, things change." I gave her a half smile and pointed to the weight rack. "Pick up some tens, I'm gonna put you through an intense arm circuit, then we're going to do a Tabata."

"Tabata?" she repeated. "Is that some sort of dance?"

"Oh, sweetheart." I laughed. "You'll wish."

To her credit, she didn't complain once, she never gave me any of the nasty looks I was used to when I put someone through a high-intensity training workout. She just did what she was asked.

Watching her do squats and spotting her was pure torture. We'd quickly moved from upper body to lower body, and now I was watching her ass go slowly down and up, down and up. Perfect form, perfect thighs.

"Is this right?" she called over her shoulder.

I jerked my head to attention, made a noncommittal noise that sounded like I was choking on something, and then squeezed out a hoarse "Yes."

I did this for a living.

I had loads of female clients, all of whom tried to hit on me at one point in their training. Yet one innocent back squat from a woman who wasn't even trying to tempt me was going to be my downfall.

"Alright." I cleared my throat. "Let's do three more."

I squeezed my eyes shut for a few brief seconds then watched, I watched like it was my last meal, and I wondered yet again how my brother had gotten so damn lucky.

I helped her rack the weights and tossed her a towel, my mind a chaotic mixture of curiosity and jealousy. "Tell me something you remember about us."

She gave me a funny look.

"I mean before all of this."

"Ah, you mean before the trust funds and fancy cars. You've always had money, you just didn't have access to it. It didn't mean you didn't have the nicest car on campus or most expensive clothes I've ever seen." She frowned and patted her sweaty chest with the towel while I sucked in a shaky breath and waited for more words, more clues into how this even happened. "My favorite memory is how we met."

"Oh?" I was dying with curiosity. "I want to hear the story from your point of view . . ."

She laughed softly. "You rarely travel down memory lane, you sure you want to do that now, with me all sweaty and you . . ." Her voice trailed off as she swallowed slowly and looked away. "Also sweaty?"

I smirked at her obvious discomfort. Excellent, at least I affected her. "I think we can handle it. We are adults, after all."

"Let's hit the showers, and I'll tell you." She skipped toward the immaculate bathroom connected to the workout room while I stood woodenly in place. When I didn't follow right away she poked her head around the door. "Julian, you're seriously acting weird. I know how you get if I don't wash your back, and I'm sweaty too. It's just a shower."

She left again.

And I muttered under my breath, "No, it's definitely not."

I forced myself to go through the motions as I slowly stripped out of my clothes. I gave myself a million pep talks, then opened the steamed-up glass shower door and joined her.

Naked.

She was so naked, her perfect ass facing me while she rubbed soap all over her body and between her breasts.

I quickly turned on the second showerhead and started thinking about every single depressing thing possible.

And then I thought of my mother.

And her sickness.

And the fact that it had been almost four weeks since I'd seen her face to face.

And suddenly I wasn't in the mood to shower, to talk, to do anything except call her and make sure my dad was keeping his end of the bargain still.

"I thought you were an arrogant prick," came Izzy's voice.

I whipped my head around. "Come again?"

She laughed and tossed a pink loofah at me. "You heard me. You were so arrogant, so aloof, everyone on campus knew who you were, who your family was. And since we'd gone to high school together and you'd sort of . . . taken me under your wing when I was dating Ryan, well, we just kind of clicked. Plus it's not like we hadn't been study partners before, I mean our senior year was the best, right?"

Shit. I had no idea if it was the best, because I had no fucking clue if she was even telling me the truth. Then again, she wouldn't lie, would she?

"Sorry, I'm still focusing on the 'arrogant prick' comment," I teased, sidestepping the entire question. "I expected you to say something like 'And then I fell at your feet, because holy fuck, it's Julian Tennyson.'"

She made a face. "You curse more now, you know that?"

"I almost died, you know that?" I deflected with a wink.

"Touché." She grinned. "And no, I didn't fall at your feet, but after all that trouble with tuition and my parents dying, it just . . . I don't know, it was so natural turning to you, to your father. You guys gave me everything and I was so thankful that I had family who cared when I thought I had nobody. You guys stepped up in a huge way." Darkness clouded her vision. "Things change, though, don't they? When you get older and realize the world isn't the place you thought it was?"

"Yeah, sadly they do." I grabbed her smooth shoulders and turned her around so I could get her back. "Do you miss it, the before?"

"Yes," she said without thinking. "And no."

"Why no?"

"Because I wouldn't be here in the shower with you if I hadn't bumped into you that day in Human Anatomy, if we hadn't recognized each other, gone to get coffee. We were inseparable after that."

She actually made my brother sound like a savior rather than a cheater. I was suddenly ravenous for more information on his life, like it would close the chasm of resentment between us. I had so many questions I didn't even know where to start, and I didn't know how much I could push without sounding suspicious.

"So what you're saying"—I rubbed the loofah over her smooth skin—"is that I wasn't always a jackass?"

"You've always been a jackass, just a manageable one, and then—" She stopped talking, her body stiffened.

"And then?" I stopped washing and waited.

"We grew up." She sounded devastated. "We left childish ways behind, when cheap Chinese takeout and passing finals were the only things we worried about. But the world doesn't care about that, not the Tennyson world. This world demands perfection. Sometimes I think you regret bringing me into it. Other times I think you'd rather kill me than let me leave it."

She moved away then shut off her showerhead and grabbed one of the towels.

I saw a flash of skin through the steam billowing around her body.

And I realized I'd pushed too hard too fast.

What the hell sort of man was my brother? Was he the monster? Or was he just as trapped as she was?

Was he the controller or was he just as controlled?

What the hell had I gotten myself into?

It wasn't as if I could ask him. I wracked my brain, slammed my hand against the wall, then shut off the water on my side.

By the time I toweled off and got back to the kitchen, she was gone, leaving a note saying she left to grab coffee.

I was alone in the apartment for the first time since stealing my brother's life.

I eyed the office I hadn't set foot in. It was technically mine. She wouldn't be thrown off if she saw me in there. But something about being in here felt wrong. Just as wrong as kissing her.

I thought of her flinching when she saw me, of the anger rolling off her body, of the way she looked bloody and beaten even though she had no physical wounds or scars. And my justification was easy.

I was the good guy.

I was the knight.

I walked into the office and shut the door behind me. Everything looked as if it had just been cleaned. A large dark-wood desk sat in the middle, bookshelves lined both walls, picture-perfect windows overlooked the city, and there was a wet bar and cigars next to a wide leather chair and ottoman.

Clearly, my brother liked the finer things if those crystal decanters were anything to go by.

I rounded the desk and sat back in his leather office chair, then tried opening the right drawer.

It didn't budge.

I tried the middle. It at least moved, but all I saw were pens, pads of paper.

I had all his passwords on my keychain. I sat at the ominous desk and woke up the laptop, then gently started typing in the login, the password popped up and autofilled. His screen came alive, and what faith I had in him being what he said he was went completely out the window.

On the main screen, I saw an account with a fifty-thousand-dollar initial deposit.

The same amount as the check I'd ripped up last year.

He'd created a fund for me and our mother, with deposits made every fucking month of enough money to . . .

I squeezed my eyes shut.

Guilt descended like a choking fog.

Years ago I'd promised my brother I'd protect him.

And I had failed.

Only to find out that during the last year, he'd been trying to protect me.

Chapter Eighteen

I needed air. I thought walking in the rain would make me feel better, more like myself. Instead, I still felt the awareness of Julian's gaze and the way he didn't stop watching me that morning when we worked out together, when we showered together.

I'd seen the man naked more times than I could count, and for some eerie reason it felt like the first time when we were in the shower. I'd probably acted like a lunatic when I jerked my gaze away from his six-pack.

He'd always had a fit body, and I'd always been attracted to him. It seemed like every woman was attracted to him, but this . . . the butterflies in my stomach were threatening to explode out of my body when he watched me, when he teased me.

I smiled to myself as I rounded the corner and made my way toward the apartment. From my pocket came the ring of my cell phone just as the doorman opened the door.

I waved him off with a smile and answered. It was the hospital.

"Isobel!" Annie always sounded so excited to talk with me. She was in her late twenties, loved her nursing job, and always had a ready smile for everyone she saw. She'd been my first friend when I started volunteering and we'd just clicked, maybe because with Annie what you see is what you get. There was no manipulation, no rules, just friendship. "When are you coming back? The nurses miss you, the kids keep complaining that the other volunteers don't read the stories right, and about half the nursing staff won't stop asking about that sexy fiancé of yours."

"He is sexy, isn't he?" I laughed into the phone, feeling freer than I had in months, like a girl on her first date getting wooed again. The trepidation that had been weighing me down over the past few weeks was slowly dissipating as Julian and I fell into more of a partnership, more of what we had before his father started giving ultimatums. "We have the banquet tonight with IFC. Everyone at Tennyson Financial will be there plus loads of celebrities and influencers. I'm semi-free after that, so I think I'll come back Monday? I can't stay late, though. Julian will officially be named CEO on Monday, and I want to be there when he gets home."

"Mmm, I just bet you do," she teased.

I let out a small laugh. "You know this is all he's ever wanted, to finally be CEO, and between you and me, it seems like he's finally, I don't know . . . realized that there's more to life than Tennyson."

"From your mouth to God's ears." Annie was one of the few people I'd ever confided in, and even then, I didn't tell her everything, only enough for her to know that the last six months had been a severe strain on our relationship.

"Right." I stared up at the apartment building and took a deep breath. "I need to get ready, but I'll connect with you Monday, okay? Let the kids know? And tell the nurses on the children's wing that Julian has made a full recovery."

"And when you say full?" I could almost see her eyebrows narrowing as she waited for juicy details.

"He's still injured, Annie . . ."

"Hey, even injured, this is Julian Tennyson we're talking about."

"True." I laughed and then frowned. He hadn't . . . touched me, had he? I mean he'd been healing, but he'd only kissed me, and only once with any heat to it.

I almost dropped the phone on the concrete.

Julian was a lot of things, but at home, without people watching us . . . I mean when he was home, he at least kissed me. In fact, he was the most attentive when it was just us.

"You still there?"

"No, I mean yes." I touched my mouth with my fingertips. "Sorry, just thinking. Monday?"

"See you then!"

"Bye!" I hung up and tapped my phone against my thigh as I walked into the elevator. The doors closed.

I was still thinking about it, which was ridiculous. Maybe he was just giving me time after the maid incident.

That would make sense, right?

When I made it back to the apartment, the familiar sound of CNBC filled the air along with Mozart. It had been years since Julian listened to Mozart. In fact, he used to complain about a friend he had in junior high who did nothing but play classical music to torture him.

I'd thought it was cute since Julian rarely shared his past with me. It was like he refused to go back to middle school and relive any moments in his life before then.

Even asking about his mom was off limits.

When I asked about his past, about his real mother, it led to another fight. He'd told me she was the one thing he wouldn't discuss.

And I'd loved him enough to drop it. We all had our things, right?

I walked down the hall and past the office, then backtracked. The door was open and there he sat. It was such a familiar scene that I paused. He had whiskey in his right hand and was staring at the screen in complete concentration.

Julian through and through. I'd found him countless times asleep in his own office because he worked so late. It could never be said that Julian was lazy. If anything he was a workaholic.

"Hey." I knocked lightly. "The Glam Squad should be here soon." I crossed my arms and waited for him to nod his head and dismiss me like he often did when he was working. Surprise burst through me when he wiped his hands over his face instead, looking like he was more exhausted than he'd ever been in his entire life.

"Glam Squad?" he asked after taking a long sip of whiskey. "Like the Kardashians?"

I squinted at him and smiled. "I guess if that's the comparison you want to make, yeah, we have the banquet in a few hours and they always come here and make us both up so we look perfect."

He made a face. "Are you saying I'm not already perfect?"

I rolled my eyes. "At least your ego survived the crash, hmm?"

He smirked. "Disappointed?"

"Never." And I wasn't. His confidence, his arrogance, they were what made him . . . *him*.

I turned around just as he said, "Guys don't wear makeup." Though it was more of a grumble than anything.

"Ah, you'd be surprised." I smiled. The man wore makeup for every photo shoot, every TV interview. It was what was done. He knew better than anyone. No fresh faces, and if they were fresh they were made to look that way by, you guessed it, makeup.

"Can I ask you something?" He stood, towering over the desk. Why did it suddenly look so small next to him, and when did he become so intimidating?

"Of course."

"Why are you marrying me?"

I was too stunned to answer. Was this a trick? Another way to get under my skin or to see where I was at so he could manipulate me?

His eyes focused on mine like he was afraid to turn away.

And I found that I couldn't lie to him, not anymore. "Because a long time ago I fell in love with a boy who told me everything was going to be okay. And I believed him. And when that boy grew into a man, I lost a piece of him every single day. I said yes, because the stupid girl in me thought it would bring him back."

"Thank you. For being honest," he said softly.

I nodded my head. "I learned a long time ago honesty rarely changes anything and usually gets you into more trouble."

"I appreciate it just the same. Besides, it's not like either of us has a choice, do we?"

I flinched a bit. "Are you saying you have no choice but to marry me? Romantic. Now if you'll excuse me . . ."

"Wait." His massive body moved around the desk and then he was in front of me, cupping my face between his hands, staring at me like I was the answer to everything. "Ask me."

"Ask you what?"

"Same question."

"Are you trying to punish me?" Tears filled my eyes. This was the old Julian, this was cruel. I didn't want his answer, I couldn't bear it.

"Trust me."

Shaking, I finally gave in, because I wanted out of his arms, out of that room. I wanted to forget how easy it was for him to hurt me. "Why are you marrying me?"

He tilted my chin up with his forefinger and whispered, "Because I want to spend the rest of my life trying to figure out how to not just make you happy but set you free."

I gasped. Had he said he loved me, I wouldn't have believed him. Had he said I was beautiful, it would have fallen on deaf ears.

But he said he wanted my happiness. My freedom.

"Does that mean you plan on doing just that? Setting me free?"

"What if being free means you stay with me?" He smiled and pressed his body against mine, reminding me yet again how good he used to feel, how good he did feel. "Just like this."

I sucked in a sharp breath when he jerked me against his chest. I leaned up on my tiptoes, but he didn't meet me halfway. "Julian?"

"Hmm?" Every muscle was taut. His jaw was tight like he was trying not to clench his teeth, trying and failing. "Why aren't you kissing me? Why haven't you been kissing me? I mean *really* kissing me?"

His eyes flickered with something that looked like sadness when he said, "Maybe I don't feel like I deserve your mouth, not after what I've put you through, not after the last few months. Not after . . ." He swallowed. "The shoes."

"This isn't about shoes."

"No," he whispered, tucking my hair behind my ear. "This is about you coming to me when you're ready. This is part of freedom, Izzy, giving you the choice, not forcing it on you."

His words were like a balm to my soul. I stood up on my tiptoes again, ready to kiss him senseless, to thank him for saying that, for finally getting me, for understanding, when the doorbell rang.

He sighed. "We could pretend we're not home, make out instead."

I grinned, my fingers gripping the back of his neck, touching his skin, wondering why it felt so much better than before, being this close to him. "Do that and kiss your position as CEO goodbye. This is important to the company, so we'll go, do our duty, the one bred into you since your dad used to lock you in your room, and get it done."

Julian's face paled. "What did you say?"

It was my turn to give him a funny look. "Don't tell me the accident repressed that memory too?" The doorbell rang again, I started walking away, but he grabbed me by the wrist and held me there. It was another topic he rarely discussed, because it was painful, embarrassing, because it showed me why it was so important for him to prove himself.

"He called you weak, remember?" I whispered, unable to look at him. "You were going through a really hard time. It was your sopho-more year of high school, and you started going through this rebellious stage, experimenting with drugs, staying out late, and he started locking you in your room. When you didn't stop, he pulled you out of school for the rest of the year, got a private tutor, and told you to your face that you would never make him proud, and you've made it your mission to prove him wrong."

God, I hated telling him this.

I hated rehashing it.

"I remember." Julian didn't sound convincing. "It's okay to hate him as much as I love him, right?"

"Honestly, I don't know." The doorbell rang again. "I need to get that, okay?"

"Yeah." He didn't look even remotely okay, but we needed to get ready and we needed to do our jobs. Funny how we used to have pep talks back in the day, mainly him telling me that everything was going to be fine. And today of all days, when his future was finally within his grasp, I was the one having to do the convincing.

Strange, strange world.

Chapter Nineteen

I smiled tightly at all the right people as we made our way past the paparazzi. Julian clung to me like he'd forgotten how insane these events got. His eyes were a bit wide, and he kept licking his lips like he did when he was nervous. It was probably the fact that he looked like he'd been in an accident too; even makeup couldn't cover the bruising on his face or the way he limped next to me.

The press was having a field day, yelling questions and accusations about someone trying to hurt him before the buyout. It was all speculation, and it wouldn't be the first threat that the Tennysons received over money. In fact, every new assistant was vetted by a private security team, especially for the corporate officers closest to the family.

Money made people crazy.

It made us all a bit crazy, didn't it?

And stupid.

And weak.

My stomach dropped to my knees as Julian smiled at my side, his confidence growing with each step as we finally made our way inside Old New York Museum. Every year the company held the Tennyson

Charity Gala, and every year they turned celebrities away from the invitation-only event.

I used to walk into places like this with stars in my eyes.

Now I just felt tired.

"Lots of people," Julian finally muttered so only I could hear as he grabbed two glasses of champagne from a passing waiter. "I wonder if Father understands that blunt-force head trauma doesn't exactly make you want to party the night away. I'm more likely to pass out in one of the water fountains than I am to have a conversation about stocks and shares."

I smiled at that and clinked my glass with his. "You used to thrive in this environment, like a honeybee going from group to group, the life of the party with all the perfect little party tricks."

"Are you saying I'm boring now?" He grinned down at me. I found myself getting lost in his easy smile and the way it made me feel warm all the way down to my toes.

"Pretty much." I sipped my wine.

He burst out laughing, earning the attention of a few people standing nearby. They gasped like he was the villain in a horror story, which only made the situation more unbelievable. Julian was always the hero, always the one people wanted to talk to, women wanted to marry, men wanted to be.

"Ah, Julian." Edward made his way toward us with a few board members I recognized.

They all looked like pale vampires, at least that's how I saw them. Only they were completely harmless, hardly talked, and looked at Edward like he created the earth in six days. I mentally rolled my eyes while smiling prettily at each and every one.

"Son, we were just discussing the buyout of IFC."

"Of course you were," Julian said in a bored tone that I'd never really heard him use with his father or in front of board members. "I thought this was a celebration. It's in the bag. I hope none of you have any concerns?"

Edward's eyes flickered with something I'd never seen before. Pride? Anger? I couldn't tell, but it made me want to run in the opposite direction or just throw my champagne at him to get him to stop looking at Julian like that, and at me, for that matter.

"Yes, well . . ." Edward lifted his glass to his lips and sipped, then winked at Julian. "My son"—he said *son* in a way that made my skin crawl—"is as always correct. We should be celebrating, not discussing business. After all, he's still suffering from his injuries, but you're feeling like your old self, aren't you, Julian? I would hate to hear otherwise."

Julian looked ready to commit murder.

The board members started whispering among one another.

This was bad.

Was he calling him out?

"The day of my accident, stocks fell thirty percent. The moment news caught wind that I was, in fact, going to survive what should have been catastrophic injuries, they doubled and then split, making every single one of you millions richer. No offense, *Dad* . . ." He spat the word. Who was this man? "But I highly doubt we'd have the same results if *you'd* come back from the dead, do you?"

Edward turned a shade of purple. The board members seemed to sigh in relief as if they were waiting for Julian to take the reins, to show everyone that Edward might own more shares but Julian was in control. It was a strange thing for Julian to do, but I respected him for doing it, more than I would ever be able to express.

"Now, gentlemen, we have much to discuss. Next week, once my signature as CEO is on that document, we can move forward. Until then, I suggest you find someone beautiful to dance with, but you'll have to excuse me, my future wife and future partner in Tennyson Financial is currently taken."

We swept past smiling board members. Some chuckled, others lifted their glasses in the air like Julian could do no wrong, and for the first time in months I wanted to lift my glass and say something like *Same.*

Edward stood there glowering like an angry stone statue while Julian grabbed both of our glasses and put them on a nearby table, then pulled me onto the dance floor in a perfect twirl.

"You're either suffering from something mental, or you've just found out your heart and balls are actually bigger than you thought," I said, trying to look bored while inside I was dancing a little jig. "Do you realize who you just said that in front of?"

"My father?" Julian shrugged.

"Not just your father, but board members who control the entire company. If they had taken that confrontation the wrong way—"

"But they didn't, and trust me, even if they did, they won't."

He twirled me again.

When we faced one another, his expression was unreadable.

"What do you know that I don't?"

"A lot," he said quickly. "I was studying files on my computer and found some things earlier, things that make it look like I've been . . . um . . . planning something . . ." He smiled at someone nearby and whirled me in the opposite direction. "I spent hours going through documents, and everything points to a plan for me to truly take over everything. Did you know Dad sold off some more stocks last year? He's no longer the majority shareholder, he wanted IFC bad enough to do something that he wouldn't normally do."

I almost tripped. "What exactly are you saying?"

He just grinned. "I'm saying that I hold all the cards, and for once in his life, I think dear old Dad is scared."

"How many shares do you own?"

He opened his mouth then shut it like he wasn't sure. "Let's just say once I sign those papers on Monday, I'll own a third of the company and the board owns another third."

"And the last third?"

"Silent investor." Something flickered in his eyes. "Someone Dad didn't want anyone to know about. I got his name and information, and I'm gonna set up a meeting . . ." He looked away. I hated that he wasn't looking at me, especially since he was actually talking about overthrowing Edward of all people, the only man in the world he ever did anything for.

I cupped his face, tears in my eyes. "You've really changed."

He sighed. Our foreheads touched as he twirled me around again and dipped me, then pressed a searing kiss across my neck.

"Ladies and gentlemen . . ." Edward took the microphone as the music softly played in the background. "We are so thankful for everyone attending tonight. We've raised over a million dollars for our nonprofit, Green Tree. We will put food on thousands of tables during the holidays, and we couldn't do it without you."

Clapping ensued while Julian clung to me.

"This evening we're celebrating more than a buyout of IFC, a partnership with one of the largest financial firms in the country. Slowly and surely we will change the world." People worshipped him with more applause and it made me sick. I touched my stomach and waited for his eyes to drop to us, and they eventually did. "We're also celebrating something else. Julian, my son, would you bring your fiancée on stage?"

Julian beamed as he put his hand on my back, leading us both up the stairs. We faced the crowd, hand in hand while Edward grabbed a glass of champagne and lifted it high in the air. "I also couldn't be happier to announce my son's miraculous recovery." People cheered so wildly it was like we were at a rock concert. "It's caused the whole family to reflect on what's most important, and I'm happy to announce he and Isobel Cunningham will be married next week Saturday at the York Country Club. It shouldn't come as a shock, just look at them, young, in love, and heirs to a billion-dollar company. Aren't they just wonderful?"

Julian lifted his glass in the air like I did, like we were expected to, and for a few short moments it all felt so real, the fairy tale Julian had promised, the life we had both talked about having.

A family.

Us back together, working toward being stronger than ever.

My eyes filled with tears as people started shouting, "Kiss! Kiss! Kiss!"

Julian turned to me and dipped me back, pressing a hungry kiss on my lips. I wrapped my arms around his neck and deepened it. He tasted like strawberries and champagne, his lips were hot, needy. When we finally stopped kissing, it was to hollering and more cheers.

Edward gave the microphone to Marla, and she thanked the guests. Then he turned to us and winked. "Didn't think you had it in you, Julian. I think this is going to be the beginning of something lucrative for all of us, don't you?"

It was impossible to miss the hatred flashing in Julian's eyes, hatred I'd never seen there before.

I made a mental note to ask him later what had changed.

Was it the accident?

Or was he just tired like I was? Tired of pretending, tired of faking it, just damn tired of the Tennyson life and ready to screw them all?

I hoped for both.

And I clung to that hope more than a girl who knew better should.

Chapter Twenty

BRIDGE

Exhaustion hit hard and fast. I didn't remember even taking off my clothes before crash-landing on my bed that night. At least I had a better understanding of the hoops Julian had to jump through, and my respect for him rose a notch after having my picture taken so much and having to look happy when I was so tired I was seeing double.

I was confused about what I was going to do.

It didn't help that my mom texted first thing the morning after the banquet; she was back in the ER.

The minute Izzy left the room, I shut the bathroom door. I sat on the tub, my old phone in hand, and called her. I'd been careful about keeping it on silent and hiding it in the back of the closet. I needed that connection with Mom, though. I tried not to imagine the worst. Did her feeding tube fall out? Was something infected? I'd been trying so hard to keep a calm façade with Izzy that I completely dropped the ball with Mom, but I couldn't be two places at once.

At least not with Julian still fighting.

She answered on the third ring.

"Mom? Mom, are you there?"

"Oh, honey, hi!" She sounded as tired as I felt. "I didn't want to worry you, I'm sorry. That's why I texted. My feeding tube fell out and apparently the incision site got infected. It was all red and angry."

I winced just thinking of the pain she was going through. Mine was nothing compared to hers. "Can they give you anything for the pain?"

I knew the answer, but I still asked the question, hoping for a miracle.

"Oh baby, you know they can't. They did try a morphine drip, but my blood pressure dropped so low I blacked out."

"Shit." I hung my head in my hands. "I need to come home."

"Don't you dare."

"Mom—"

"Bridge!" She raised her voice, which was completely out of character. "What you're doing, what you've done . . . I've been sleeping, it's a miracle, but it's like I'm not afraid to close my eyes. I've even gained five pounds. This is a minor setback. I'll be fine."

"Five pounds?" I clung to hope. "Mom, that's incredible!"

"I know." She seemed happy even though she still sounded tired. "Trust me, this is nothing. The doctors said they'll get me out of here once the infection is cleared up. I'm on some antibiotic cream, and it's already helping."

"Good."

The line went quiet.

"Saw you on TV last night," she whispered. "She's beautiful."

And there it was. "Yeah."

"Does she know?"

I swallowed more guilt. "No. Not at all. Though I think she likes me more." I could have sworn I heard my mom rolling her eyes.

"I rolled my eyes," she stated almost immediately.

I barked out a laugh. "Yeah, figured you did."

"And Edward?" She always sounded like she was in so much pain when she said his name, like it was a wound that would never fully heal. "Is he treating you okay?"

"Sure, if being forced to marry your brother's fiancée is okay, then yeah, I'm peachy."

"Oh, son." She sounded so sad it broke my heart. "I was going to ask, but figured it was just another one of the clauses he put in that damned contract, just another way to control you."

"Yeah." My voice cracked.

"And your brother? How's he doing?"

"I saw him almost a month ago. I don't know, Mom, I had so much resentment toward him, still do, but I'm learning some things . . ."

"Things?"

"He set up a trust for us."

"That sounds like Julian," she said softly. "I imagine he deposited that fifty thousand dollars for the check you tore up and stomped on?"

I smiled sadly. "Oh yeah, plus a few more zeroes. He has over two million in that account, Mom, with our names on it."

She was silent and then whispered, "He's your brother. That means the part of him that is good, the part that you loved, the part I still love is there, honey. You know he never knew how to express himself well, and your father wasn't exactly nurturing. None of us are perfect."

"He won't even come see you!" I roared. Pain flared to life in my ribs as I jumped to my feet. "He pretends you don't exist."

"He did." She said it quietly, shamefully.

"He did what?"

"Visit." She sniffed. "Last year. You were at work. He brought cash during Christmastime, that's how I got you the new flat-screen. I'm sorry, I just wanted you to have something nice. He said he would bring more money. He started calling every week, and then he told me that he had to wait for some deal to go through, said he needed to talk to you. I'm so sorry." She sobbed harder. "It's my fault. You were just so angry with him, and he said it was important, and then I got sicker. That was a week before the accident."

"You think he was worried Dad was gonna try something?"

"Your father is a dangerous man. Now that he's aging, he's worse than before. He has two brilliant sons ready to take over and make something great, and I think he's afraid. And fear is never a good sign."

"I'm safe, Mom, I promise, and I'll tell—" My voice cracked. "I'll tell Jules you said hi."

"I love you, son." She sounded like she was crying. "You tell him to fight, alright?"

"Alright." I choked up. "I love you . . . so much."

She ended the call.

I stared at my phone.

And then jerked to my feet when the bathroom door shoved open, revealing a pissed-off Izzy. "You love who exactly?" She paced in front of me, hairbrush in hand. "I can't believe I took you for your word! Who was it this time, the same maid? Different one? Marla? Hmm? I'm such an idiot!" She threw the hairbrush, narrowly missing my recently healed eye.

I ducked and then grabbed her around the waist. She elbowed me in a few ribs I knew were still broken, driving me to my knees in pain.

"Good. I hope you hurt! You promised!"

"Izzy," I wheezed. "That was my mom."

"What?" She froze. "You never talk about your mom. In fact, the last time I asked about her you left midconversation and went into your office to pout!"

Damn it, Julian, why didn't you talk to her?

It wasn't like Izzy was hard to talk to!

"Dad pretends that she doesn't exist. I reconnected with her right before the accident." Partially true. "I found out she's really sick, and I wanted to help out. Last night she texted me that she was back in the

ER." The only way to keep the lie straight was to tell the truth. My chest felt heavy as I relayed the information.

Izzy shook her head, her eyes narrowed. "So you've kept her from me for almost our entire life together? And just now want to reconnect? I'm calling your bluff. Wow, the girl must have a magical v—"

"I'll put up with a lot, Izzy, but talking about my mom in any way that's negative . . ." I stood to my full height. "I won't allow that. Ever."

Izzy looked at me, really looked at me. "Say I believe you. Does your father know?"

"What do you think?" I spat. "He knows. He just doesn't fucking care. He cheated on her, she left, end of story." I ran my hands through my hair. "He's finally paying for some bills, but he doesn't actually care, no."

Izzy held out her hand. "I want to FaceTime the last number called."

"Trust runs deep," I muttered, praying to God my mom would not only answer but know exactly what to say as I handed Izzy my phone.

She hit the FaceTime on the screen and waited.

One ring.

Two rings.

Three rings.

"Bridge? Is that you?"

Izzy glared at the screen. "Bridge? No, this is Julian's fiancée. I'm calling from his phone. Who the heck is Bridge?"

Mom's mouth dropped open, and then she pasted a blank expression on her face. "I'm so sorry, honey. Bridge is a nickname I used to call Julian. When he was five he peed his pants on a bridge because it was so high, and the nickname kind of stuck."

Son of a bitch! Thrown under the bus by my own mom? Granted, the story was true, but it was actually about me, not Julian. I shifted uncomfortably on my feet.

Izzy stared, and stared, and then burst out laughing, wiping tears from her eyes. My mom joined in while I glared at both of them. "That's the best thing I've heard all day!"

"You should have seen him when he discovered he had a pee-pee. Was so proud of that thing he whipped it out in the grocery store!" I hadn't seen my mom laugh that hard in a really long time, the only reason I wasn't losing my shit. Her smile always did me in. Every single day it was her smile I lived for, I fought for, I wanted to earn.

Izzy took a deep breath. "I'm sorry for just calling like this. It's just, I walked in, he was saying I love you, and—"

"Oh, sweetheart, don't blame Brid—I mean Julian, for that. It was too painful to bring up. On top of that, his father never wanted the public to know about me, especially now that I'm dying."

Izzy put her hand on her chest. "Is there anything we can do? The doctors in the city are the best. I volunteer at Manhattan Grace. I can call someone and—"

"No, honey, I have the best care now thanks to, thanks to Julian and to Edward. I'm sorry for keeping this secret, but sometimes it's the best when it comes to a high-profile family. Sadly." And she sounded sad, like she understood that she was sacrificed in a cruel way, because she was forgotten, by everyone but me.

And apparently now my brother.

I wish I had known.

Maybe the hatred wouldn't have run so deep.

Maybe I wouldn't have been so hell-bent on agreeing. Then again, there was nothing I wouldn't do for Mom.

I felt conflicted.

Like I was stealing his life without knowing all the facts, and I wondered what he would do if he was in my position. Would he be the bastard I'd always believed him to be? Or would he try to make it right? Would he kiss my fiancée?

I ran my hands through my hair, not realizing that Mom and Izzy were both giving me funny looks. "Sorry, just thinking." I flashed a smile I didn't feel. I could see the sadness in my mom's eyes, because she knew the toll this was taking on me even though I didn't admit it. I was never brought up to be a liar.

And that's exactly what I was doing.

Every day.

Lying to get money.

Tennyson through and through.

"Thank you for answering," Izzy said softly, and the inflection in her voice rang true. Odd that I would know that about her already, that when she said *thank you* in that voice it meant she truly was thankful.

"I'm sure this won't be the last time," Mom said cheerfully, and just like I knew the meaning behind Izzy's tone, I knew the warning behind my mom's.

My gut twisted because this, this was what my mom had always wanted, for me to settle down, for her to know that when she left this earth I had someone by my side.

It killed me to think she might die watching her son live a lie.

Chapter Twenty-One

I was furious when I'd heard him say "I love you" to someone else. He hadn't said that to me in . . . I refused to count because it was depressing thinking about how long it had been since he'd looked into my eyes and said those words, the words I needed so desperately to hear.

And then to find out he'd been talking to his mom.

I still felt betrayal and anger, but I at least could understand why he would keep her a secret from the press. I just couldn't get over him keeping it from me.

"Why?" I crossed my arms. "Why hide something this huge?"

"Izzy . . ." Julian let out a rough exhale and mimicked my movements, crossing his arms and leaning against the sink. "My father . . . let's just say things didn't end well between them when I was a teen. I know it's not possible, but I blame him for her sickness. I always thought that when he broke her heart he also broke something inside her, making her weak enough to get sick. The truth is—" He looked angry in that moment and cursed furiously, then locked eyes with me. "The truth is, he didn't want anyone to know about her because it would make him look bad, that would make the Tennyson family look bad. He's been remarried three times, which seems to escape his notice when it comes to having a stellar reputation. And I made my mom a promise when I was fourteen. To always keep her safe. And sometimes keeping people safe means pretending they don't exist."

My heart slammed against my chest. "Julian, pretending someone doesn't exist doesn't make their existence any less true."

"I know that, don't you think I know that?" He moved toward me, his eyes angry, his muscles straining against his simple white T-shirt. He was predatory in a way I'd never experienced before, aggressive. "But you know how this family is, sometimes you aren't given a choice. I did the best I could with her . . ." He sighed. "And with you."

"Ohhh, so you cheated on me all those times to protect me, gotcha," I snapped.

His face fell.

I looked away. "Sorry, you didn't deserve that. I'm just . . . I'm processing."

"Yes, I did deserve that, and I know it's a lot to take in," he whispered sadly. "I need you to keep it to yourself, though, Izzy. My father may be paying for her treatments right now, but anything could set him off, and we have the buyout papers to sign and the wedding and who the hell knows if Ju—"

He cut himself off abruptly and cursed. It almost sounded like he was going to refer to himself in the third person. He'd been pretty arrogant but never done *that* before, not in his entire life.

"Just trust me on this, okay?"

I breathed in and out, I studied his muscular form and the way it towered over me. His green eyes raked across my skin like he wanted to permanently burn me with his stare. "Alright," I whispered. "Any other skeletons I should know about? Long-lost sisters? Brothers? A great-aunt who inherited a duchy?"

His lips pressed together in a grim line.

"I was kidding, Julian."

His smile was forced. "Yeah, I know. I'm sorry, I'm just exhausted, and last night was longer than I imagined it would be."

"Tell me about it," I agreed. "Why don't we just watch a movie and hang out later this afternoon?"

His grin was wicked as he responded. "Izzy, are you asking to Netflix and chill?"

I burst out laughing and then covered my hot face with my hands. "I know I'm red, like really red. I guess I am?" I peeked through my fingertips to see longing on his face as he pulled me into his arms and kissed the tip of my nose.

Another new Julian thing.

He rarely kissed me on the mouth anymore.

Always on the cheek, the forehead, the nose, the guy even kissed my hand last night. In public he had kissed me, and I could feel the women in the front row shoving each other out of the way for a chance to glimpse his perfect ass and biceps.

"Where'd you go?" Julian whispered, still holding me tight. A thrill washed over me, and it almost felt like we were getting a second chance, like this was new, and then every time I'd get excited I'd remember his cryptic words about breaking my heart and wonder why he was so doubtful of this connection between us.

"Sorry, I was just thinking too hard, about everything."

"That's fair." He wrapped an arm around me and led me out of the bathroom. He was still limping a little bit. He grabbed a chilled bottle of white wine from the fridge, and two glasses, then walked me over to the couch and helped me sit before he did the same.

Such a gentleman in his own home.

Then again, Julian had been a lot of things, but he always opened doors, he always had perfect manners. Maybe that's why I had slowly been going insane.

Everything was controlled with the precision of a surgeon's knife.

There was no freedom in perfect manners and polite smiles.

Only heartache and gilded cages.

"So . . ." I poured us each a glass and reached for the remote at the same time he did.

His hand covered mine.

And I stared.

And stared.

Unease trickled down my spine. "Julian?"

"Yeah?" His chest heaved as he looked down at our joined hands. At the tattoo that was on his thumb that hadn't been there before. A *T* with an *X* through it. What an odd thing to put on your body.

"That's new. When could you have possibly done that without me noticing?" I rubbed my thumb over it. Why did his hand suddenly feel so foreign?

After a long pause, he exhaled, rubbing his fingers back and forth across mine.

"Relax, Izzy." He grinned and gave me a shrug. "We've been looking into purchasing a small company called Inkbox that makes temporary tattoos. They went viral online, and we were testing the product to see if it actually worked. The day before the accident I did a few, and they seemed invisible. But I noticed them the other day. I'm sorry I didn't say anything, I promise it's not a big deal." He squeezed my hand.

I released a breath. "Sorry, I'm being ridiculous. I just . . . things have been so different since the accident. You're different."

He tugged me closer to him and pulled my feet onto his lap. "Bad different or good different?"

I licked my dry lips. "Honestly?"

"Always."

"Good different," I confessed. "You seem happier, but not just that. You seem stronger, more willing to stand up for yourself." I sighed. "To stand up for me."

"That's what I wanted to hear." His eyes darted from my mouth to my eyes and back down to my mouth. The low hum of the TV filled the room, images flickered, but all I saw was him. My old Julian, the one who used to stare at me the way he was now, it was almost like amidst the greed and chaos, he'd finally found his way home.

Finally.

Tears filled my eyes. "It's really you."

"It's me." He cupped my face and pressed a soft kiss to my mouth then started pulling away. Maybe insanity was taking over, maybe I just needed to feel his mouth longer. I hooked my arms around his neck and pulled back.

He moved on top of me, probing my lips apart with his tongue as he dug his fingers into my hair like this was the first real kiss he'd had in forever. He kissed me like there had never been other women, just me. Only me. There was something so fulfilling about having his weight on me. I could feel how thick and muscular his thighs were as he pressed our bodies into the creamy suede couch. He angled his head as his hands grazed my ribs, slowly and delicately lifting my shirt higher. His touch singed my skin in a way it never had before. I was addicted to his taste. It wasn't like coming home, not this time; it was like discovering something hidden that had been burning between us. It exploded in hundreds of soft touches and kisses and was now this uncontrollable tether. I refused to let go of his shirt as I bunched it in my hands. He straddled me and kissed me harder. A charge of excitement swept through me as his brazen hands moved to my jeans. I circled his neck with my arms as his lips spread out into a smile against my mouth. He didn't unbutton my jeans. He didn't move his hands under my shirt. He was trying to go slow, and I had no idea why.

That was out of character for him. At least when we were having sex and he wasn't cheating, he was aggressive, he was always solely focused on us and only us, on finding release.

This version of him was focused on kissing.

I couldn't decide if I liked it or if I was ready to strangle him and threaten him if he didn't give me more than just a kiss, but his body, his hands were everything.

"You have the perfect mouth." He pulled back, his eyes a bit crazed, his breathing heavy. "I could kiss you all day."

"I can't remember the last time we've kissed that long before sex."

"No sex," he said quickly. "I just want to enjoy you, enjoy this without making it about sex."

My lower lip trembled as he cupped my chin and let out a little growl before tasting me again, before rocking his hips against mine. Little bouts of pressure hit me between my thighs. I arched a bit, rubbing my body against his as he kissed me deeper, held me harder against the couch. His hand came down on my shoulder, pushing me into the suede as he moved against me. He moaned and managed to pick me up to a sitting position so I was straddling him, legs on both sides, knees forced into the cushions while he kept kissing me. I could feel his erection straining against his pants, could feel his need for release like it was my own, because it was. Nothing but flimsy clothes and heat separated us, and yet he just kept kissing.

"You're going to make yourself miserable," I moaned against his mouth when he adjusted himself against me.

"Mmm . . ." was his only answer. And then, "Worth it."

"Doesn't have to be like this," I said when he pulled me roughly against him.

He didn't answer, just mimicked the movement again and clenched his teeth before devouring my mouth like it was his next meal, almost licking his way down my tongue, and then his hand cupped between my thighs. My body gave such a heightened jolt of pleasure that I couldn't control the whimper that followed his touch or the next as he rubbed with the palm of his hand, so rough and so tender at the same time.

"Please don't stop, this is crazy, please." I clutched his shoulders, digging my fingers into his shirt and skin, holding on while I rode his hand, while I chased more pleasure with my clothes on than I'd ever had with them off. He coaxed and teased, I cried out, his name on my tongue. He kissed me like he didn't want to hear it, like he wanted to make the moment more than that, and I let him, I let him drink in my next few words, my sentences as my heart hammered in my chest.

We broke apart, our eyes searching each other, his full of wonder, mine full of euphoria.

And I knew in that moment he'd somehow given me freedom, just like he promised.

Selfless.

I reached for him.

He grabbed my hand and squeezed it. "This is about you, not me."

"But—"

"I'm not stupid enough to believe I deserve something as special as your touch, Izzy. I'll wait until you're ready to trust this. I want you willing, not keeping track."

What? We'd always kept things equal, in the bedroom, out of the bedroom, and then his father had happened, and college ended and, well, things just weren't the same, because I was afraid to let him into the very same bed I'd found someone else in.

"Julian." I placed my hands on his chest. "I don't know what to say."

He grinned at me. It was a different sort of grin. It reached his eyes in a way his other smiles never had. In fact I'd never seen him look at me like that, both playful and possessive.

He gripped me by the ass and squeezed, then set me very gently next to him on the couch. "So, what do you want to watch?"

"Don't you think . . ." I eyed what seemed to be the biggest erection I'd ever seen, and that was saying a lot since I knew the Tennysons were proud for a whole 'nother reason. It was maybe why it was so easy to cheat. They were reputedly well endowed, but this, this was . . . Did I really turn him on that much? More than I ever had? "Shouldn't we . . . ?" I pointed.

He batted my hand away. "That's really not helping, Izzy."

"Sorry." I laughed.

"Neither is the laughing."

"Sorry!" I covered my face with my hands, feeling a hot blush stain my cheeks. He very gently pulled my hands down and kissed the insides of my wrists.

"I've survived worse. I'll just be over here thinking about CNN and world hunger while you decide what you want to watch."

A few seconds later, when I'd settled on some sci-fi fi movie with Channing Tatum, I glanced over at Julian, whose teeth were clenched right along with his fists.

"How's that working out for you over there? All that world hunger thinking working?"

He grabbed himself and cursed. "Fucking perfect, can't you tell?"

"You're bigger everywhere, aren't you?" I teased.

He whipped his head toward me as a pleased smile crossed his face. "Izzy, you have no idea."

And I wondered if I did.

I would look back on this moment and realize I ignored the signs on purpose because it was the first time in years that I went to sleep with a genuine smile on my face.

I would learn too late that the smile was only temporary and that heartache can last forever.

I laid my head on his chest and fell asleep to his heartbeat an hour after our make-out session on the couch.

And when I woke up later that afternoon from a bad dream, Julian pulled me into his arms and held me tight.

I fell asleep to the fake tattoo on his hand and the foreign one on his biceps that also looked like a *T* with an *X* through it.

And I embraced the lie that I was falling in love with a stranger, a very beautiful stranger that would one day take me away from here.

And I woke up with sadness knowing that this was only the fantasy of a girl who'd had her wings clipped too soon.

Chapter Twenty-Two

BRIDGE

I left her a note and went for a walk to the offices, my offices, to be exact. It was a Saturday, and most people wouldn't be in, but that didn't mean business just stopped running. I hoped I'd see assistants and interns. None of the bigwigs would be in on a weekend when they could be golfing, right?

I scanned my ID across the metal and walked past security to get into one of the twelve elevators.

Tennyson Financial occupied the top fifteen floors. And my shining office was on the top. My hands shook as the elevator climbed. I tried to focus on Izzy's smile, on the little sounds she made when she found release, images of her lips parting, her eyes unfocused and aroused.

She was magnificent.

She was also his.

I'd touched what was his.

I'd pleasured what wasn't mine.

And I wondered if that was exactly what my father wanted, for me to play right into his hands, to want her so badly that I'd be willing to do anything, just like I was with my mom.

The thought scared me.

What scared me more was the fact that I didn't know if my brother was alive or dead, and that my father had thousands of reasons and millions of dollars why Julian's death would be welcome.

Was I just his replacement?

Something wasn't adding up. Then again, nothing ever added up when it came to my father, he was an evil enigma who wanted one thing. World domination. I used to laugh when people said that, but now it just made me uncomfortable with how true it was.

A man like him should never hold the keys to the kingdom.

And he didn't just have the keys. He had the crown, the heirs, the fucking iron throne.

The elevator doors parted. Both of my secretaries, Kelsey and Amy, gasped as I walked in. They were wearing too much perfume and were in all white. They looked like they belonged on a Virgin Atlantic flight with their perfect hair and bright-red lipstick.

"I'll just be a minute," I said, casually walking by the one on the right. She stepped forward and gave me a seductive smile that had my stomach rolling.

"Julian." She said my name like she knew me intimately, and I got even sicker. "I think we should talk." She followed that with a wink.

"I'm not in the mood to talk," I said through clenched teeth, ignoring her completely as I walked into my office and shut the door behind me.

I barely had time to register the massiveness of the room or the view of the financial district before a knock sounded and the annoying woman let herself in and shut the door behind her.

She clapped her hand over my mouth and slammed her hand against the door. "Yes, right there. I missed you so much, baby, so much."

My eyes widened as I shoved away from her. "What the fuck!"

"Shh!" she snapped and then grabbed me by the arm and dragged me around the corner to the couch. "She needs to think we're having sex."

"She?"

"Amy." She rolled her eyes. "Receptionist number two, dumb as a bag of rocks and useful because she distracts old board members, mainly your father."

"Too much information." I held up my hand. "And what do you think you're doing? You can't just—"

"I know you're not Julian," she said softly, her eyes searching mine like she was waiting for confirmation.

My mouth snapped closed. I was not prepared for this. I abruptly stood and paced the room. "You need to leave now. That's completely false."

"You look like him, but he's leaner. He's also better at playing this game than you are." She sighed. "Use your passwords to unlock the computer, I'm sure by now you know something's not right. Before the accident, Julian found out that your father had created a trust for you but wasn't going to release it. Julian joked about using it as leverage one day. Not only would it set you up for life but it would give you a one-third ownership of the company. It was just what Julian needed, the power he needed, both of you owning your shares so you could take over the company." She opened her hand. On it was a tiny USB flash drive that was shaped like a tube of lipstick. "I've been helping him access files as much as I can without getting flagged, but he had big plans once he became CEO, and now that he's in a coma, I figured he would want you to continue making them."

I grabbed it. "Trust me, I know. Edward showed me the papers and used it as a bargaining chip over the upcoming wedding, knowing I didn't want to get in this deep." I sighed. "There's nothing I can do, not with Julian still in a coma."

"His toes moved." She said it slowly. "I overheard your father on the phone when I was bringing papers to sign into his office. He distinctly said, 'Toes moving doesn't mean anything, I want more results.'"

It made me a horrible person, didn't it? That my relief was mixed with dread, dread that he would walk in and pick up right where he left off.

The company I didn't care about.

Izzy, however . . .

I looked up. "What was Julian planning?"

She pressed her lips into a thin line. "Look, just go over the documents he drew up, the letter to the board members, the business plan for the future of Tennyson Financial once the buyout was completed with IFC. I think you'll be impressed."

"Does my father know?"

She shook her head. "No, but a week before the accident I found him in Julian's office rummaging around, typical for Edward since he has no personal boundaries, but still."

"Shit." I groaned and leaned against the couch. "I wasn't prepared for this level of insanity. I thought Julian just wanted to be CEO."

She shrugged. "Of course he wants to be CEO, because it's the only way he wins."

"Come again?"

"You don't know your brother very well, do you, Bridge?"

"No," I rasped. "Apparently not, but I'm here, aren't I? I'm trying with everything I have to give him what he's always wanted."

She licked her lips and looked away. "I think what he always wanted is standing in this office . . . I think you should keep praying for more toe wiggling, because he's going to have a lot to say to you."

"How did you even know about me?" I crossed my arms. "According to the records my name is Bridge Anderson."

She grinned. "Who do you think helped draw up all the paperwork? Your father trusts me, and shouldn't. Julian, however, trusts me with his life, even the one people don't know he has."

I groaned into my hands. "And the cheating?"

She frowned. "Julian? Cheat? With me? You're crazy, but how else could he get all this done without his father stomping in here? We may have at times let him assume the worst. It was only supposed to be a cover until he got the board on his side. He's been working tirelessly on something for months."

"Shit, shit, shit, shit." I was going to say *shit* at least a dozen more times before the day was done. "Does Izzy know about any of this? I'm assuming not?"

She made a face. "Isobel?"

"Yeah." I felt exhausted, suddenly so exhausted as the pretty blonde watched me warily. "My fiancée, same one."

"He was going to talk to her the day of the accident. He knew she was upset but was trying to fix it. Honestly, I think he thought Isobel would forgive anything as long as they were together in the end."

Fuck me.

"Gotta go." She gave me a sad smile. "He'll wake up, have faith, alright?"

Why was it that she'd just voiced my biggest fear?

Shame choked me like I was dangling by nothing but a tie.

Because I knew the minute he woke up, Izzy would know the truth, and from what I'd just gathered, it wouldn't take much confessing for him to tell Izzy everything and beg for forgiveness. He would have no way of knowing I was falling for her.

That I wanted her.

That every night sleeping next to her was pure hell.

The door shut behind Kelsey.

I shoved the USB into my pocket, not trusting the company computers not to have any tracking on them. I knew that there was a good chance the company would be able to see everything I did.

So I purposefully calmed myself the hell down, sat at his desk, and wondered what he would do if he was awake and moving.

Take our dad down?

Get married?

Drink?

I would sign papers Monday as acting CEO for Julian.

I would marry Izzy Saturday, as Julian.

And I knew, as I locked up the office and rode the elevator back down, that my father had genuinely fucked me.

Because I wasn't standing in for my twin during that wedding.

No. I was supposed to become him, for the media, for the pictures, for the world.

I rubbed my eyes and hopped out of the taxi I'd called when it was back at the apartment. Another elevator.

Another ding.

Another bout of heaviness rested on my shoulders as I let myself in and saw Izzy baking cookies.

It was so normal I smiled.

I needed normal after what I'd gone through that day, more than she would ever realize.

I wanted to punch Julian as much as I wanted to hug him and tell him I was sorry for misjudging him.

It was more than that too. It was deep-rooted jealousy over the life he had. The life that was now mine.

He had hurt her.

I deserved her.

My thoughts swirled around in my head, tempting me to look the other way. It would save Mom.

It would save Izzy.

If I just gave in, told my father that I'd do whatever it took to keep them both, he would be waiting in his high tower with another ironclad contract and a pen filled with my blood.

And he would win.

I couldn't let that happen.

Even if I wanted the fantasy of Izzy to be true.

She would eventually find out I wasn't my brother or my father, and it would ruin us just like I deserved.

"You look rough." She dipped a wooden spoon in the batter and handed it to me. "It's your mom's recipe. I may have stolen her number from your phone. Hope that's okay. I just wanted to check in now that she's part of our life."

She said *our life* and my resolve cracked a little bit more. "That's more than okay. She needs someone other than me to talk to. I'm boring as hell."

Izzy's cheeks pinked. "Not true."

"Okay, I'm boring as hell when I'm not making you c—"

"Nope, I'm already red enough, I can feel my face heating." She looked shyly away. "So how's the dough?"

I licked the spoon and watched her nervously tuck her hair behind her ear. She was in black yoga pants and a long loose sweater that looked easy enough to peel from her body. It was light blue, and I could see skin through it, including her black sports bra and perfect breasts.

"Dough?" I repeated dumbly. "The dough's good, sorry, I was just looking at your outfit. It's . . . a little too tempting for a Saturday, don't you think?"

"As opposed to a Sunday or a Monday?" She took the spoon back and stirred the dough again, then added some chocolate chips.

Part of the sweater fell off her shoulder. "Damn."

"What?" Her eyes sparkled when she looked up.

I did that.

Me.

Bridge.

Not Julian.

I was the reason she was baking cookies, so why the hell was I not saying anything?

And then it hit me, like shame typically does, it doesn't creep up and reveal itself slowly. No, it rams you in the chest and steals your next few breaths right along with the beats of your heart.

I, Bridge Anderson, was just like them. Because I was too selfish to tell her the truth even if it meant saving her.

Well played, Father, well fucking played.

Chapter Twenty-Three

It was the best weekend of my life, followed by the longest Monday in the history of Mondays.

Julian took me to brunch Sunday. We talked about the wedding, and I fielded calls from Marla asking me to stop by for a few dress fittings.

In a week, my life would change forever.

But it finally felt like I had my partner back, ride or die. That was us. I'd sworn to him when we were in college that I would never abandon him, and I hated the sad look he had given me when I vowed my loyalty. It wasn't one of excitement or relief; it was one of total devastation.

We'd fought over it, and I wondered if he felt guilty over pulling me into his family.

He brought up his father again.

And I should have known, should have seen the signs then, that his father's talons were already in, already causing hemorrhaging that even our love and friendship couldn't stop.

I sent Julian a quick text of encouragement. He hadn't seemed excited to be headed into work, but at the end of the day, he would officially be the CEO of Tennyson Financial. The only peculiar part of the scenario was this whole silent investor, who still had a third of the company. Who the hell would Edward trust with that much of the stock? Furthermore, you'd think the board wouldn't like it.

It would take a lot to remove Edward from the company, which Julian reminded me that morning over breakfast, like he was actually thinking of attempting the impossible.

He said he had a plan.

And I almost puked.

It was almost identical to the conversation we'd had weeks before he got into his accident. It was a business dinner, and I'd left the table and cried in the bathroom because Marla yet again was hitting on him in front of everyone. Edward didn't seem to mind since he was with one of Julian's assistants, the blonde pretty one who actually looked like she had a good head on her shoulders, one meant for more than designer makeup and red lipstick.

He'd knocked on the stall, begged me to come out, then held me while I sobbed, while my sharp nails made a mark in my clenched left hand.

"Izzy, I need you to pull yourself together," he whispered in my ear while *I was having a meltdown. "Can you do that for me, we're close, so damn close to getting everything we want."*

Right. Everything he wanted.

"You're a monster," I muttered. *"And I still can't walk away from you, from us. What happened, Julian? How do I stop this?"*

He tensed and then cupped my face. "Just a little longer, Iz, alright? I need you to walk out there and look like the perfect doting fiancée. I need you to smile like you've been taught, I need you to be a Tennyson now more than ever. If my father assumes I'm just like him then he'll finally trust me. Things will be different once I take over. I promise. The flirting means nothing."

"Don't you dare patronize me!" I roared. "I've done everything for you! You couldn't even let me leave the house today without making me change into this." I pulled at my revealing dress. "What? Am I supposed to whore out for you now?"

"That's enough!" he snapped, his eyes cold. "This is bigger than you, bigger than just a job. Do you know what I could do with this position? I would have the power to change lives! To make an empire bigger than my dad. Like I said, this is bigger than us. This is more important than any one person." He looked away.

"Money generally is." I glanced away. It was the first time in a long time I'd raised my voice at him, the first time I didn't care that he could hurt me or leave me destitute. I wanted to yell, I wanted to claw at his face and beg him to kiss me and make it better.

"Deep breaths." Julian gave me that perfect smile, the one I loved, and then he kissed me softly on the mouth. "We'll get through this, we always do. Money is power, Iz, never forget that."

"You don't need any more money."

"That, sadly," he murmured, looking away, "isn't the point. It's never been about the amount, it's about who holds all the cards."

I followed him two minutes later, makeup fixed, fake smile present, and I watched women flirt with him. I watched him flirt back and drink like I hadn't just had a meltdown.

And at the end of the night, I watched him clink his glass with his father while they laughed about a stripper one of the board members had invited to the bar for drinks later.

He was just like him.

And my hate rivaled my love.

I shook my head like I was trying to get the memory out and gazed at our text exchange.

Me: Good luck today. Everything is going to be fine.

Julian: Who needs luck when I have you? Promise to send me pictures of the lingerie you pick out from your shopping trip this afternoon?

I frowned down at my phone.

Me: What shopping trip?

Julian: Marla said she was taking you shopping after lunch. I just found out, assumed you planned it.

Me: I'm screaming but you can't hear me. Ugh, I'm volunteering at the hospital afterward too, so I might be late. Have I mentioned I hate her?

Julian: Play nice, and I'll let you eat cookies off my chest later.

Me: Who are you?

Julian: Just me. :)

I grinned down at my phone. And typed back.

Me: Give them hell today, okay? I'll make my visit with the kids fast. I want to celebrate when you get home, and when I say celebrate what I really mean is . . . Netflix and chill again.

Julian: If I could drive home right now, I would. Miss you, Izzy.

I stared at my phone for a few minutes, trying to figure out why the nickname he'd been using sounded off. It was so natural. In public he called me Isobel just like everyone else. But in private, Julian used to call me Iz.

He hadn't used that name once in the last month.

Maybe I'd ask him when he came home.

I really was losing my mind, wasn't I?

I sighed and dialed Marla even though it was the last thing I wanted to do.

"Yes?" She answered on the second ring. "I'll be there in a few minutes."

"And you thought it was better to just spring this on me rather than asking permission?"

"I ask for forgiveness, not permission. I'm wearing white today, black should suit just fine."

The conversation was over.

The line dead.

Luckily I was already in a sleek black YSL number. I grabbed my Ray-Bans along with my blue Prada clutch and locked up.

It was going to be a really long afternoon.

Chapter Twenty-Four

BRIDGE

I was wearing a suit that was too small, surrounded by men twice my age clapping me on the back as I signed page after page after page of a document that would officially make me CEO.

"I trust this will all stay in this room." My dad lit a cigar while one of the board members, Harry Wilde, handed out more Cubans to the rest of the members.

There were thirteen of us.

We were missing one important person.

Julian.

I signed my name, my real name, Bridge Anderson Tennyson. And I hoped to God I wasn't screwing my brother completely.

"Won't leave the room," Harry announced with a wink in my direction.

I sighed and kept signing.

Father watched from his end of the long marble conference table. He had a gleam in his eye, and the more pages I signed the sicker I felt.

I was becoming CEO.

To the board I was Bridge, the long-lost son finally coming home to claim my rightful place.

To the rest of the world, I was Julian Tennyson, becoming one of the richest CEOs in US history.

The only thing keeping me sane was the fact that Julian and I would have enough shares together to take our father down.

I just had to marry Izzy in order to get my shares.

I wasn't sure how much work Julian had already done, but looking around, they all seemed pleased I was the one sitting there, which made me wonder if they saw the writing on the wall.

And if they did—I had to wonder if my father did as well.

I had to win them over, every one. I had to do a damn good job and do the one thing Julian had been trying to do all along.

Make our dad proud.

Another page was pulled.

They talked about yachts and private schools and expensive vacations.

Money ruled their world.

And if money stopped making it turn.

I snapped my head toward my dad and smiled.

His eyes narrowed.

I was going to take him down.

And I was going to do it with a smile on my face.

The unexpected sound of champagne popping had me dropping my pen on the last page. I picked it up and finished my signature. I'd sealed our fate, I had saved my mom. I had saved thousands of jobs.

I was CEO.

I had what Julian had wanted his whole life.

I had it.

Please, God, wake up . . . because I was never meant to sit in that chair, overlooking that kingdom, that was Julian.

And the longer I sat there, the more I wondered if my dad hadn't counted on being able to suck me in too.

Both of his sons, leading by his side.

I'd only glanced at the USB once, saw so much information I wanted to take a nap, and then felt like everything was already slipping through my fingers, mainly Izzy. I jerked it out of the computer and haven't looked back. Since then it had been burning a hole in my pocket.

And I also knew that when he woke up.

Izzy and I were done.

I accepted a glass of champagne and lifted it toward my father.

He lifted his right back and looked happier than I'd ever seen him, and smug as ever.

"To Tennyson Financial." A board member whose name I couldn't remember raised his glass in my direction. "And to our new acting CEO, Bridge Anderson Tennyson!"

Cheers erupted around the room, reporters waited outside the glass doors, one from *Forbes*, another from the *Times*. When I walked out there, they'd yell Julian's name, not mine.

"Gentlemen." My father stood. "If you'll excuse us, I'd like a private moment with my son."

They slowly exited the room, slapping each other on the back, while I stared out at the cityscape, a city that felt like I'd helped him own, now that two of the largest finance firms had merged. The sick feeling didn't dissipate; if anything it worsened the more I stared.

"You saved a lot of IFC jobs today, a lot of money, a lot of speculation." He moved to stand right next to me. "You were firstborn, you know. This was always supposed to be yours."

"Don't patronize me," I spat. "You chose him because you couldn't control me and you knew it."

He was quiet, and then, "Had I known you'd grow up to have bigger balls, believe me, I would have chosen differently. He pretended to want this, but I saw through it. He was always angry with me. He has so many ideas, most of them good, but he's too eager to please me, too eager to do whatever I say, and it drives me batshit crazy."

"I wonder why," I said tersely, then took another sip.

"I see the world differently, and I'm willing to sacrifice whatever I need to earn my cut of what it has to offer." He didn't sound the least bit apologetic. "Tell me, are you enjoying Isobel?"

"Is she my door prize?" I snapped, angry that I was falling for her, angry that he saw that too, possibly planned on it.

Father smiled and put his hand on my shoulder. "She was going to break off her engagement with him, Amy overheard the conversation. He would have let her. A kingdom needs its kings and queens just like it needs its pawns. A broken engagement would have looked bad. It could have seemed like the family was unstable and it could have leaked into the news, and as much as you doubt my next words, I do care what happens to her. She's been loyal to the family and deserves what we have to offer, and if she's willing to play the game why not let her have some winnings?"

I shook my head. "Why won't you let her go?"

He frowned. "Why would she want to leave?"

The man was delusional. "Is this a pride thing again—"

"Enough," he snapped. "Julian's worked hard. It's only natural that he gets to have the girl in the end. Besides, she has no one, we basically adopted her into our family, the media loves a good sob story. So I ask you again. Why would she want to leave?"

I had no words.

I stared at him.

"I don't have to worry about that anymore anyway, son, she'd never leave you. I saw the way Julian treated her, he's cut from the same cloth as his old man. He's not a one-woman man. I expected her to walk, but everything's worked out as it should. We have over seven hundred billion in assets, the girl's back in love with you, we have a wedding that would make royalty jealous. Everyone wants to be you, don't you see? You have everything at your fingertips, why would anyone run away from that?"

I needed him to stop talking. I needed him to make the relationship not sound like a business transaction.

"And if I walk? You could run things behind the scenes, you know, they don't need to see my face. What if I walk and take Izzy with me, along with the trust fund and all my shares?"

His smile faded. "You walk, you get nothing, and I'd think before walking away from all of this, you'd have to consider the thousands of jobs that depend on you, son."

Sickness took over, and I almost hurled my champagne all over him. "Ah, so this isn't about you, it's about other people now? What? You suddenly care about your employees more than the money they bring in?"

He flinched.

It was barely there.

Maybe he had a small sliver of his heart left, or maybe he just had the hiccups.

I was going to go with the hiccups.

Pain filled his eyes. "A father does what he needs to do to protect his family even if it means he's protecting them from themselves."

"Bullshit." I set down my glass. "I'm gonna go see Julian tonight, talk to him, see if there's any progress."

"He moved his toes and fingers the other day. The doctors are concerned there may be brain damage. You have to understand, son, Julian may wake up a completely different person, or he may wake up a vegetable."

I froze. "What do you mean? You said you had the best doctors."

He looked away, but I saw the flash of guilt. "I'm not God."

"No shit."

"I want him to live, I need him to live."

I eyed him skeptically; was he getting emotional over this?

"I'm controlling the pieces I can, Bridge, and letting the universe take care of the rest. If he's moving his fingers and toes that's a good sign. If he wakes up and can't resume his responsibilities as both husband and CEO, I expect you to do the right thing, the thing he would want more in this world." He put his hand on my shoulder. "And take your rightful place."

Fuck. Me.

I didn't say anything.

Because there was nothing to say.

Nothing I wouldn't do for Julian.

And now? Nothing I wouldn't do for Izzy.

"You're a Tennyson, you can't run away from that."

He started walking toward the glass doors, when I turned around and asked the dreaded question that had been occupying my mind. "Did you plan it? Me falling for Izzy? Or were you just hopeful?"

"She's beautiful." He didn't even glance over his shoulder. "And starving for attention. What do you think?"

"I think this is fucked up."

"Welcome to corporate America." He opened the glass doors and started answering reporters' questions.

And I stared out at the kingdom one more time and whispered, "Please, wake up."

Chapter Twenty-Five

Julian wasn't answering my texts. Not that I blamed him; he had interviews to conduct and people to celebrate with. This was huge news: Tennyson Financial now had a monopoly over investing in a way no company ever had. They were untouchable.

I was proud of him, proud of everything that he'd done to get to this moment even if it meant that this moment included Edward and an accident that nearly cost Julian his life.

"I like the red. It's very couture," Marla said, taking a sip of her white wine while I spun around for the designer who was currently pinning fabric around my hips and having her assistant take Polaroids.

"It's a bit tight," I pointed out. "Around the thighs."

"Go on a cleanse and you'll be fine," Marla piped up. "Besides, it's not like you'll be in it long, not with a Tennyson standing around you."

"Can we not talk about Julian?" I said with clenched teeth. "He's my fiancé, and you're married to his father. Remember him? The one with the beer gut well on his way to developing gout?"

Marla gave me a scathing glare. "Jealous? Edward is one of the most powerful men alive, so what if I have to close my eyes and imagine your fiancé's face when we sleep together. It's not hard to imagine what it would be like with the real thing."

I sucked in a sharp breath of air and promised myself I'd keep the tears in. Amazing how I couldn't even imagine him cheating after this last week together.

The man I was with now wasn't a cheater.

What did that even mean?

That he'd found God during that accident and decided to keep it in his pants?

Had she touched him? Seen him naked? I couldn't bear the thought of it.

I'd smelled him on her.

"Excuse me." I batted the designer's hands away and walked briskly into the dressing room, slamming the door behind me.

With shaking hands, I called Julian's office. I needed to talk to him, to hear his voice, to know that this wasn't all a dream, that what I felt between us wasn't my imagination.

"Tennyson Financial, Julian Tennyson's office." Amy's voice was way too chipper.

"Amy, hi, it's Isobel, is Julian available?"

She sighed like I was a burden she never asked for, she'd always treated me that way and Julian always allowed it. "Actually no, he finished conducting interviews for CNBC a couple of hours ago and then left. I don't know where he is."

"Okay, I'll just call later." For some reason, my mind flashed to the tattoos. That was one of the companies, right? "Amy, one more thing."

"Yes?"

"Are they going to go through with purchasing Inkbox?" I wasn't sure why I asked. I don't usually inquire about their business deals.

"Inkbox?" she repeated. "I have no idea what you're talking about."

A chill blanketed my body. "The temporary-tattoo company that Julian said went viral online? The last few weeks?"

An annoyed sigh followed. "Look, if we're buying them out then I'd be the first to know because I take all of Julian's notes in those meetings. In front of me I have ten companies he and the board will be looking at over the next calendar year, and not one of them is called Inkbox. Maybe he hasn't presented it yet, but that would be really out of character since he always runs everything by his team first."

"Out of character," I repeated. "Right."

"He's not here and the media is still clamoring around the offices. He won't be back for at least an hour. I'll leave him a note like I always do and tell him to text you, alright?"

"Thank yo—"

The line went dead.

I slowly changed out of my dress, my body feeling more and more numb as I tried to put two and two together. He could be looking at the company on his own before telling his assistant and Edward. It wouldn't be that out of character, would it?

I picked up several shopping bags containing items I'd been given earlier that day, bags of expensive lingerie I was going to wear on my wedding night, provided to me by every single designer in the city who wanted free publicity, and then I grabbed my purse.

"I don't feel well." I walked past Marla, past the security standing at the doors, and down the street to the waiting town car. I heard Marla call out my name but I didn't care, I just wanted to leave.

"Miss Isobel?" Belford, my driver, looked at me in the rearview mirror. "Sorry, I was expecting you to be another hour. Where to?"

"The hospital. I promised I'd stop by so I could start to get back to my regular schedule."

Belford nodded and took me directly there. Within minutes, I was on the third floor surrounded by the nursing staff and Annie with her pink scrubs and black cropped hair opening her arms wide.

I stepped into them and sighed.

"You've been busy." She pulled back and winked. "Now, we've all taken bets. Are you guys getting married this soon because it's a shotgun wedding?" I could have sworn everyone looked at my stomach and speculated: heavy lunch or baby?

"Guys!" I rolled my eyes and laughed. "It's more of a publicity thing for the company. The accident shook a lot of people up, Julian included, and honestly, we just want to be married."

Weird how true that was.

I smiled to myself.

"You literally can't stop smiling," Annie pointed out with a grin of her own.

"I'm happy." I lifted one shoulder and let it fall.

"Yeah." She shook her head at me like it was almost unbelievable "You really are, aren't you?"

"The accident seemed to change him, his outlook on life, on me, on everything. Let's just say it's been a really good month and leave it at that."

"In bed or—"

"Sorry, you lost, Dave, I'm not pregnant," I laughed as he handed Annie fifty bucks. "Maybe next time?"

Groans erupted around the nursing station as money exchanged hands over the shotgun wedding / pregnancy bet.

"Right, right." He grabbed a clipboard. "Did you want back on the schedule? Annie said you'd be coming in today to get things situated, but I wasn't sure what your hours would be like because of the wedding."

"Oh, I'm sorry. I honestly wasn't even thinking of that."

"Her head's too far up in the clouds," Annie teased.

I winked as I took the clipboard and looked over the schedule. "Let me check if I can come back tomorrow and the next day. Then I have the rehearsal dinner to prepare for and all the other things a Tennyson bride has to do." I said the last part with my nose scrunched up.

"Poor"—he lifted the clipboard out of my hands with a smirk—"princess."

"Annie." One of the new charge nurses walked up with a grim look on her face. "I keep trying to get new bedding from the sixth floor, and it's been hours. I have two kiddos waiting, and both Josh and Sarah just took their breaks."

"I'll go." I put on my badge and shrugged. "I still have at least an hour. What else did you need?"

"Oh, thank you, Izzy!" She handed me another clipboard. "Everything on this list. We just had a few accidents with the little ones, and I swear ever since they brought in the patient who shall not be named, it's like pulling teeth to get anyone in the old ICU to talk to us."

"Old unit?" I repeated. "Why would they put anyone there?"

"Security." Annie rolled her eyes. "There's another bet if you want in on it. I keep saying it's George Clooney, someone else swore it was Kanye. You know how celebrities are. They think they need not just one special bed, but the entire floor. They moved him up a floor a few weeks ago. His agent, or whoever the man was, came in with a check for the hospital and that was it."

"Strange," I agreed. "Alright, I'll be right back, then."

"No peeking!" Annie called after me. "That's not a fair bet."

"You can't peek on patients," I called back in a hushed tone.

She just shrugged.

I didn't realize how much I had missed her friendship; she was just so positive and full of life. I was still smiling when I made it to the floor and slid my card through the slot then waited for the door to open.

"Yes?" came the disembodied female voice over the intercom.

I looked at the number on the clipboard, 7808, which would match the identity of the patient I was visiting or the department I was from. "I'm coming in for supplies, not to see a patient, or the patient. It's Izzy."

They should know me. But I said the number anyway.

A few more seconds went by.

Everyone knew me there. Then again, this could be someone new. The door buzzed, thankfully.

I walked through. Nothing was more eerie than an abandoned ICU. A doctor was at the old nurses' station surrounded by three other nurses who I'd never seen before.

"Hey." I handed the clipboard to the lady at the computer. "I just need some bedding and a few other things on the list. It's a bit crazy in the pediatric cancer wing."

Her eyebrows shot up as she looked behind me and sighed. "Yeah, well, it's been a bit crazy here too."

I smirked at that. "Celebrity?"

She just snorted. "Only the doctor knows who it really is, though I don't recognize the name, so who knows."

"The name of the celebrity?"

"Yeah." She stood. "Be right back."

The doctor and other two nurses walked over to the closed door, knocked, and let themselves in.

I shouldn't have looked.

But I did.

I looked.

Inside that room, standing, was Julian.

My fiancé, Julian.

What the hell?

I ducked behind the desk and nearly wept when the room numbers were on the main screen along with the names.

It was easy to find.

Because he was the only patient in that part of the wing.

Bridge Anderson.

The name didn't sound familiar.

The only thing that did sound familiar was that Julian's mom had joked about calling Julian Bridge.

But Julian was standing right there. I just saw him.

What sort of secrets was he keeping?

My stomach sank a bit. And then I ducked even farther when the door opened again, and my fiancé swept out of the room and walked down the hall, his expression grim.

Chapter Twenty-Six

ISOBEL

"Home."

"Alright."

The drive was short. I didn't even remember walking into the elevator with my bags or dropping them at the door. I kicked off my shoes and walked toward his office.

His very private office.

I was never allowed access to his computer. Too many business dealings that could go wrong, and though he trusted me, it was a hard pass, especially after college.

I went over to his leather chair and sat as the memory unfolded.

"Iz, I need you to promise me something, alright?"

"Anything." I was too enraptured with our penthouse apartment, the expensive sofa, the drapes. I'd never had drapes before, and now I couldn't stop staring at them; they were electronic and pulled across the windows with a button that had me reeling. In fact, everything was run through a control system with buttons, the showers, music, even our iPhones were connected.

"Iz, focus." His lips pulled into a tiny smirk. "Can you do that?"

"Huh? Yup, sorry." I put down the remote and faced him. He looked nervous and a little bit sad, but I figured he was just going through the same disbelief I was. He was now a senior VP at Tennyson Financial, and all our dreams were finally coming true. We'd start having kids right away, I'd continue my volunteer work, and we'd never have to worry about money ever again.

He finally had access to his trust fund. It felt like something out of a fairy tale, and I was living it!

"I'm going to be given access to a lot of private information, information that if leaked could take down companies, get people fired. I trust you, I do, I just, I need this to be our one rule. I'll buy you whatever laptop you want, but my computer is mine, alright? I don't want secrets, and I don't want you thinking I'm keeping you out because I'm password protecting everything, but this job is really important to me. And protecting you is more important."

"I know, Julian. You've always protected me, even when I was annoyed with you. I never had to worry about life getting me down, because you were always there to pick me up."

His eyes flashed with something before a smile erupted on his beautiful face. "You know exactly what to say to make everything better, don't you?"

"Uh-huh, it's why I'm your girlfriend and you love me." I wrapped my arms around his neck and kissed him softly.

He groaned. "I'll never get tired of this, Iz, of us, of you. I can't wait to start a family with you. I can't wait for what the future holds."

"It's gonna be an adventure," I agreed.

And never went behind his desk.

For three years I'd kept my word.

And now I was tapping my fingers on the mouse trying to wake the computer up and praying that his passwords were saved.

Sometimes he wrote them down next to the computer.

Other times he put them in his phone.

I placed my hands on the desk and patted around for a sticky note or something that would help. He had document after document of generous donations, which was just like him.

My hands came up empty, which meant I'd have to confront him when he got home and ask for the one thing he'd always promised me.

Honesty.

Because even when he cheated, he didn't lie.

Even when he hurt me, he didn't sugarcoat it.

I got up from the desk and tripped over the rug beneath his chair. I quickly grabbed the side of the desk and knocked over a picture of us.

Thank God the glass didn't shatter.

I picked it up and stared at it.

We were happy then, just like we were now.

I tilted my head as he smiled at the camera.

And then I squinted.

He looked so much more composed in that picture. It was taken over a year ago, which made more sense, but something else about it didn't quite make sense.

With a sigh I put it back down on the table. There was a sticky note where the picture had been.

On it a phone number.

And the name Bridge Anderson.

Chapter Twenty-Seven

BRIDGE

I needed a drink. Maybe ten.

After the conversation with my father, I endured several hours of interviews, and my stomach was eating itself from hunger.

I hadn't been prepared for the flirting.

All the flirting.

Every single woman who interviewed me seemed to think that I was still on the market. That was the most confusing part of the entire day, did he flirt with everyone or did he just use his flirting to get things done? He had more women than men working for him, and they all seemed to be on a first-name basis.

"What the hell, man?" I whispered under my breath. "What were you thinking?"

I was in over my head and had no help. It felt like drowning in a really expensive suit that had a life jacket only Julian knew how to access.

After the interviews, I went immediately to the hospital. The doctor said that Julian could still wake up at any time and that the swelling was going down, but the longer he stayed under, the more concerned they were that he wasn't going to wake up.

The doctor left to go talk to the nurses.

And I had stared at him.

My brother.

His face was almost completely healed except for a few new scars that plastic surgery would have to fix, and the machine was still breathing for him.

I felt so much guilt I couldn't speak.

And then I knew I had to.

Maybe he would wake up, maybe I could piss him off enough for him to react.

It was worth a shot.

"Hey, man." I grabbed his hand and held on. "Just thought you should know that you have the prettiest fiancée I've ever seen and that she said my hair was softer than yours."

His fingers flickered.

I jerked my hand away and let out a small laugh. "Didn't like that, did you?"

No response.

"Well, at least this means maybe you can hear me, maybe you'll stop sleeping on the job and get your ass in gear. The world thinks you're healthy and the CEO of Tennyson. The board knows the truth, that I stepped in to stop widespread panic over one of the biggest buyouts in history." I sighed. "I don't want your life, Jules. I swear I don't. But I'm starting to panic. Okay, I'm already panicking. I need you to wake the fuck up. Dad is . . . he's breathing down my neck about Izzy. You have a fiancée." My voice cracked. "A life." I hated myself so much. I wanted her as much, maybe more than he did. I would fight for her, cheat death for her. "A wedding."

This time his fingers jolted.

I grabbed them and squeezed.

"I don't know what to do," I whispered. "I am completely in over my head and from the looks of it, you were too before this happened. I don't know what your plan was, but I saw your computer. I know I have a trust fund, I know I have a third of the company, so I need you to wake the fuck up so you can tell me what we're supposed to do with this info." I cursed again. "Dad said he wouldn't sign the shares over to me unless I did something, something that would hurt you. Something that would hurt me too." I dropped his hand and stood. "I need your permission. God, this sounds idiotic, but I need your permission to marry Izzy, to do the right thing by her. I haven't told her yet, but if I do and she's upset, which she has every reason to be, then Dad won't sign over the thirty percent I know we need."

A soft knock sounded at the door.

Dr. Perkins walked in with an unreadable expression on his face. "His vitals are good, but we still don't see any meaningful brain activity beyond basic brainstem function. His Glasgow Coma Scale score remains at three."

Impatience grew inside me. I didn't know what any of that shit meant. "Look at him." I pointed at my twin, my heart twisting. "He looks like he could wake up any minute. He's moving his fingers, he even got mad at me and did it twice when I provoked him."

"Mr. Tennyson." He settled his hand on my shoulder, and I clenched my jaw. "He needs time to heal. We assume patients can hear us, but we also know that sometimes their movements can be a trick of the nerves trying to heal. Don't lose hope, and we'll keep doing our best, alright?"

"Yeah," I croaked. "I won't give up on him."

"Good." He smiled and held out his hand. I shook it and then turned to my brother and leaned down to kiss him on the forehead. "I'm sorry I didn't protect you, Jules, and I'm sorry for what I have to do to make sure I never make that mistake again."

I walked out of the hospital just as helpless as before. My brain was clouded with confusion as I drove a car I didn't even own, a brand-new Maserati, back to the apartment and parked it in the garage.

I still had the USB in my pocket, but it seemed meaningless without Julian, because I couldn't act without him. I couldn't act by myself, and from what I'd already seen, I needed him in a huge way.

And unless a miracle occurred, I was truly stealing his life come this weekend—no, not just his life, possibly the love of his life.

And maybe the love of mine too.

Shit, how did it get to this?

When the elevator doors finally opened to the apartment, I was welcomed with the smell of spaghetti and bread.

My feet carried me to the kitchen, where Izzy sat with a glass of wine and a small grin on her face.

She was wearing nothing but black lace.

My brain refused to function past the fact that she was in lingerie and I was still dressed.

"Damn." I was almost nervous to speak. "You look incredible. And here I thought I wasn't going to get a preview." *Because I didn't deserve one, because my brother had you first and I want to hate him for that, no matter how unfair it is.*

"Thank you." Izzy trailed her finger down the lacy strap of her bra and grinned. How the hell was I supposed to keep my hands off her? "Long day?"

"You have no idea." I groaned and tried to think of more words to say, but my brain was misfiring, reminding me that she wasn't mine to unwrap. "It smells amazing." I sidestepped her and grabbed my own glass of wine and put the kitchen island between us, I needed some sort of barrier before I threw her on the counter and licked my way down her body.

"Julian?" I flinched at the name. Not today, not now. I would do anything to hear her say my name, anything. I hated that this was what it had come down to, me wishing she knew how much I cared and her thinking she already knew the truth because I was Julian. "You look tense."

"I am tense." Sexually repressed and tense, emotionally drained and in need of her legs wrapped around me. "It was just, I know signing my name on all those dotted lines saved a lot of jobs since IFC was going under. I get that it was good for the economy, for us, but it just felt . . . selfish and like we were never going to come back from this, like my dad just had one more thing . . ." I shook my head. "It's just a lot to process." I thought of Julian and me fighting over CDs, of him taking my shit and me getting annoyed and then having the thought that I would never treat him that way. It was like our roles had reversed at the worst possible time. Only this time, I was the one taking and he wasn't the sort of guy to just let me have things.

"Julian?" During my mental breakdown, Izzy had somehow walked around the island and was now standing in front of me, nearly naked. I could touch her, I wanted to touch her. I couldn't, I just . . .

I leaned in and kissed her on the cheek, my lips hovering near her mouth, tasting the wine in the air. "Sorry, I was just thinking. It's been a really long day, like I said. Why don't we sit and have something to eat?" I stepped around her and walked into the living room, grabbed a blanket and wrapped it around her shoulders. "Don't want you to get cold."

The blanket whispered down to the carpet. "I'm not cold."

Fuck.

"No? Because you're nipping out a bit there." I palmed her breast, hoping it would be enough that she'd kiss me and I could escape without totally ruining her life.

She'd stayed.

She was loyal.

I was taking that from her without her even knowing it.

Maybe I was the villain after all.

The monster. Just like my father.

Because I wanted to take without looking back, and I was suddenly starting to think that leaving without her wasn't an option.

Her eyes closed as she leaned in and wrapped her arms around my neck, her body pressed firm against mine, soft in all the right places. I slid my hands down to the curve of her hips and tried not to think of how good it felt, how right it felt, having her in my arms.

A lesser man would have taken her.

I needed to be more than that. Besides, even though I didn't know her as well as he did, even though I didn't deserve this, somehow this felt out of character for her. She'd still been somewhat shy with me. More playful, yes. More responsive when I held her at night? Absolutely, but I would have never pegged her as a seductress.

Weeks ago, she had looked like she wanted to murder me. Something wasn't right, but I was still a guy, and I couldn't take my eyes off her.

"Izzy?"

"Hmm?" She started kissing my neck, her lips moving up and down my skin, leaving a trail of sensations that had me ready to black out. Was this a test? To see if I was really Julian? If I would respond?

I was suddenly worried she knew something she shouldn't.

Something that would destroy what fragile relationship we had between us.

"I just want you to know, I think you are the most beautiful woman I've ever met, and I wish—"

She stopped kissing.

"I wish that—"

She backed away. "I wish we were already married."

"What?" It came out louder than I meant it to.

She smiled at me, and then reached for my dick.

I was going to hell.

She palmed the front of my trousers while I bit back a curse and whispered, "Izzy, don't you want to wait until this weekend? It's more romantic that way, and I told you, I want you willing, not because you feel like you have to."

There was no way out of this unless he woke up.

And that was the annoying part. If he woke up, I didn't get her, and if he didn't, I did. I was stuck between wanting both futures.

Izzy's eyes narrowed. "So just to be clear, you, Julian Tennyson, are turning down sex?"

I was mentally strangling myself, and my balls were in the process of removing themselves from my body, they were so disappointed in the rest of me.

I hung my head. "Yes, but only because I respect you so much."

For the love of God, those words just came out of my mouth, didn't they?

"And I want you to trust me," I added.

Something shifted in her eyes when I said *trust*.

She smiled. "Trust, hmm? So that means you'll tell me the truth, no matter what? From here on out?"

Fuck. "Yes."

She smiled then, a beautiful smile, bent over, and picked up the blanket and then piped up with "I guess we should eat, then."

My eyes narrowed. "Izzy, what's going on?"

"Food first." She pointed toward the bedroom. "Get comfortable, and I'll plate everything, alright?"

"Sure."

Something was up.

Did she know?

I stared at her a little harder.

Her look was one of complete innocence. I shook my head and went into the bedroom, shut the door, went into the bathroom, shut that one, and texted Mom on my old phone.

Me: Is it public information? That me and Julian are twins?

Mom: What?

Me: Can you google our family and see that we're twins?

Mom: Everything about you is under the Anderson name, not Tennyson. Trust me, your father made it very easy for people to forget us, though I'm still listed as his first wife and mother of Julian. It's hard information to find, especially with all the new Tennyson information popping up everywhere.

Me: She's acting suspicious. Izzy.

Mom: Because you may look the same on the outside but you are two very different people on the inside. You have more of your father than I'd like to admit and Julian, well, he had a lot of me. He cares, sometimes too much. I never did understand how your father thought he could turn him into a ruthless monster.

Me: I want to still hate him.

Mom: He hurt you deeply. He hurt me as well. We hadn't spoken to him in over a decade. It's okay to be angry. I'd like to think he had his reasons, that he was somehow protecting us.

Me: Or he's just selfish.

Mom: That too. Then again, that would be the pot calling the kettle black, now wouldn't it? Who are you marrying in a few days?

I sighed and nearly dropped my phone into the toilet.

Me: I like her.

Mom: I know.

Me: Tell me what to do.

Mom: Pray he wakes up.

A knot formed in my throat. I didn't have the heart to tell her that a part of me wanted the best of both worlds, him waking up and giving me his blessing to steal his only reason for living. My heavy thoughts consumed me as I went back to the closet and hid my phone—making a grave mistake in the process by forgetting to double-check it was on silent.

Chapter Twenty-Eight

ISOBEL

He didn't touch me.

And for some reason all I kept focusing on was the damn tattoo on his hand. I lay next to a man I was going to marry in five days, and the more time I spent with him, the more concerned I was that something was going on.

And the more I didn't want to know.

Did that make me a monster?

A horrible person?

For wanting to squeeze my eyes shut, hum loudly, and pretend that this was forever, that Julian was himself again, that he didn't care about the money, the fame, the power, that finally Edward would step down and let us live our lives.

I wasn't stupid.

Edward had controlled everything about our lives since college. Why would he stop now?

And why the hell was Julian visiting this Bridge person and keeping it a secret? I wanted to demand answers, but I was also a coward.

Because I was enjoying him so much I was afraid that if I asked the question, he'd revert back to the man he was before the accident.

It was stupid.

But it was still there. That sinking feeling.

I turned on my side and put my hand on Julian's back and then jerked it away. There was another tattoo on his left shoulder. It was small, and looked tribal, or maybe it said something in a different language? Either way, he would have had to have someone use the Inkbox material on him rather than doing it himself, based on where it was located.

What the hell was going on?

I traced my fingers over the writing.

And felt my stomach sink to my knees when I felt the ridge from the ink.

His tattoo was real.

I knew every inch of him, even though sure, these last six months we hadn't slept together a lot, mainly because I was still hurting from his actions. Would he really get a tattoo without telling me?

Furthermore, why would he lie about it?

I rubbed my fingers back and forth a few more seconds. It felt so foreign, his skin. My eyes traced down his insanely built body.

And in my soul, I knew there was something I was missing.

And I was transported back to the day of the accident, when all I wanted was to be set free from this life, from the control. When I was thankful that he was in a coma, when I realized that I was just as bad as the Tennysons, because I wasn't praying for a miracle. I was praying for freedom.

I sighed when Julian turned over and faced me, his eyes sleepy, his smile casual. "Can't sleep?"

"Why did you get a tattoo without telling me?"

His face gave nothing away, but his body tensed, his biceps flexed, and I could see the tension in his shoulders as he stared me down. "I'm sorry?"

"Why would you be sorry? Does Inkbox even exist?" I was going to go crazy before the week was over. "I mean isn't that something you would talk to your future wife about? 'Hey, I'm permanently putting ink on my body'?"

He kissed my forehead and grabbed his phone, pulled up a website, and showed me. It said Inkbox, and true to his story, they had temporary tattoos that lasted close to three weeks so people didn't have to commit.

"And you're looking into purchasing them? Seems a bit off brand for us, don't you think?" I was challenging him; I never challenged him, never questioned, because he never let me, he always ended the conversation first, he always asked me to be reasonable.

Not anymore. Instead, this old or new version, however I looked at it, wanted me to challenge him, welcomed my arguments as if anything else would be a disappointment.

"You're right. It is off brand, but I think the brand is moving in a new direction, especially now that we have more control over what we can buy out." He tucked my hair behind my ears and pressed a kiss to my nose. "You're just exhausted."

"Don't patronize me!" I snapped. "This feels . . ." I shook my head. "I went into your office."

No reaction.

No anger.

Nothing.

"And?" He tilted his head like it wasn't a big deal.

It was suddenly getting hard to breathe in that room, in that bed. "You're not mad?"

"Why would I be mad? You're my other half."

Things I would have killed to hear weeks ago, years ago.

"I knocked over a picture of us." I was feeling hysterical. "You've put on at least ten pounds of muscle since then, maybe more. Your smile is different. It tilts to the right not the left. You have tattoos, three that I can see, that I've never seen before. And you're . . . you're . . ." Tears filled my eyes. "You're different. But you see me. And now I think I'm losing my mind, and maybe I am, maybe after years of being under the Tennyson rule I'm just losing it all. We're getting married in five days, and the man who went into that hospital is not the man who came out."

His eyes darted to mine then locked on like he was afraid to look away. "You're right. The man who walked out of that hospital isn't the same man. I told you, I've changed. I'm in this, Izzy." He cupped my face with his hands. "All you need to know is that I'm in this with you. Okay? I won't abandon you. I won't leave you. I'm going to fight like hell for you even though I know you don't deserve the man who went in that hospital or the one who walked out. Do you understand what I'm saying?"

I gulped. "I saw you today. At the hospital."

His body completely tensed, and then he pressed a heated kiss to my mouth. "Promise me that tonight I can taste you, and tomorrow you can ask your questions?"

"Why?" Tears filled my eyes.

"Because I'm a fucking selfish bastard, and I want you, just you, right now, without secrets, without questions, you." He dipped his head and kissed me so hard my head spun.

I clung to him because I needed something to be real and true, and when he kissed me it felt like everything was going to be okay.

He growled against my neck then pulled down my silk boy shorts and jerked my legs apart, disappearing under the covers. I let out a surprised gasp when I felt his tongue between my legs, when his hands dug into my skin. My hips bucked with each flick of his tongue. I gripped the sheets in my hands as my body pulsed with each climbing sensation. I was engulfed in emotion as the image of what he was doing burned into my mind and pounded as the aching tension mounted until his agile fingers took over.

"Julian." I grabbed his hair. "Now, I need you now." My thighs quivered as he drank from me, sucked and breached every defense or argument I had just thrown at him. My brain wouldn't focus. All I felt was him, and all I wanted was more as my cry of release filled the entire room, maybe even the building. It was drugging, the way the waves of my climax rolled over and over again as if my body was still trying to relive and squeeze out every minute.

Julian's tongue slid across my thigh as he pressed one single kiss there and then hovered over me, his biceps muscles bulging in the moonlight.

"I won't ever deserve you," he rasped. "Doesn't mean I won't try every damn second of every damn day. You're special, never let anyone tell you any different. You're a fighter, stronger than you think. No matter what happens, Izzy, remember that."

He turned on his side while I was still recovering, my breathing heavy.

My heart sad.

Because that was exactly how the old Julian would have solved the argument, by making me forget, by using my own body and love for him against me.

I didn't let him see the tear that slid down my cheek, I wiped it away too quickly. And I didn't let him know how badly he'd hurt me by doing something he thought was a favor when I would have taken the truth instead.

Tears burned the back of my throat as I tried to piece it all together, and when I knew he was finally asleep, I walked into his office and stole the piece of paper with Bridge Anderson's name on it, right along with the number.

Chapter Twenty-Nine

BRIDGE

I woke up feeling like I had done something irrevocable. I'd promised myself I wouldn't touch her, and I'd done just the opposite. Worse, I'd done it in a way to prove to her my own worth rather than making it about her.

Selfish didn't even begin to cover it.

And I could feel it in her posture when she lay down and closed her eyes, when she thought I was sleeping and I could hear her softly weeping.

I had done that.

I'd made her sad.

Not Julian.

I, Bridge Anderson, had done that.

And I couldn't undo it.

And I couldn't tell her why because then it would all be for nothing, wouldn't it? I had no recourse other than to march forward and marry her, ask for forgiveness after the fact, and pray that Julian woke up, soon.

Did it make me a horrible person that when I eventually had sex with her, I wanted her to scream my name, not his?

I rose from bed and went over to the walk-in closet and grabbed a pair of trousers. I carried them with me to the bathroom. While I quickly got ready for the day, I stared at myself in the mirror. I looked just like him, didn't I? But Izzy knew, she knew something wasn't right, and I wasn't sure I could keep my lies straight, wasn't sure I wanted to.

I looked down at the tattoo on my hand. Mom had let me get it when I was sixteen. I had told her I wanted nothing to do with the Tennyson name, and still I wanted it on my body to remind me of who I was, and who I wasn't.

Cursing, I pulled the lipstick USB out and stared at it. Why did it feel so heavy? Like a loaded gun or bomb about to be set off. The heaviness of it felt like a bad omen as I weighed our future in my hand.

I never asked for this responsibility.

All I wanted was for my mom and brother to live.

And now I was stuck in some sick love triangle that my own brother wasn't even aware he was participating in.

Things were fucked up, and I only had myself to blame. We wouldn't be so desperate for money if I had just worked harder to be there for Mom, if I had just swallowed my pride and contacted Julian, hell, if I hadn't ripped up that check.

If I had just told Izzy the minute she opened the door and sworn her to secrecy and let her fall for me, not him all over again.

I was officially disgusted with myself.

I quickly went to the adjoining closet and put on one of Julian's many suit coats; this one was gray. I didn't put on a tie because I didn't give a shit. I shrugged into the too-tight jacket and made my way into the kitchen.

Izzy was already dressed, sitting at the breakfast bar, sipping her coffee, and checking her phone.

The minute I walked up, she slid the newspaper toward me and then followed it with a cup of coffee. All black.

I grabbed it and added some cream and a packet of stevia.

She looked up from her phone. "You don't want black coffee anymore?"

I froze. "Just felt like something sweeter this morning."

"The last time you had any sort of real or artificial sweetener was years ago."

I gulped. Shit. She knew, she knew something was off, she was finally putting it all together, and all I was doing was throwing more lies at her.

"Well"—I sipped the sweetness—"maybe I just want something that reminds me of what you taste like while I'm suffering at work."

Her eyes narrowed. "Interesting."

"What is?"

"The fact that you're suddenly left-handed. Weird, since I didn't notice it before. Is that another one of the aftereffects from the brain injury?"

Fuck. "One of the many, I'm afraid. If you're concerned, I can get you a list of all the crazy shit I'm bound to do while my head is recovering from all that swelling."

"No." She sighed and then frowned back at her phone. "No, sorry, I'm just—last night was—"

"I'm sorry." I moved around the counter and grabbed her hand. "That was me being a dick and not thinking about you. You wanted to talk, and instead I just took over, and that's not fair to you, alright? I don't want to be that guy."

"What do you mean?" She gazed into my eyes.

God, she was one of the prettiest women I'd ever seen. I wanted to protect her from everything—me included. *Damn it, when did this get so complicated?*

"I mean I don't want to be the guy who doesn't hear you, doesn't see you. The one who fixes things with orgasms and easy smiles. I want to know your concerns, and I want to talk even if it means I stay up all night. I want to be that guy because that's the way I was raised. And that is the truth."

"Edward didn't raise you that way."

"I know," I whispered. "He didn't." I felt myself giving in, sinking into the sand as her eyes locked onto mine. It was the perfect moment to confess to her, to ask for her help. To apologize.

I hated that we were having a wedding in a few days and she still thought everything was fine.

"So you're saying your nanny did that?"

"I had my mom before the divorce," I whispered, while my brain chanted *Lie, lie, lie, you still have her.* "I know how to treat the woman I love."

It was the first time I'd said *love* to her as Bridge, but it wouldn't be the last.

I was doing this, wasn't I?

I was keeping her.

And if he was alive, he would hate me forever.

My gut clenched as she slid off the barstool and wrapped her arms around my neck. "I love you too."

Wrong, so wrong.

Did she love him? The new him? Me? Who did she love?

Did it matter?

I kissed her then, softly, and then more urgently as she took the cup of coffee out of my hands and spread her palms across my broad chest.

Mine, she was mine.

I lifted her onto the counter, my hands on her hips as I walked between her legs, our tongues twisting as she clutched my hair and pulled. Everywhere I touched was like heated silk.

"You'll"—she kissed me again—"be late for work."

"Let me be late."

"Julian."

I stopped.

I stopped because it was his name.

And I hated him more, maybe in that moment, than I ever had.

My jaw flexed. "Right, you're right, I'll see you tonight for dinner?"

Her face was sad. "Yeah, Julian."

I needed her to stop saying that name.

"I'll see you tonight."

And like I needed another strike against me, I muttered under my breath. "Isobel."

I heard her soft gasp before the door shut behind me.

Chapter Thirty

My hate was back. Or maybe it wasn't hate, maybe it was hurt masquerading as hate? The minute the door shut, I locked it, just in case, and ran toward his office. I slid my fingers along the computer keyboard, waking it up, and grabbed the piece of paper. I wasn't sure when he would notice it was missing. And that's when I noticed that the screen was still open, frozen, actually.

I could feel my heart in my throat, still pumping, still reminding me I was breathing and okay, as I moved my fingers over the track pad.

In glaring black-and-white typed script, I saw the name Bridge Anderson Tennyson.

It was a trust fund.

For $2.5 million.

And 30 percent of Tennyson Financial.

I don't know how long I stared at it.

Julian had a brother I didn't know about.

A brother named Bridge.

Maybe that's why his mother slipped earlier when she called him Bridge?

Oh God.

Is that why he'd been acting so weird?

It was time to ask him questions.

Time to get answers and grow a backbone.

He'd been at the hospital visiting his brother.

I wanted to know why.

Chapter Thirty-One

BRIDGE

I deserved to rot in hell.

That was really the only thing that came to mind when I sat in that board meeting, while my father kept smiling at me.

That he had somehow won.

Because I'd called her Isobel on purpose, to make her think I was him, out of desperation, because I wanted to save her, because I wanted to save both of them.

My heart lodged in my throat.

I was out of control.

"Now . . ." Father rose from his chair. "As you know, Bridge is CEO, and while we are all so thankful that he's here and able to run the company, I think we should discuss what happens if Julian doesn't wake up. Obviously, things will go on as usual. But if it does get leaked in the right way, Bridge will look like a hero. I just want us to be completely prepared for the worst." He sighed. "I talked with the doctors, no more movement."

Harry sighed. "Sorry, Edward, I know how much Julian means to you, to all of you. I—"

"Sorry for interrupting." I stood. "But can we not talk about my brother as if he's already dead? He's in a coma, healing, that's all that matters. Now if you don't mind, I'd like to get back to business. IFC had over six thousand employees that we're now responsible for, employees who, without us, would be out of a job. I want this transition to be seamless, but you know what happens when you start working with a new company. Things slip through the cracks and, gentlemen, we can't afford to let that happen."

My dad's jaw looked like it was ready to fall off his face, and then he muttered the most shocking thing I'd ever heard him say. "You're absolutely right, son, I'm sorry, let's get a letter drafted to the VPs and management."

Harry nodded while another board member looked over at me and smiled. "Two days in and you're already busting balls, hmm?"

"It's my job to bust balls and to make sure you guys stay rich, so should we move on to the next few acquisitions I'd like to look at, including a temporary-tattoo company that's been extremely lucrative over the past year? If you'll just pay attention to the screen, I'll be quick."

The lights lowered.

And two hours later, I actually felt better about the day. I was giving Julian this; I was giving him his company.

And I refused to fuck it up by not doing a good job.

I had a long day ahead of me and was suddenly thankful I had a secretary who could feed me copious amounts of Starbucks throughout the day, because I knew I was going to have an even longer night.

Izzy.

Damn it, it always came back to Izzy, didn't it?

I dismissed everyone and silently made my way back to my office, his office, the line was blurring too much for me to process.

I made it a few steps down the hall when my father caught up with me.

"You did well in there." He seemed so proud I wanted to hurl. "I mean you overstepped since I'm still the boss, but you did real good. Your brother would never have—"

I stopped walking and glared at him. "Comparing us is only going to make me more angry."

"Kind of hard not to compare you. He works his ass off, and I can tell it doesn't come naturally to him. He's the guy you bring to parties, the one that people adore without even hearing him speak. Put him in a boardroom, and he can make anyone believe anything, but thinking about the employees the way you did today, getting down to business instead of talking about golfing and—"

I held up my hand. "I get your point, and since you're so impressed, let me make mine."

Dad's smile faded.

"I have shit to do." I said it with a smile on my face. "And a fiancée I really want to get home to, so this conversation is done. Compare me to him again, and you won't like the outcome."

I took maybe five steps before he caught up with me again and put his hand on my shoulder. "Don't for one second think she won't compare you to him too. Because one day, maybe even soon, she'll know the truth. If I were you, I'd think about how truly excited you are for your brother to wake up from that damn coma and take everything back with a smile on his face while you sit in the background . . . again."

My nostrils flared. "I want him to wake up."

"Huh." He shook his head and laughed. "I almost believed you."

He left me standing in the hall seething.

And not because he was wrong, but because he saw the desire I had to do a good job, because he saw the feelings I had for Izzy.

I was well and truly screwed if he didn't wake up.

Because my father just discovered that he had me.

And that I wouldn't go anywhere, not with Julian's legacy to continue, and not with Izzy still here. I kept a good pace on the way back to my office, and jerked my head at Kelsey, she knew things I didn't.

I ran my hands through my hair as she closed the door behind her.

"I need enough coffee to stay awake for the next few hours without getting a panic attack. Can you also very discreetly call the hospital and check in on Julian for me? He has—" I started pacing. "He used to love heavy metal music, the screeching kind, maybe see if they can play some for him once a day, and—"

"Bridge." Kelsey smiled warmly at me. "You're doing a good job, everyone says so."

"That's the damn problem," I whispered sadly. "I want to do well so when he wakes up he has this." I spread my arms wide. "I need him to wake up."

"I know you do." She looked like she was going to say something else.

"What?" I crossed my arms. "You look like you have a question."

"If Julian was here right now and he told you to walk away from this, from his life, would you be able to?"

"I don't really feel like answering that question without being mind-numbingly drunk."

She laughed. "It's okay to be good at this, you know. It's okay to be a little bit like him, as long as you don't turn into the other Tennyson. Give yourself permission to be successful, alright?"

I gulped. "Alright."

"And I'll get all the coffee for you."

"You're incredible."

"Hah, you're the one with the power to give raises, just throwing it out there."

"Hilarious." I rolled my eyes. "Oh, and that other receptionist, the grumpy one who I've heard is rude to everyone on the phone, including Izzy?"

"Amy?"

"Yeah, send her in."

"Right away." She walked out and opened the door again as Amy swept into the room, looking every bit the haughty sort of receptionist my father would try to seduce. Her blouse was too low, her lipstick too bright, and she looked minutes away from asking me if I wanted a striptease.

"Amy." I said her name with indifference. "I'm going to need you to pack your things. I'll give you four weeks' severance, which is really generous considering you're actually being let go."

"Excuse me?" She gawked. "Wait, you're firing me?"

"Firing sounds too aggressive. Let's just say I'm asking you to stop working for me in hopes that you'll start working for someone else. Also, Izzy's my fiancée and the future daughter-in-law to Edward Tennyson. Learn who to be a bitch to. Now grab your things."

It was probably the first time in my life I did something that resembled my father's behavior and also the first time I didn't even mind.

She stomped out of the office.

And when she started throwing shit into a box, I had security escort her off the premises.

Kelsey returned with two huge coffees and winked. "Keep doing things like firing freeloaders and you're going to become the new superhero around here."

"Did he . . ." I almost couldn't ask it. "Did Julian ever . . ."

Her face softened. "No, not for lack of trying on her part, but he never caved."

I sighed in relief. "Good. Thanks for the coffee."

"Anytime, Julian." She said my name with emphasis, which made me laugh.

Amazing that weeks ago I was training in the gym and bartending. And now . . . I turned around and sighed . . . running a multibillion-dollar company.

I felt less imposter and more anxious.

That I was living a life I did nothing to earn.

I sent a quick text to Izzy.

Me: I miss you today.

Izzy: I miss you too. I'm headed to the hospital to do some reading with the kids then I'll see you tonight?

Panic seized my lungs.

Me: Sounds fantastic, love you.

Izzy: Love you too.

I buzzed Kelsey back into my office.

"Okay, when I said anytime, I didn't mean every few minutes after you fire the only other person who answers phones," she teased and then did a double take when she glanced at my face. "What's wrong?"

"Call the hospital. I don't care what we have to donate, tell them nobody, not even volunteers or nice grandmas, gets into the old ICU wing."

"Right away." I knew she didn't need an explanation, but I gave her one anyway.

"Izzy's headed there."

"Say no more." She speed-walked back to her desk and the door shut behind her.

And all I kept thinking was *Let it be over.*

Let it finally be over.

Izzy texted me throughout the afternoon and acted completely normal. It was still early, but I missed her and I was nervous about her being at the hospital, so I texted her to let her know I was headed back early.

Me: Coming home early, how are you?

Izzy: Good, I have questions.

Me: Questions?

Shit, shit, shit, she saw him at the hospital. She knew.

Izzy: I would wear a cup.

I started to immediately sweat. I was torn between being relieved and being panicked that I would lose her.

Forever.

Did I ever even have her, though?

Me: What's going on?

Izzy: I may tie you to a chair.

Could this day get any worse?

I let out a rough exhale and typed back.

Me: Just make sure not to break any more ribs, I'm in short supply.

Izzy: No promises.

Shit! What the hell happened at the hospital? Did a nurse talk? Did they let her in despite the free lunch we delivered along with another heavy donation?

I hated how much I actually needed my brother in that moment, would have done anything to reach out and punch him in the face then ask him why, why did he bring me into this? Was he planning on contacting me? Was he going to tell me about the trust fund?

My mind wandered to when we were kids.

"Julian, come get me!" I yelled and ran through the backyard while Mom watched us play hide-and-seek. I quickly found a tree and hid behind it.

He chased and tripped over his feet and then started crying.

I rushed over to him. "Jules? Jules, you okay?"

"It hurts, it hurts!" He rocked back and forth while Mom came running.

I grabbed his hand and held on. "I'm your big brother. I'll always keep you safe, always."

Tears fell from his eyes as he looked up at me. "Promise?"

"I promise. I'll always be there for you, even when it's weird."

He laughed at that. "You're weird."

"You're weird!"

By the time Mom made it to us, we were both laughing even though his ankle was turning purple and blue.

Our father chose that moment to come out of the mansion and yell at us to come inside. "Hide-and-seek is for babies, get your asses in here, your mom has coddled you enough."

I stiffened. So did Julian.

"Will you protect me?" he asked in a small voice. "Even from him?"

He'd never alluded to our dad being anything but nice to him. I was the one that he treated like dirt.

The tears were back in his eyes.

So I nodded. I made that promise. "Even from him, Julian, even from him."

"Forever?"

"What?"

"Say it, say forever.*"*

Mom was quiet as we talked.

"Forever," I whispered, gripping his hand in mine as I helped him limp back to the house.

I looked up at Mom just in time to see a tear fall from her face.

And true hate for Edward Tennyson was born.

The car pulled up to the apartments. I didn't know what to expect. All I knew was I was going to be on the receiving end of something I probably hadn't done, which meant that after I somehow got us out of this mess, I was strangling my brother.

I needed to keep thinking he was waking up.

Because when I didn't, I couldn't swallow.

I couldn't breathe.

I couldn't live.

I made him a promise, one I'd conveniently forgotten, and I'd let that hate for my father seep into him.

The elevator moved slowly.

The front door was unlocked.

Taking a deep breath, I stepped inside. Izzy wasn't in the living room. I checked the master and spare, and then called out. "Izzy?"

"Office."

I squeezed my eyes shut. Shit.

When I walked in, she had her heels on my desk and looked so sexy in a black sleeveless dress that I wanted to sweep off the contents of the desk and have my way with her across it.

"Rough day?" I asked, already knowing the answer.

"Why?" She held up a glass. Oh good, day drinking. I could get on board with that after my day. She took two long sips. "Why did you do it?"

"Do what?" I had no idea what she was even talking about.

"You know what!"

"No, Izzy, I really don't. Let's just talk. What are you so upset about and how can I fix it?"

"You can't just fix everything, Julian!"

"I know that!" I roared. "Don't you think I know that? I'm trying, I'm fucking trying, Izzy! Do you think I enjoy this? My only goal right now is to keep you safe, and I'm even failing at that because I'm a selfish prick just like my—" I cut myself off and shook my head. "My father."

"You're not him."

"I'm not him, but I am a Tennyson, and apparently we don't know how to think about others first, because when I walked into this room all I wanted to do was fuck you against the table and ask questions later. How's that for selfishness? When I know you're clearly upset with me, that's what I'm thinking about."

Her jaw dropped and then she narrowed her eyes. "It's the dress."

"It's not the dress, Izzy, it's you."

"Your computer screen, it was frozen." The words tumbled out one after another. "Who the hell is Bridge Anderson Tennyson, and why do you have a private trust set up for him for over two million dollars?" She leveled me with a glare. "Furthermore, why is he currently in the hospital in a wing nobody's allowed to go into but you?"

"That was . . ." I took the whiskey from her hands. "A shit ton of questions."

"Well?" I hated the look of mistrust in her eyes, almost as much as I hated the fact that if I told her the truth I would never get to touch her, she'd be dead to me, just like she was to Julian at the moment.

I didn't want to lie.

I wanted the lies to stop.

I handed back her glass and whispered, "My brother, my brother is in the ICU."

Her eyes widened in shock. "I figured he was family, since he currently owns one-third share of the company you're now CEO of. What I want to know is why you keep hiding things from me. You never told me about a brother, you never told me about your mom still living. In fact, the more I think about it, the only off-limit topic was your family, and now I'm finding out two of them are still living. This is a huge deal!"

"Both are still living," I corrected with a rasp in my voice. "But both are fighting for their lives."

Her face fell. "Julian—"

"Don't fucking call me that." It felt like a shout even when it was a whisper. I stood up on wooden legs and made my way into the kitchen, blindly reaching for alcohol, fully aware of what was coming down the pipeline.

I would tell her.

Because not telling her was killing me inside.

"Wait!" She chased after me and nearly collided with my body when I was standing stock-still in the kitchen. She moved her hands around my back to my stomach and held me, kissing the back of my suit. "Is this conversation the one we need to have? Is it going to change things?"

"Irrevocably," I whispered.

"Will you still be the same person?"

"That's a complicated question."

"It's really not."

"Shit, you have no idea, Izzy."

She sighed and released me while I paced in front of her then finally met her gaze. "Get comfortable, it's going to be a long night."

Chapter Thirty-Two

ISOBEL

If he wasn't acting like himself right after the accident, then he really wasn't acting like himself now.

Julian enjoyed whiskey; he sipped it slowly and didn't approve of people taking shot after shot of something so expensive.

Meanwhile, this version of him was pouring half the bottle into a juice glass.

"Julian?"

"Like I said, don't call me that, not now," he muttered. "I just—I need some time, Izzy. To process, to . . ." He cursed again. "To try to explain." And then he burst out laughing. "Yeah, this isn't going to go well, is it?"

Was he talking to himself?

"Go change, Izzy, I'm gonna tell you again, you'll want to be comfortable," he barked in a tone I hadn't heard him use before. It wasn't mean or even threatening. No, it was filled with disappointment.

He took another swig directly from the bottle, abandoning the glass, while I wondered if I should call his mom.

This wasn't him.

Not at all.

Had I ever known him?

I walked back into the master bathroom and started changing out of my dress.

Ugh, what was wrong with me? He was acting crazy, there was money in a trust fund for a brother I knew nothing about, and now he was asking me not to call him by name?

I jerked my bra off, causing a flicker of paper to fall from it. I snatched it up. It was Bridge's phone number, I never meant to use it, just to wave it in front of his face and demand he tell me what he'd been hiding.

I was prepared for war, but he'd given up immediately.

It still didn't make sense, none of it did.

After quickly changing, I walked back into the kitchen, where I'd left both Julian and my cell.

He looked up at me, pain in his eyes, like he didn't want me to do anything except tell him everything was going to be okay.

This wasn't just different. It felt heavy with sadness, and I had no reason to feel that way. Neither did he, right?

I picked up my phone while he watched me.

And I dialed the number to Bridge Anderson.

The first ring felt fake, like I'd conjured it up somehow. The second ring was like a bomb going off in the apartment.

And Julian still didn't move as he stared me down like he was waiting for me to ask the question that seemed ridiculous to even ask. His eyes were wide, his skin pale.

Why the hell did he have Bridge's phone in the closet?

I felt like I aged ten years as tears filled my eyes. I slowly walked back into the master bedroom, and into the closet. There was an older iPhone 8 tucked under a few pairs of sweats.

I picked it up and held it in my hands.

I felt him behind me then.

In that too-small closet.

I squeezed my eyes shut.

I didn't know what to think.

"I can explain," Julian whispered.

"Why do you have his cell phone? Planning on suffocating your own brother at the hospital? I'm trying to understand, I really am, but you have to give me something."

"He's alive, you should be thankful for that."

"Who? Your brother?"

"No," he whispered. "Your fiancé."

Slowly I turned around. "What the hell are you saying?"

He swallowed slowly and then said thickly, "My name is Bridge Anderson Tennyson. I'm Julian's twin."

Chapter Thirty-Three

BRIDGE

"Say something." I gripped her by the shoulders, needing her to tell me that she knew the truth, that it was okay, that she felt the way I did, that this thing between us was real despite being based on lies.

She stared at me in stunned silence and then her voice cracked, breaking my heart in two. "You, you hit your head, Julian! You don't know what you're even saying. God, I'll-I'll get a shrink, a therapist, a—"

"Izzy . . ."

She wasn't having it. She jerked away from me, tears in her eyes. "No, you listen! You're the crazy one, you don't have a twin brother. This is like something out of a soap opera! You just had a really bad accident, and now you're trying to do right by someone else who's suffering. It happens all the time, survivor's remorse and—"

"Survivor's remorse?" I let out an ugly laugh. "Really? You want to talk about guilt? I'm living his life!" I spread my arms wide. "Didn't you ever wonder why the suits were too tight? Why I have tattoos that I lied to you about? Come on, Izzy! You're a smart woman!"

Her nostrils flared. "No, I can't . . . Why would you do this? Why would you pretend to be him?" Tears filled her eyes then streamed down her cheeks. "Why would you do this to me? Both of you? How could you be so cruel to give me hope that—"

My face softened as I reached for her.

"Stop!" She shoved at me. "Don't touch me!"

"Izzy." I reached for her again.

She burst into tears. "You made me love you again!"

Fuck. Me.

Even though she hit at me, I pulled her against my chest while she sobbed. I let her hate me, while I loved her, and in that moment I'd never hated my own father more in my entire life.

"Will you please just listen before you start saying things like I made you fall in love again when the entire time I was the one falling?"

She clung to me like I was hers.

And I held her like she was mine.

She went rigid in my arms. "How would I even know that's true? You've been lying this entire time!"

"Lying to save a company, to save Julian's position as CEO. The board knows I'm the stand-in . . ." I gulped. "In more ways than one."

"What do you mean in more ways than one?"

I grabbed her left hand and lifted it between us. Her giant rock sparkled like the expensive diamond it was.

She let out a gasp. "You were going to marry me!"

I expected her to slap me.

She didn't.

"Edward didn't want you to know."

"Ohhhh, Edward didn't want me to know, fantastic! So you made a deal with the devil, why? Because you love your brother who never even talks about you so much that you'd take over his entire life!"

I inwardly cursed. "When you put it that way . . ."

She crossed her arms.

I let out a sigh and ran my hands through my hair. "Like I said, it's complicated. Will you please just hear me out before you strangle me to death or shove me off the balcony?"

"Poison," she said in a deadpan voice. "It's quicker."

"Good to know, Nurse Ratched, good to know!"

She glared.

I glared right back.

And then because I had already lost my mind, I slammed my mouth against hers in a punishing kiss then pulled away.

She shoved me back and touched her hand to her lips. "Please don't kiss me, not now, not like that."

"I've been wanting to do more than kiss you for the past month." I shook my head. "Believe me, I should be sainted for my self-control."

"You're a lunatic!" She spread her arms wide. "Do you even hear yourself? Sainted for your self-control? For not kissing your brother's fiancée—"

"Ex," I pointed out. "Ex-fiancée."

She immediately looked away, but I continued. "I wasn't the only one lying, so don't pretend for one second you didn't go along with this because things felt different. My father told me about Amy overhearing you breaking things off, and Kelsey indicated that things weren't right between you and Julian."

"I hate you right now."

"Good, that makes two of us." I rubbed my hands down my face. "Now, can we please go back to the living room, away from the guns hidden in the safe?" I eyed the safe in the corner. "And closer to the alcohol so if I have to get mind-numbingly drunk in the next hour it's close by?"

She swallowed and then nodded her head. "Yes."

"Thank God."

And since all pretenses were gone, I chose that exact moment to completely strip out of the idiot penguin suit I was wearing while she gawked at me like she wasn't sure if she was invited to watch or should turn away.

I grabbed a pair of joggers and a hoodie and then sighed in relief. "Better."

"Is it, though?" She eyed me up and down and then gave me a cheeky grin.

I may have given her the finger with both hands.

Which only made her laugh through her tears.

I loved that sound.

"What do you even do for a living?" she asked as she followed me into the living room.

"I torture people," I said with a shrug.

I could hear her soft intake of breath.

With a grin, I looked over my shoulder. "Tabata ring a bell?"

Her eyes narrowed.

"I'm a personal trainer, Izzy."

"Ohhh, so that's why—" And then rage replaced curiosity. "You asshole! I showered with you!"

I couldn't wipe the grin from my face. "Oh, believe me, I'm well aware."

"You sick bastard!"

"If I'm so sick why are you still smiling?"

"I'm not." She looked down and wrung her hands nervously. "I was just . . . in shock."

"Uh-huh." I took a focused step toward her and tilted her chin up with my fingertip. "For the record, you have a fantastic ass." With that, I slapped it with my left hand, grabbed the bottle of whiskey on the table, and then sat on the couch. "Time for a story."

"It can't get any more unbelievable than this."

I let out a chuckle. "Strap in, Izzy, strap the hell in."

Chapter Thirty-Four

BRIDGE

I took a deep breath, then I took two shots and handed her the bottle.

She sipped from it, wiped her pretty mouth with the back of her hand, and gave me a look of disgust. "I prefer wine."

"I know you do."

"Now you're going to pretend to know everything about me?"

I wanted to touch her, to tell her I knew everything worth knowing, to tell her my feelings were real, but she didn't trust me, and she had good reason not to.

"The truth is, I know more about you than I should, not because I was given a manual on Izzy Cunningham but because from the minute I walked into this apartment, I was fascinated with everything about you, from the way you'd flinch and treat me like you hated me one minute to when it seemed like you loved me the next. I'm confused as hell as to what kind of relationship you had with my brother, and at the same time, I want to strangle him for hurting you. That's the truth."

Her expression softened. "Yeah, well, it's complicated."

"Want me to go first?"

She nodded. "Please."

I took a deep breath. "Julian and I were best friends." I sighed. "Until the divorce. Mom got me, and my dad got Julian. So I went from having the best of everything, private school, tons of money, friends, a best friend in my brother, to living in Jersey going to public school, and then my mom got sick with a disease that didn't have a cure."

Izzy put her hand on my bicep and kept it there.

I drew strength from her touch and went on. "I swore to Julian I'd protect him, and up until the divorce I did. I shielded him as much as I could from our dad, from his evil, controlling side. I'd put on music when our parents fought, I'd let him borrow my shit just to see him smile." My voice cracked. "I always promised to take care of him and then my hands were tied. We had email, but part of me thinks that my dad controlled that too. When we lost touch, I blamed Julian, thought he just didn't care."

"If I know Julian, he cared," she said softly. "He just . . . his only motivation is trying to prove himself to the man who's always told him he wouldn't be good enough."

"Yeah, I see that now." I put my hand on hers and kept it there. "He sent a check last month, and in all my stupidity and rage, I ripped it up. I was working two, sometimes three jobs to take care of Mom's hospital bills, and I let my pride speak for both of us, when he was just trying to make something right."

Izzy tilted her head like she was thinking. "So the trust fund with your name on it? From Julian?"

"I was uncomfortable with fifty grand, so he did what Julian does, he dumped in the fifty and added another zero then just kept adding. I don't know what his end game was, but the point is, he cared enough to do that, and now he's in the hospital and he's not awake, Izzy, he's moved his hands and toes and—" I squeezed my eyes shut. "When it counted most I failed him."

"You haven't failed him." Izzy moved closer, then cupped my face with her soft hands. "Jul—" She shook her head. "I mean Bridge, look at me."

Muttering a curse, I looked into her perfect green eyes, as bright as emeralds shining with tears. "You're here now, right?" Izzy asked gently.

"I'm here, he's not, Izzy. I'm living what he's supposed to be living, I'm taking his place, I'm just the stand-in until he gets better. *If* he gets better . . ."

She flinched at that. "It's bad then."

"It's very bad."

"And Edward? How did he get you to do this? You don't seem like the type of person who just says yes to that man."

At that I smiled. "No, in fact we're both lucky I'm not in prison for his murder."

She laughed, and in that moment, I would have done anything to keep that laugh going, to keep the smile on her perfect face.

And it felt damn good to know that she was smiling at me, not Julian.

Shit, I was a horrible excuse for a brother.

"He offered to pay all of Mom's medical bills, and he dangled a ginormous trust fund in front of me, with thirty percent equity in the company. Julian has thirty, I have thirty, and with the board's shares we have complete control." I sighed. "If he wakes up."

"He has to wake up," she whispered under her breath.

My gut clenched. "If I tell you something, will you promise not to judge me?"

"Maybe."

I didn't look at her, just stared straight ahead. "Sometimes I wonder what life would be like if he didn't wake up, and I hate myself for it. I wonder what it would be like for you to say my name, not his, I wonder what it would feel like to earn you, and not feel like I have to make up for all his mistakes."

She sucked in a breath. "I didn't tell you about the broken engagement because a part of me thought the man I'd fallen in love with . . . had come back."

She burst into tears, crumpling against my body. I pulled her onto my lap, rocking her while she cried.

"I'm sorry, Izzy, so fucking sorry, I should have told you sooner. I just—I was thinking of my mom, I was thinking of Julian, of Edward backing out, I'm so sorry . . ." I continued to rock her while her tears soaked my shirt, while the heat of our bodies started to make me sweat. "For what it's worth"—God, I didn't want to defend him—"I think the reason these last six months were so hard was because he was fighting this internal battle of loving you, but also wanting to please our father in the only way he knew how."

"By cheating?" she sniffed.

"From what I've gathered, it sounds like he may have actually cheated once, and gotten hit on a hell of a lot more than that."

"What about the maid?"

"That I can't answer," I said honestly. "All I can say is this. When people noted the difference at the board meeting, it was because I wasn't a bullshitter, whereas Julian could charm a nun out of her gown. So maybe that's the difference. People are just drawn to him, both the right and wrong people. It doesn't help that he's rich."

She laughed. "No, no, it doesn't."

"Why did you stay, Izzy? Why did you put up with it? If you were that unhappy? That upset?"

Izzy pulled back and looked into my eyes. "Because I made Julian a promise too. A long time ago, I told him I would always stand by his side, no matter what, and I refused to go back on my word. We were best friends who became so much more, and I knew he was struggling to gain your father's approval. And he—he said he was sorry about the cheating, and he seemed so sorry about it, and then the closer he got to becoming CEO the more distant he became until I couldn't handle it anymore. I was suddenly faced with the stark realization that my universe was him, and I didn't really have an identity outside of him. I was afraid. Afraid to have someone as powerful as Edward come after me. I had no money, no job. Everything I have on this earth belongs to Julian."

"And your heart?" I asked. "What about that?"

She chewed her bottom lip. "I'll answer that if you answer this. Was any of it real?"

"Every moment, every single one was real. Why do you think I tried to keep myself from kissing you? Because every kiss took more of me and I knew it would kill you when you found out." I squeezed my eyes shut. "I'm not him. I won't ever be him," I admitted sadly. "I'm not your real fiancé, or the man you fell in love with in college."

"The man I fell in love with in college took my heart, and he never gave it back, Bridge. He kept it close even when he hurt it, even when he knew it was breaking. Julian may own this apartment, he may own my car, but he doesn't own me, not anymore, and the day of the accident, when I was giving him back his ring, when he was trying to put me off again, I made a choice, to walk away from this, from him, with what was left of my heart intact."

"I'm sorry."

She looked up at me with bright eyes. "Don't be, you're the one who nursed it back to health."

And then she kissed me.

I didn't wrap my arms around her.

I was afraid to move.

Afraid to shatter the moment.

Still feeling guilty but wanting her more than anything in this world. Her tongue touched my lower lip and then slid inside.

I opened my mouth to her.

I wanted to give everything to her.

Our hands found each other then, entangling, holding on for dear life as we sat in the middle of the couch, both broken, just something else my father had tried to destroy.

Izzy pulled back and then moved to straddle me.

I had my hands on her back just below her waist. I was petrified to go any lower. We were both too vulnerable. I didn't want her caught up in the moment.

I wanted her caught up in me.

"For the record . . ." She licked her lips like she could taste me there. "Every night, when I went to sleep, I'd pray for more time with this version of Julian. What I didn't realize was that I was praying for more time with you, Bridge Anderson Tennyson."

I sucked in a sharp breath. "What are you saying?"

"I'm saying . . ." Our foreheads touched.

I held on to the moment, her in my arms, knowing it was me, not him.

"I'm saying we should probably watch a movie and order takeout because I'm exhausted and I know you are too."

"Yeah." I was disappointed, and I had no reason to be. She was being rational, and I was acting like a fool in love.

Chapter Thirty-Five

Emotionally I felt like I'd been run over by a train. Physically I didn't know how to react. We were familiar and yet we weren't.

He was a stranger.

One I'd kissed.

One who'd held me.

Showered with me.

Slept in my bed.

It was bizarre to try to process and yet I still yearned to see Julian to make sure he was okay, to sit at his bedside and confess all the ways I had failed him, even though he failed me first.

I wanted to recite my sins one by one.

Worst of all, I wanted to confess that I fell in love with his brother, while he was healing.

Now that I knew Bridge wasn't Julian, I felt like an idiot for not realizing it sooner, then again it's not normal for people to walk around with unknown identical twins taking over their lives, but there it is.

Bridge was sitting on the couch, his arm draped over the back, and his hoodie clinging to his muscular body like a second skin.

He was the rugged version of a very polished Julian.

Where Julian was smart suits and flirty smiles, Bridge was loud and argumentative, sarcastic and at the same time sad, more sad than Julian, like he'd purposely taken the weight of the sadness for both of them and volunteered to carry it so Julian wouldn't have to.

Julian had never been weak. His biggest fault was trying to earn the approval of a man who would never give it.

And Bridge? His biggest fault was resentment over his father separating them while his brother continued to live and die by Edward's approval.

"You're thinking awfully hard over there," Bridge called out. "Don't you just press a button for popcorn? Or did you need a manual?"

I rolled my eyes and grinned. "You know you could get off your ass."

"I could." He turned to look at me with that same smolder Julian had, damn it. "But then I wouldn't get to stare at you while you walk all the way back over here with the bowl, and when I dropped a piece I wouldn't get to watch you bend over to pick it up."

"You're crass."

"Thank you." He grinned.

Heat flooded my cheeks as I tossed in the popcorn and waited for it to pop while I stood in front of the microwave.

And I knew he was watching me.

I liked it.

I suddenly didn't want to ask about Julian. I would go see him, I would hold his hand, I would confess everything.

But right now, I just wanted to sit with Bridge, with no secrets between us, eating popcorn.

I jumped when the microwave dinged. And just like he said, Bridge watched me walk all the way back to the couch, and when I handed him the bowl, he took one kernel and tossed it to the floor then gave me a look that said, *Well? Pick it up.*

I scowled while he grabbed another piece and tossed it on the carpeting.

"I can't decide if you're just really bad at flirting or still stuck in middle school."

He barked out a laugh. "I slayed in middle school."

I picked up the popcorn and shoved it into his mouth and kept my hand over it while he chewed. His skin even felt good. I could keep my hand there forever.

"I bet you did."

"Not as much as Julian, though, he has better hair."

I smiled at that. "He does have nice hair. Then again, so do you." Before I knew what I was doing, I put the popcorn bowl down on the table and ran my fingers through his hair while he wrapped his arms around my waist and pressed his face to my stomach.

Butterflies erupted.

His touch was everything.

Not just that, but the way that he seemed to sense that I wanted to be held, touched, treasured.

"Come here." He pulled me onto his lap and grabbed a blanket, then covered both of us with it. "Try to relax, alright?"

Relax? My heart was thundering out of my chest.

This was the man who had brought it back.

This man.

Not Julian.

I pressed my head against his chest and whispered, "What happens if the wedding day comes and he's not awake?"

He went completely rigid and grabbed my left hand and squeezed it. "I don't really think we've been given that choice, Izzy."

"Am I a bad person?" I wondered out loud.

"Why would you say that?" He played with my hair then kissed the side of my head while I struggled with the right words.

"At the hospital, I could have fought more to see him, I could have yelled, I could have done so many things, but I just . . . I don't know, Bridge. I felt so damn relieved that it was over, that our engagement was done, that I was done walking on eggshells, done being hurt by a man who said he loved me."

"Izzy, that makes you human."

"A bad human."

"A fantastic, intelligent, wonderful, sexy human," he added with another kiss. "Your heart was bruised, you were in pain. All you wanted was relief."

I turned my face into his chest, loving the way he smelled even if it was similar to Julian. It was still different enough that I clung to him tighter. "I needed to hear that."

"I'm not leaving you, Izzy."

I smiled against his chest. "Good."

He moved a bit and then his lips were on my ear. "We can talk more about him tomorrow, about our plan, but for now, can we just be two people on a couch, watching *Space Jam*?"

I jolted and turned around. "*Space Jam*?"

"Kidding." He smirked. "I just wanted to see your face."

I smacked him on his muscular shoulder. "You have HGTV on."

"I like nice things." He winked and then pressed the softest kiss to my lips I'd ever received. "Why else do you think I want to hold you tonight?"

My heart thumped wildly, and then I tucked myself next to his body and fell asleep with a peaceful smile on my face.

Chapter Thirty-Six

BRIDGE

I woke up with a beautiful woman in my arms.

One I wanted to call mine.

One I couldn't claim.

It was the worst feeling, knowing I'd found someone who I could love for the rest of my life—who currently belonged to someone else who looked just like me.

Shit, it was messed up.

I asked her if she wanted to see him, and she said yes. I knew we needed to be careful and would obviously need to swear the staff to silence, but I figured if money could get him an abandoned ICU wing then I'd just throw more at the hospital to get Izzy in.

There wasn't anything I wouldn't do for her, which I repeated that morning when she came into the bedroom wearing nothing but a towel.

I eyed her up and down and said, "I think I prefer the towel off."

Her eyebrows shot up. "I'm sure you do."

"There may be a towel shortage in the future, fair warning."

"Good. I'll just use your clothes to dry off and then throw your favorite sweatpants over the balcony."

I gaped. "That's rude."

"Don't steal my towels." Her gorgeous eyes narrowed into tiny slits.

"What about you?" I countered with a serious expression. "Can I steal you?"

She'd stared at me with such a stunned expression I immediately felt like an asshole for asking.

And then she'd blushed, her cheeks going bright pink as a slow smile spread across her face. "You should get ready."

"I was waiting for you to shower."

"Funny, since you never did before . . ." She got me there.

"Right, but you assumed I was him, ergo, it would be weird if I closed my eyes every single time you changed, just as weird as not noticing the little birthmark on your right ass cheek and—"

That earned me a pillow in the face. I caught it midair and grinned while she burst out laughing and made her way into the closet. "Get ready, Bridge, or I'm leaving you here."

"Yes, Mom," I teased.

And then I felt a stinging slap to my ass and jerked around. "Call me Mom again, and I'm grabbing that appendage you're so proud of."

"Like big things, do you?"

"You're impossible!" Her blush grew.

I just shrugged. "Hey, this is me. If you want me to act like him, I can give you a stern expression and hole up in the office."

Her face fell. I realized my teasing may have gone too far.

"Izzy, I'm sorry. That was uncalled for." I moved toward her.

She shrugged. "Only because it's true and I hate that instead of talking with me he'd go work."

"Izzy, people grow apart, it happens, even to people who love each other." I wanted to smash my face against the nearest blunt object. I didn't want to be defending him, but I felt like I had no choice. On top of that, I wasn't sure where the boundary was for me and Izzy. Was I allowed to touch her? Kiss her? Last night we'd kissed, but we'd been emotional and I knew she'd needed comfort.

Izzy sighed and put her hands on her hips. "Passing ships in the night, that's what it felt like at the end, being reminded of all my appointments, checking on him while he worked, and feeling my heart break every single time he kissed me on the cheek and told me he'd be late to bed."

"Look." I searched for the right words and knew I would fail in being sensitive, but I wasn't the sensitive one. "I know this is going to come off wrong but I'm just going to say it. He's an idiot for ever letting you lie in that bed alone. If you were mine"—our eyes locked—"I'd never let you fall asleep without my arms around you, without my lips teasing you, and that's the truth." I sighed. "Let me just jump in the shower real quick."

"Bridge." She reached for me, her hand resting on my shoulder. "Thank you. For saying that."

"I know it doesn't change anything. I just don't want to lie to you anymore." I smiled sadly and slowly stepped away from her and into the bathroom. I needed space before I did something I couldn't undo, something that would not only change my relationship with her, but my already unsteady relationship with him. "Be ready in five."

She opened her mouth to say something.

I shut the door.

Shutting her out.

Knowing it was probably the wrong choice, but also very aware of my need to touch her, to kiss away her pain.

Disgusted with myself, I quickly took a shower, grabbed a pair of clean jeans and a T-shirt that was again way too tight, and then put a beanie on over my hair.

I really didn't care if I looked like the evil twin. I just wanted to be comfortable and look like my old self. I snatched a pair of his aviator Ray-Bans and made my way out into the living room.

Izzy stared at me. Hard.

"What?" I frowned, putting on the sunglasses. "Are you okay?"

"Uh." She grabbed her purse, dropped it onto the floor, grabbed it, dropped it somehow again, then finally adjusted it under her arm. "Yeah, sorry."

"Nervous?"

She gulped. "Not to see him."

I frowned and walked toward her, grabbing his wallet and his cell from the counter and shoving them in my pocket. "That's cryptic."

She shuddered and then reached out a shaky hand and pressed it to my chest. I instantly reached for her hand and held her ice-cold fingertips tight.

"You're beautiful." It came out as a whisper, and then she looked up into my eyes. "It's not really fair."

I couldn't help the grin that spread across my face. "Are you complimenting me instead of threatening to poison me now?"

"Maybe." She licked her lips.

I leaned down and kissed her, damn the consequences.

She stood up on her tiptoes and wrapped her arms around my neck, returning the kiss, opening her mouth to me. I spun around, pressing her against the kitchen countertop. Our bodies moved against one another like we couldn't get enough.

"Bridge." She said my name like a plea, and I wanted to give her everything that plea implied, right there, on the kitchen counter if it came to that. "I like you."

I smiled against her mouth.

It was a start.

Especially after all the confessions last night. "I like you too."

"I'm scared."

I pulled back. "Of what?"

"Us. This."

"Nothing to be afraid of. I've been with you for the last month and two days, I'm with you now, Izzy. I won't leave your side."

"Swear?"

"Swear." I kissed her forehead. "We should go before I lose what restraint I have left."

She smiled up at me and winked. "Yeah, wouldn't want you to lose out on that sainthood."

"Smart-ass," I grumbled, smacking her in the ass and making her jump as I went to the door and opened it for her. "No matter what happens, Izzy."

"No matter what happens," she repeated in a strong voice.

We took a town car to the hospital.

I let the office know I was sick and would be coming in later that afternoon after seeing the doctor—it wasn't a total lie, I was going to the hospital.

Dad had called my phone twice already.

I told him I had a stomach flu and that I would be in as soon as I was done puking, and then I had coffee sent to his office along with enough donuts to make everyone on the floor happy and distracted.

It was a Wednesday, and I didn't have any meetings scheduled until later that afternoon, which freed me up to take Izzy to the hospital. Not only didn't I want her to go alone, I knew she wouldn't get in to see Julian without me—too much security—too many family secrets.

Izzy held my hand the entire drive. She had her black sunglasses pushed high on her nose, her hair pulled into a messy bun on the top of her head, and she was wearing skinny jeans, heels, and a black sweater.

To her that was casual.

She looked beautiful, so I didn't comment. That was her flying under the radar.

Skinny jeans.

The car pulled up to the hospital too soon.

"We'll be a little while," I said under my breath.

"Got my book." The driver held his book high and grinned.

"Good."

He shut the door after us and then got back into the car. I grabbed Izzy's hand and squeezed it. "Ready?"

"Nope." She sighed and held on to my arm. "I don't know how to feel right now."

"Just allow yourself to feel, Izzy, that's all I ask," I said quietly as we walked into the hospital. If people recognized us, they didn't say anything. The elevator was blessedly empty when we walked into it. I hit the old ICU floor.

The doors opened.

My heart thundered in my chest like it was trying to warn me.

I didn't want her to see him. Not really.

Because she would hate me when she saw how much he was suffering in that coma, she would hate herself for spending time with me.

I felt like I was screwing myself.

But I had no other choice.

Hand in hand, we walked out of that elevator and toward the two blue metal doors. I hit the comm. "It's Julian Tennyson."

I felt Izzy tense next to me.

The doors buzzed open.

We walked down the hall.

One of the charge nurses that I'd talked to last was at the desk along with another nurse whose name I could never remember. She was always coming in and checking on Julian, and always talked to him like he could hear her. She was sweet.

We stopped in front of his room. "You want to go in by yourself?"

Izzy shook her head no.

Shit.

I opened the door. She took a deep breath and walked in while I closed the door behind us.

The machines buzzed in the tense silence.

His chest rose and fell with each breath as the machines breathed for him, his face now showed only a few pink scars from the stitches across his jaw.

His arms were at his sides, lifeless.

"Julian." Izzy let go of my hand and rushed to his side.

I felt the loss of her warmth immediately.

Just like I felt the loss of her by my side.

I was an idiot to think I could hold on to her when Julian was the one who'd saved her in college.

Julian was the one who'd proposed to her with a rock I could never afford.

Julian was the hero even if he was also the villain.

I hung my head and tried not to let bitterness take root, as resentment pounded against my heart like it wanted me to let it in and take over so I didn't hurt, so I didn't feel like my chest was about to crack open.

"Julian." She sat in the chair next to the bed, scooted it forward, and grabbed his hand between hers. "You need to wake up."

I couldn't breathe.

Couldn't think beyond the image that was in front of me.

What the fuck had I been thinking?

That she would leave him?

That she would love me?

She squeezed his hand tight and then pressed a kiss to his wrist. His fingers didn't so much as twitch; he almost looked dead.

I was torn between wanting him to snap those eyes open and wanting the machine to stop.

That's where I was at.

All because I wanted what was his.

I tugged off my beanie and wrestled with throwing it against the shiny white tile. I deserved to be in that bed, not him.

He had everything to live for sitting next to him holding his hand.

"I'm so sorry, Julian," Izzy whispered. "I'm sorry I didn't come sooner. I didn't know, your dad didn't want anyone to know, me especially, so when Bridge took over I just thought you were acting crazy."

Great, now I was crazy.

"We need you to wake up, Julian. We need you to wake up and fix this before Bridge fires you, alright?"

At that, I laughed a little. "Can't fire the CEO, Izzy."

"Shhh, I'm trying to threaten him."

God, she was incredible, strong, beautiful.

I walked over and put my hand on her shoulder. "Your fiancée . . ." It physically hurt to say that. "She's right, Julian, I will literally kick your ass if you don't get up out of this bed soon and help me take over the company. I don't have a clue what I'm doing, and you could wake up poor as shit, and we both know how much you like your sunglasses collection."

I could have sworn I saw his mouth move, was that a smile? Did he hear us?

"Fight, Julian, alright?" Izzy stood and kissed his cheek.

I squeezed my eyes shut.

It wasn't my moment to witness.

It wasn't my life.

"One day you're going to ask me what happened between me and Bridge, you're going to want to know how a month and a few days could completely change a person's outlook on life, you're going to ask where you went wrong, and you're going to hate both of us." I sucked in a breath as she kept talking. "You rescued me when I was a girl . . . and then we grew apart. Life happened, and the girl you rescued turned into a woman, a sad, lonely, resentful woman. Bridge saved the person I was starting to lose, the person I'd always wanted to be. He makes me feel like myself, he makes me feel safe, and loved, and cherished. I hope one day you can forgive me, forgive us, for falling in love while you were dreaming . . ."

I was rooted to the ground.

Unable to speak or do anything except stare at her in shock as tears rolled down her face onto Julian's lifeless body.

And then she turned to me. Tears filled her eyes as she walked into my arms and sobbed. "I'm the worst human being on the planet."

"No, I think I took the trophy on that, Izzy."

She clung to me. "What are we going to do? We can't just . . ." She pulled back. "I mean he's going to wake up, I know he is, and when he does . . ."

My stomach sank. "Izzy, you don't have to do this, not now, you just found out he was in a coma, you don't have to make any decisions."

I was too distracted by the sadness on her face to hear the door open.

Or to turn and see that it wasn't a nurse or the doctor, but my own father.

"What a vision, both of my sons in the same room together, with a girl who must have a magic—"

"Finish that sentence, and I'm throwing you out the window," I said through clenched teeth.

Dad held up his hands. "Knew you weren't sick."

"Oh, I'm sick alright," I spat.

"Isobel." He eyed her up and down. "Wasn't one son enough? You had to take two? Greedy little thing."

I caught her as she lunged for him. "Not worth it."

"I own you, both of you." He grinned. "Better get back to work, Bridge. Wouldn't want any speculation about our new CEO."

I hated that he was right.

Things had to appear normal.

For Julian.

"I'm doing this for Julian." I didn't sound very convincing.

"Funny." Dad had a gleam in his eye. "Because one might say you're actually enjoying the challenge. Taking over his life shouldn't have been so seamless for you, Bridge, and yet look at you. I had two board members call me this morning just to say they're impressed, heard you fired Amy . . ."

I rolled my eyes. "This isn't the place."

"Amy?" Izzy's head jerked in my direction. "The flirty rude one?"

I nodded.

And then I received a hug from her while my dad snorted something under his breath. "Nobody finds out about this, Izzy, or it's your head that rolls."

"Fine." She paled. God, I hated how afraid of him she was.

I hated even more that I couldn't do much about it, not with Julian still in his coma.

Dad adjusted his tie. "Really looking forward to that wedding this weekend."

With that, he opened the door, stepped out, and shut it.

We had our answer.

We were getting married.

I knew it.

She knew it.

But hearing him say it, that even though she knew I was Bridge, it didn't matter to him, because it was all about money and appearances.

And I felt like a complete ass that I hadn't told her the rest of the story, that I needed to marry her to get my trust. That he was dangling it over my head, that even though I would do anything to be married to her—I was still using her.

I was too distracted with my own thoughts and a shaking Izzy to see it then.

The movement from the bed.

I would look back on that moment and hate myself more than I could possibly bear, knowing that my brother, the one I meant to save.

Heard every fucking word.

And worse.

Saw me kiss her hard on the mouth before leaving the very room that had been his prison.

Chapter Thirty-Seven

ISOBEL

I didn't know what to think.

About anything.

Seeing Julian had been physically painful. Knowing he'd been in the hospital that whole time while I was playing house with his brother, falling in love with him, felt so cruel that I couldn't even process anything beyond what to do for the rest of the day.

I needed to talk things through.

No, I didn't need more talking.

I needed, I wanted Bridge.

I was halfway to the apartment when I asked the driver to turn around and head to the offices. Bridge was there, under orders by Edward, of course.

Maybe I really was a bad person because I wanted Bridge to tell me it was going to be okay, that we hadn't done anything wrong.

That it just happened.

"I'll text you when I'm coming down," I told my driver as I hopped out of the car and made a beeline for the large building nestled in the middle of the financial district. They occupied the top fifteen floors, and now that they were expanding again, would own the entire thing.

I scanned my security guest pass and went into the elevator that would take me to the main offices.

Julian's office.

Bridge's office.

Funny how last time I took that elevator to Julian's office I was ready to puke because I was ending something.

And now? Now I wanted to puke because I was starting something, really starting it, with both feet in.

And needing now more than ever for the other person to tell me that he was in too, that I wasn't crazy, that even though the situation wasn't the best, we would be okay.

When the doors opened I speed-walked down the familiar hall and toward the receptionist's desk. "Hi, Kelsey—"

"Go right on in." She smiled brightly. "He's on the phone, but I'm sure he'll want to see you." Something seemed different.

My eyes narrowed.

Her eyes narrowed.

We had the stare-down of all stare-downs.

Did she know he was Bridge not Julian?

I almost opened my mouth to ask, but then she said with a quick smile, "He's been making some great changes."

"As opposed to before when there were no changes?"

She just smiled. "He likes to get things done, and not just that, Isobel, he's having HR do an analysis of every position's salary and benefits to see where he can give raises. I haven't had a raise in three years."

I sucked in a breath. "Wow. Can he do that?"

"He's the CEO. He can do whatever he wants." She looked down at the phone. "Looks like he's off."

"Right." I took a deep breath.

"Relax." She smiled. "Oh, and bring him this." She grabbed a hot cup from her desk. "He's already on his third."

I rolled my eyes. "He's going to need a tranq to come down from that tonight."

"Oh, I think he'll manage" was all she said, and then she put her hand on my arm. "This is the first time I've seen you in this office with a real smile on your face. I like it."

I felt tears burn my eyes as I looked away and thought back on my confessional phone call with Annie, who I called as soon as we dropped Bridge off at the office.

"I'm a horrible person."

"No. You're human," Annie fired back. "I'll take this secret to my grave, and I'm honored you even told me in the first place. Just know it's going to be okay, and I truly think everything happens for a reason."

"I care for him."

"I know you do."

"But I'm also a mess."

She just laughed. "Welcome to humanity."

Annie always had a way of pointing out the good in a situation, so her words combined with Kelsey's observation were on my mind as I straightened my shoulders and smiled when I set eyes on Bridge.

Looking every inch the CEO, even though he was still in his jeans from earlier, pacing in front of the window with a Bluetooth attached to his ear. He must have picked up another call.

"No, if we can't give them benefits like that then the turnover rate is still going to be that high. Gym memberships and health care for every IFC employee that comes over, they keep their vacation, and we have thirty days of sick leave and if you argue with me one more time about parental leave for dads, I'm going to fire you." He sighed. "Great, keep me posted."

He turned then.

I almost dropped the coffee and jumped into his arms.

Instead, I held it out, my jaw still slack.

He smiled at me. "This is a nice surprise. Didn't I just see you, oh, I don't know, an hour or so ago?"

"Yeah, well, now that you're stuck with me . . ." I beamed. "Heard you've been hitting the hard stuff already."

He lifted the coffee in the air. "Yeah, well, I don't know how he ever made it through a day without constant coffee."

"It made him jittery." I offered the information freely. "And since caffeine made him shake, he didn't want people to think he was nervous or irritable, so he drank decaf tea."

Bridge made a face. "Poor guy."

"Yeah, well, he did still have his one cup every morning."

"I hate that we're talking about him like he's not coming back, like we need to talk about his memories because he won't have any more to make." Bridge set the coffee down on his desk and crossed his arms. "Are you okay?"

"No." I nodded. "Yes." I cursed myself. "I don't know, I just, I needed to see you. I know some of the things I said to him sound crazy, and I'm just all over the place, and I thought if I saw you then I would—"

He interrupted my ridiculous speech with a soft kiss. He held me in his arms, and I felt myself instantly relax. He wasn't telling me he had to go to a meeting, or that I needed to schedule time with him even though I knew he was busy.

By holding me in his office.

By giving me time.

He was giving me the world.

And mending a heart that had been ignored and set aside for too long.

"If you ever, and I do mean ever, ask me to make an appointment to see you, I'm kicking your ass." I mumbled it against his shirt and smiled when his laughter shook both of us.

"Noted. Anything else?"

"I'm making dinner."

Bridge's eyes softened. "What were you going to make?"

"Well, I hadn't gotten that far yet but I thought I'd call your mom and . . . maybe get some of your favorite recipes, and—"

That earned me another kiss, this one more punishing as his tongue pushed past my lips while his hands moved to my hips pulling me against him.

We broke apart, panting.

I reached for him again.

This time he pulled away. "I really, really don't think you understand how much I want you, Izzy."

Oh, I could tell alright.

His shirt wasn't the only thing that was tight.

"Hurry home, then?"

Bridge cursed. "You're making me want to take a sick day so I can crawl into bed with you."

"A few hours won't kill you."

"It might," he said through clenched teeth. "Izzy, this needs to be your choice, alright? Because right now I'm not really thinking clearly. All I see is you, all I want is you, and I'm selfish enough to take whatever you offer me, so you have to be sure."

I let out a shaky breath. "I know."

"We won't come back from this, it's the one line . . ." He bit down on his lip and looked away. "It's the one place we can't come back from, the one thing he won't ever forgive us for."

My eyes welled with tears. "I know."

"Okay." He kissed my nose. "I like you, Izzy."

"Like you too." I kissed his cheek one last time and left the office, this time with a giant grin on my face and a huge sense of foreboding hovering over every step I took.

Hours later, I was still thinking about the scene at the office, so much so that when Bridge walked in the door, I was staring into my empty wineglass like it was some sort of crystal ball.

"Drunk already?" came his familiar voice.

Warmth rushed to my cheeks. "We're lucky I'm not perpetually drunk after the last few days I've had."

"True." He kissed me on the top of the head like it was normal, like we'd been living this life for a while, like I was cooking for him after a hard day at work, and he was getting ready to ask me about my day.

It was normal.

Not forced.

And I couldn't help but compare it with all the nights I'd fix a meal and Julian would be an hour late, apologetic and all smiles like it wasn't a big deal, when it was.

Or the times he'd take his plate into his office because he wasn't finished and there weren't enough hours in the day to take over the world.

"Izzy?" Bridge put his hand over mine. "Something wrong?"

"What?" I gave my head a shake. "No, sorry, do you want wine?"

"Sure." He slowly eyed me up and down. "I like this apron . . . I don't like the clothes behind it, but I understand . . . the apartment can get drafty at times."

I rolled my eyes, secretly loving his teasing. "Immature."

"Very," he agreed, after grabbing the glass I'd poured him. "It smells incredible in here."

"Homemade lasagna," I announced.

Bridge set down the glass and stared at me. "Did you just say homemade lasagna? As in you made it yourself? And it's in the oven? And I get to eat it?"

"Wow, your mom said you'd lose your mind, but I didn't think—"

"I have exactly twelve lasagna recipes. All of them are perfected. This is a test I hope you pass."

I burst out laughing. "She also said you got territorial when it came to your lasagna recipes, so I found my own, nothing wrong with a little competition."

He gaped. "You realize I'm never speaking to you again if you win, right?"

"Ah, and he's a sore loser, good to know."

"I haven't lost yet."

"Have you smelled that lasagna?" I teased.

"God, have you looked in the mirror and seen how beautiful your smile is recently?" he countered, making me almost drop my wineglass. "I'll let you win if I can kiss you right now."

"You're making it too easy."

"And you're making it extremely . . ." He hesitated and grinned. "Hard."

"I'm blushing, aren't I?"

"Like a tomato, one hundred percent. It's endearing, though."

"That's what a woman wants to hear, that she's endearing, like a bunny."

"No." He ran a hand down my back and cupped my ass. "Not like that."

I loved the way his hands felt on me.

At the rate we were going, I was going to burn the lasagna and the apartment down.

"We should eat," I whispered, staring into his gorgeous green eyes.

"We should." He backed away slowly and then grabbed two plates while I tried to calm my racing heart.

I stood there long enough for him to pull out the lasagna and bread, put huge portions on each of our plates, and carry them over to the couch, where we seemed to eat every night since he'd walked in that door.

It was like he had an aversion to the dining room.

An aversion I secretly loved.

That room always felt too formal anyway.

"This smells amazing." He dug in with his fork. While I nervously waited, he took one bite, two, three, and then leveled me with a glare. "You added vodka."

My eyes widened. "How do you even know that?"

"And heavy cream." He took another bite. "Shit, did you put some sharp cheddar in there too?"

"Yeah, you really should have gone to culinary school." I took a sip of wine with a giddy smile. "So you like it?"

"I'm probably going to marry it, sorry for the letdown."

"Well, at least you guys already have a venue."

"Imagine our wedding night." He grinned wide. "Just . . . sauce . . . everywhere, sauce on the pillow, sauce on the bed, sauce in my mouth—"

I burst out laughing. "You had to make it weird."

"What can I say? I'm emotionally attached to it already."

"You eat more than three people."

"Is that a question or observation?"

"Observation," I answered, taking a bite and enjoying the lasagna almost as much as he was.

I ate a few more bites, but my nerves were starting to take over.

And I was having a heck of a time not focusing on the way his biceps flexed as he took a sip or the way he wore that tight T-shirt like he was a man born with weights in his hands and testosterone coursing through his blood at alarmingly high levels. "Tell me more about you, please?"

Bridge did a double take then laughed. I loved his laugh. It was unapologetic, loud, masculine. I shivered and tried to think about Julian, about the target on my back, and I came away with absolutely nothing.

I wanted to trap this moment in time, hold on to it, and savor the laughs Bridge gave me. I wanted to run my hands up and down his body, explore it, search out every unique difference and memorize it.

"Are you listening to anything I just said?" Bridge's smile felt almost wicked, the way his eyes roamed over my face like he knew every dirty thought I was having about him, or about to have.

My eyes widened. "Um . . . sorry, I wasn't paying attention."

"Oh, you were paying attention alright, but not to anything coming out of my mouth." His grin widened. "Did you see something you liked?"

I scowled and then covered my face with my hands, laughing. "I was just thinking you look the same but you aren't the same. There's a lot of differences still, you know?"

"Good differences or bad differences?"

I gulped, throat suddenly dry. "Good."

"How good?" He ran his free hand up my leg and gripped my thigh. I felt his fingertips everywhere. "Are we talking really good? Or just sort of good?"

I licked my lips. "Really good."

"So . . ." His fingers crawled higher until he came into contact with my hip. "On a scale of one to ten . . ." His fingers swept past my hip and slid under my shirt.

I let out a gasp.

"Ten being really good, one being really bad . . ." His hand was right below my breasts, his fingers inching beneath my bra. "What would you say?"

Say? I couldn't even think! I was afraid to set down my wineglass, afraid to breathe, afraid this moment like so many other moments before would disappear and I'd be left with nothing.

"Ten." My answer was breathless, my body weak.

Bridge didn't move right away, his eyes were so intense I wondered how I never saw it. Saw the raw emotion there that Julian had shuttered so often from me, saw the war beneath the surface of his calm façade. Julian had stopped fighting. And Bridge?

He was a man at war.

My body pulsed and ached.

A heady tension pulled between us.

Bridge closed his eyes. "I can't—I want to—"

He started pulling his hand away.

I hated it.

I counted the seconds.

Fingers slid back down my body, leaving me emptier than before.

And I was angry.

So angry.

Maybe I was worse than all of the Tennysons, because one selfish act would break me away from Julian for forever.

One choice.

Just like the one he'd made when he started working for his father.

When he didn't value what we had anymore.

When he started making decisions for us without asking me.

So I decided I would make this choice without asking him.

And damning any future we could have in the process.

I set my wine down on the glass table, and then I slowly stood.

Bridge's lazy perusal gave me confidence that I wouldn't get turned down. I was doing this knowing exactly who he was.

And who I was as well.

He didn't move as I slowly peeled my shirt over my head and dropped it onto the floor.

His chest rose like he'd just sucked in a large amount of air because he was having trouble getting enough oxygen into his body.

"Bridge." I whispered his name, tested it on my lips. I liked the way it made me feel, his name, I liked saying it while I was stripping in front of him. I liked the way his massive body seemed to go rock hard just watching me take off something as simple as a shirt.

My bra came next.

He still didn't move.

I wasn't giving up.

I was seeing this through.

I was making my choice.

He bit down on his bottom lip and muttered a curse when my hands moved to my jeans. I kicked off my flats in the process, then unbuttoned the first button, the second, his eyes zeroed in on my fingers like he was about to devour them and me completely whole.

I shrugged them down my hips and kicked them off my legs, discarding them next to the rest of my clothes.

And still he didn't move.

All I had left was my white lace underwear because even then, I was a creature of habit and I wore white, didn't I? To please the Kingdom, I wore white.

I started to slink them off when Bridge suddenly reached out and jerked my hips toward him. He held on, his eyes never leaving mine as he fisted the sides of my panties in his hands and jerked them from my body, ripping them completely in half.

No, this definitely wasn't Julian, was it?

This man had danger lurking beneath his gaze. This man also had a simmering hatred I recognized in my own eyes.

"I never want to see you wear white again," he rasped. "Do you fucking understand?"

I nodded numbly. "My wedding dress is champagne."

"Izzy?"

"Yeah?"

"I really don't want to talk right now." And then he pulled me onto his lap, causing me to straddle him still fully clothed as his mouth met mine in a frenzy of heat and tongue that left me aching everywhere. I felt him in my lungs, I felt him in my brain, against my skin, the weight of his body between my legs. I squeezed my thighs, imagining what it would feel like when he was finally between them, when he was mine.

When I took what was mine.

My hands roamed over his solid chest and then lower as I pulled his shirt over his head.

Perfection.

Muscles everywhere.

Ink that was finally uncovered.

I raked my nails down his chest while he flipped me onto my back on the couch, never pulling his lips from mine.

He was aggressive.

There was nothing tender about Bridge Tennyson.

He was raw, feral, hungry.

Starved.

So I fed him my body, I opened up to him, I watched while he shrugged out of his jeans, kicking them down the couch.

No boxers.

"Do you always go commando?" I asked once he pulled back for air.

He just shook his head. "Do you really want to talk about my lack of boxers right now?"

I smiled against his mouth, earning me a smile in return as he deepened the next kiss, angling his head to the side while he positioned himself over me, I could feel his heat, his length even though he wasn't even inside me yet.

My body strained for it, begged for it. I was shaking, and I had no idea why this moment in time felt like everything to me. The most important thing I needed to do.

"Izzy." His neck strained as we touched foreheads. "Tell me to stop, because we can't come back from this, we can't."

"I know." I kissed his mouth and softly repeated, "I know."

"I wanted you the moment I saw you," he admitted.

"Oh, Bridge." Tears filled my eyes.

"Say it again." He clenched his teeth as his tip grazed my entrance. I'd never been so ready in my entire life. "My name, say it again."

"Bridge," I whispered, sliding my tongue into his mouth only to pull away and say it against his lips. "My Bridge."

"Damn right I am." He thrust into me so hard that my hands moved to his shoulders to hold on while he started slowly moving in me. "I'm stealing you, Izzy Cunningham." Another thrust. "You're mine."

"Yours," I agreed as he stretched me, completed me. He worshipped me with his mouth then, kissed me so deep, filled me even deeper. "Bridge!" I couldn't stop saying it, I needed it to be real, to be him, not Julian. "Bridge!"

"Yours, Izzy." He clenched his teeth then cupped my face with both hands and locked eyes on me, our movements synced, deep, fast. I was so close. "Stay with me, Izzy."

I nodded stupidly as my body pulsed with pleasure with the need for release. "I'm with you."

I clamped around him.

He let out a curse.

And then I felt it, him, me, together.

My head fell back against the couch while he kissed down my neck, breathing heavy against my skin, his mouth hot, his lips even hotter.

"You're right." I finally found my voice. "We can't come back from this. But I don't want to, Bridge, I don't want to."

His gaze focused on mine, his lips turned into an annoyingly smug grin like he knew it was never like that between me and Julian, like he knew that I couldn't remember ever flying so high with him. "Good."

Chapter Thirty-Eight

BRIDGE

I couldn't sleep that night.

I woke her up three times, twice while I was inside her, once with my mouth all over her. I had this pressing need to make sure that it wasn't all a hallucination. I felt like we were both waiting for the bomb to go off.

We had no plan other than continuing with the façade for the world to see, and getting ready for the wedding in a few days. We looked and acted like the perfect power couple. The media was camped outside our building and #weddingcountdown was trending on Twitter.

Guilt grew like a tumor in my chest.

The more hours that ticked by, the more it grew.

Because I wasn't sure how the hell I would ever face Julian, look at him man to man, and say, *I'm keeping her . . . and I'm not sorry.*

Because I wasn't sorry.

Because I was in love with her.

And she was everything to me.

And in that moment I had the most selfish thought: if my brother died he would never know I'd betrayed him, how we betrayed him in his apartment, on his couch, and in his bed. I betrayed him using his clothes, his money, his possessions, his life.

I'd done that.

We'd done that.

I'd always thought I was a good person—solid, loyal, dependable. And now?

I felt like an unapologetic thief.

I leaned over and kissed her on the cheek.

She reached for me, and her eyes opened, and then she was crawling over to me, shoving me onto my back and riding me.

I was so hard for her already that it was painful.

I cursed as she moved on top of me. I cupped her breasts, squeezed, then lowered my hands to her ass and pulled her harder against me, faster.

She leaned over, her hand on my shoulder, our eyes once again locking like we knew what we were doing was wrong, but once you've had one taste, you're fucked.

Literally.

I couldn't stop.

And neither could she.

"Nothing has ever felt as good as you feel, Bridge." Her hair tickled my face as it created a curtain of privacy as we kissed. Her body shuddered, I felt her release, and gladly followed.

I liked her on top of me.

I liked the feel of her thighs wrapped around my body.

She leaned over and kissed me again and then pulled away and rolled to her side with a yawn.

I let out a low laugh and leaned over to kiss her on the head. "Sleep, sweetheart."

"Mmm." She didn't say anything after that.

I played with her hair. I imagined a scenario where this was real life, where I was in my apartment . . . with her, living a life . . . with her.

I was such a fucking imposter.

I got up and grabbed my old phone, ready to text my mom, to ask for advice, when I realized it wouldn't do any good for her to be even more stressed.

I tucked my phone away and looked back at the bed as the sun started to slowly rise, letting light in the room.

"Please, Julian, please . . ." I squeezed my eyes shut. "Please try to understand."

Chapter Thirty-Nine

My body was sore from him.

I felt it with each step I ran in Central Park.

I felt him when I washed my sweaty body.

I felt him when I went to the market to grab food for dinner.

And I felt him when I went back Thursday night and started cooking, waiting in excited expectation for him to walk through the door.

Bridge.

My Bridge.

I squeezed my eyes shut as I thought about the choice I'd made, a man I barely knew and yet felt like I'd known all my life.

Maybe because Bridge truly felt like the way Julian used to be, before his father took over. Bridge was the man Julian was never given the chance to be, wasn't he?

I'd gone to the ICU wing that day to bring Julian flowers and was shocked when the nurses told me that the doctors said I couldn't see him. Something about a compromised immune system. So I left the flowers at the desk with a get-well balloon and ran errands the rest of the day.

And because I felt stupid waiting for Bridge to get home, I'd gone on another walk; it helped me process.

Hours later, I put my hand on my stomach and took in a deep breath as the door to the penthouse swung open.

I sucked in a breath when Bridge dropped keys and Julian's wallet onto the counter. The suit he was wearing was navy blue, his shirt white. He looked like he belonged on the cover of *Men's Journal*. Then again, one misstep and he would probably Hulk right out of those clothes.

Bridge looked at me, pulling off the aviators Julian rarely wore, setting himself apart that much more.

"Hungry?" I rasped.

"Starving." Two steps, and he was pulling me into his arms, pulling my skirt up to my thighs, and setting me on the counter. I'd never heard a sexier sound than a belt being pulled off, pants getting unzipped as he angled his head, kissing me hard, demanding I give him every inch of my mouth as my bare ass slid against the cold marble. "You're not wearing underwear."

"Thought I would see what all the fuss was about." I pulled back and bit down on my bottom lip at his amused grin.

"And?" He teased my lips with a few hungry nips. "What's the conclusion?"

I spread my legs wide, his eyes dilated. "I think if it makes you look at me like that, I'm never wearing them again."

His mouth slammed against mine. "Damn, where have you been my entire life?"

"Oh, you know, waiting for the evil twin to show up and rescue me."

He smiled against my neck. "Truer words were never spoken. Don't forget I'm the bad guy in this scenario, Izzy. You weren't mine to take."

"Yes," I confessed. "I really was."

He let out a fierce growl before kissing me harder, pulling me to the edge of the countertop, and entering me with one fluid thrust. "Thought about this . . . in every shitty meeting."

"Sex in the kitchen?"

"Sex with you." He silenced me with another kiss. "Sex with you everywhere. And then Netflix while we break, more sex, talking, whiskey, tucking you into bed, keeping you safe, more sex, followed by more protecting." His movements were frenzied. I wasn't going to last long, I dug my nails into his bulging biceps and hung on while he picked me up by the ass and sank deeper into me.

"Right there." I squeezed my eyes shut. "Oh God, I don't think I can—"

"Don't think," he commanded in a strong voice. "Just feel what you do to me."

And I did, oh man, I did.

Every hard inch of him.

I did that.

I clenched my teeth as my release hit me soon after.

He said my name.

He whispered it.

He repeated it.

He revered it.

I felt his words wrap around me softly, our bodies still linked, when he pressed a kiss to my lips and looked into my eyes. "How any man can keep his eyes, let alone his hands, off you is beyond me, Izzy. You're everything."

My eyes welled with tears. "I'd like to think it was hard for him."

"I'd like to think he's into guys and won't murder me when he wakes up from his coma."

My smile was sad.

"And I'm sure he battled it every day, Izzy. I lasted a month. A damn month. At least you know who got the gift of self-control."

I wrapped my arms around his neck. "Don't forget, I'm the one who seduced you."

"Don't forget, I was a willing victim." He smirked.

"Yeah, but I didn't know that. You just stared."

He threw his head back and laughed. God, I loved his laugh. "Izzy, I couldn't form a coherent thought beyond 'uh.'"

I loved that he admitted that to me, that he was this giant of a man, sexy as hell, and still vulnerable. "You make me laugh."

"Someone should," he countered. "Now, why don't I keep cooking"—he looked over his shoulder—"this wonderful-looking spaghetti while you clean up, grab a glass of wine, and sit on the couch with a book."

I stared him down. "Who are you?"

"Bridge Tennyson, the twin who gets that every woman should have the opportunity to sit at the end of the day with a duke and a good glass of wine."

Julian had always made fun of my romance novels, saying they were like junk food for the mind.

Bridge was encouraging me to spoil my mind with fantasies and wine.

"Hmm, evil twin knows what a girl wants," I teased.

He made a face. "Don't even get me started on the sort of books I've seen on Mom's coffee table, though." His eyes raked me over. "Not a bad way to get some tips and tricks."

My jaw dropped. "Are you telling me you read romance novels?"

"No." He pointed his finger at me and laughed. "I'm telling you I skip to the good parts, do the necessary strategizing in my head, you know, like wondering if you could actually do that sort of thing at that angle, and then I store it in my head for future use. That's not reading, sweetheart, that's fucking research."

I laughed so hard I had tears in my eyes. "You read romance novels."

"Shhhh." He clapped a hand over my mouth. "I admit nothing."

I nipped at his hand and he jerked it back. "Bet I could get you to admit it."

"Izzy . . ." His eyes narrowed as my gaze lowered.

"Hmm, maybe you should think about that while you cook, all the ways I'm going to get you to admit that deep down, you love romance."

"I'm man enough to admit I love romance. Every woman should have it, and if a guy isn't man enough to give it to her, he shouldn't get to have a cock let alone be allowed to use it." He shrugged.

"I think I like you, Bridge Tennyson."

"Thank God. I was waiting to change my Facebook status . . ." He winked. "Seriously, go, I'll finish cooking."

"Okay." On wobbly legs, I moved through the kitchen and then stopped. "Hey, I almost forgot to ask. How was work?"

He smiled so wide that I wanted to kiss him again. "It was good, we're making great progress, I won't bore you to tears, but it's good, Izzy, real good. Though as good as it was, all I wanted was to come home to you."

"Sorry."

"Don't be." He shook his head. "It gave me something to look forward to. Home . . ."

"Home," I repeated. "Funny, I never thought about our apartment as home."

He was silent. I could tell he wanted to say something against his brother, his jaw ticked like he was clenching his teeth. "I'm gonna . . ." I nodded toward the bedroom. "Try not to burn the apartment down."

"No promises. I love a good bonfire," he called back while I smiled the rest of the way into the bedroom.

It was perfect.

So perfect that I was terrified it was going to come crashing down around us in a fiery glory.

Chapter Forty

BRIDGE

"You ready for this?" Izzy sounded nervous as she clutched my hand in hers. I squeezed back. "I don't know why I'm so nervous."

"You look beautiful." I kissed her hand. And she really did. I'd helped her out of that dress three times before finally relenting and letting her keep it on. It was a slip dress that barely covered her ass, ice blue, and so soft against her curves that I was almost jealous of the damn thing.

It got to hug her, caress her, tease her, while I had to wear a stupid designer tux picked out by a few editors at *Vogue* who in my opinion slipped several times when measuring me earlier that week.

"We've got this," I whispered, pulling her into my arms and kissing her neck. "We're a team, alright?"

I could sense the tension in her body. We were standing outside the restaurant where our rehearsal dinner was being held.

For the wedding the next day.

Where the world would think I was legally making her his.

When I was keeping her as mine.

The priest was sworn to secrecy and paid off, which was disappointing for other reasons. When Julian woke up—not if—the marriage would be annulled . . . at least that was my understanding. A board member in my father's pocket would bear witness along with my dad.

And I, Bridge Anderson Tennyson, would not only steal his future bride, but his life.

I would get my trust fund.

All my shares.

And I would keep praying my brother wouldn't kill me and that when he woke up he'd understand all the reasons I did it.

The doctors said he'd been moving a lot more, which was progress, but they still wouldn't let him have any visitors.

"We're a team," Izzy repeated from her place at my side.

I smiled down at her and kissed the top of her head. If someone had told me a year ago that I'd be headed to my rehearsal dinner that summer with the most beautiful woman alive, I would have laughed.

Everything had changed.

And was still changing.

I was actually getting used to the attention, the way people took pictures of us like we deserved their notice. The constant praise at the office.

And worse, the constant attention from my own father every time I did something right.

He even admitted that he didn't think I would be able to pull it off like Julian and then laughed and said, "Well, at least I know my company's in good hands if he dies."

Laughed over it. Like my brother's life was a joke.

Making me hate him even more.

Next to me, Izzy tensed before I opened the door to the restaurant.

"You okay?" I asked.

"Bridge." She whispered my name, always careful, always protective of me, of us. "You don't have to do this, you know."

"Funny, I was going to tell you the same thing."

She grinned. "Great minds."

"I just want you to know I'm not marrying you because my father wants me to, Izzy. I'm marrying you because not having you in my life would physically hurt me. Five weeks, Izzy. It took me five weeks to fall head over heels in love with you."

"I love you, too." A tear slid down her cheek. "I love you so much."

I pressed a slow, drugging kiss across her mouth and then moved to her neck. "I think I needed to hear that as much as you needed to hear it."

She nodded. "Does it feel wrong to you? Our love?"

"Not wrong, just bad timing," I answered honestly. "But that's life, Izzy, and we both know how short it is. We never know how much time we've been given, so I'm not going to waste it, not when I have you."

Her smile was so bright as she licked her lips and then sighed happily. "You know, when you're not being argumentative you can be really romantic."

"I'm not argumentative. You just refuse to let me win."

"Because I'm always right." She winked.

I rolled my eyes and slid my hand down her ass and tapped it lightly. "Let's get this over with so we can go home and have ice cream."

We walked into the building amidst cheers and champagne, and I actually found it within myself to smile because she was by my side.

Because we were together.

Because I was actually happy despite the guilt I held in my heart, the guilt that I fed every time I kissed her, every time I was inside her, knowing he was in a coma.

"A toast!" Edward lifted his glass in the air. "To the heir of the Tennyson throne my son Julian Tennyson, and his beautiful bride, Isobel Cunningham."

Izzy lifted her glass with me. We both drank deep as people joined in.

My father gave me a knowing smile.

I shot a cocky smile right back.

At least I knew he needed me now that I was the new golden boy. Guilt gnawed when I realized that he was looking at me the way Julian would have killed to be looked at.

Damn it.

"What was that?" Izzy said from my right.

"What?"

"That." She nodded her head at Edward. "He looked almost . . . proud, not angry, not manipulative, but proud."

"Because he is," I said quickly. "I've played directly into his hands, made him richer, I'm marrying the girl he approves of . . . According to him, all is well. Now if only someone would wake up . . ."

"Part of me thinks he doesn't want him to," Izzy admitted, voicing exactly what I'd been thinking for the past week. "Julian would have killed to have Edward smile at him like that."

I hung my head. What was she? A mind reader? "You can't say that to me, not now, not when I already feel this heaping amount of guilt like I've taken everything and left him with nothing."

"What happens to the CEO position when he wakes up?" Izzy held my hand tight as we made our way around the room, smiling at guests.

"No idea."

"Would you keep it?" She pulled me in close as we moved to the small dance floor. "If you could, would you keep it?"

I felt my throat all but close up. "Can we not talk about that right now?"

"Not an option," she snapped back. "Nothing but honesty between us now, you know that."

"Shit," I muttered under my breath. "Yeah, I would want to keep it, alright? I'm enjoying myself, but I battle with this . . . sickness in me that tells me I'm just like my father, worse, actually."

"Don't." She gripped my chin with her free hand. "Don't compare yourself to him. He's not even worthy of standing next to you."

I exhaled. "Thanks, Izzy."

"I mean it."

"I know you do." I didn't deserve her. I would spend the rest of my life trying to earn her, though, with a smile on my face. "At least people won't doubt that we're actually getting married, what with you holding your purse like you're seconds away from hitting me with it." I winked.

She lowered it and glared, though it didn't last long. "You're antagonizing, you know that?"

"You weren't complaining a few hours ago when the floor below us filed a noise complaint."

She looked like she wanted to hide behind me, her cheeks went bright pink. "I wasn't that loud."

"Oh, you were." I grinned triumphantly. "Bridge, God, Bridge, deeper—"

"I'm this close"—face beet red, she held her hand in front of her eye, thumb and forefinger a half inch apart—"to following through with the whole poisoning thing."

"You shouldn't have to apologize for orgasms, Izzy."

"You also shouldn't scream so loud that the floor below you thinks someone's getting murdered."

I choked on my next sip of champagne.

She shrugged and then leaned closer to me. "Tell you what, let's make the rounds, shake hands, smile, and then make our excuses so we can go back to the apartment and see if we get an eviction notice for noise."

I held up my glass and clinked it with hers. "You have yourself a deal."

"Fabulous." She downed the rest of her drink and then smiled at me.

And I knew right then: I would never let her go.

Ever.

"Mine," I whispered under my breath so only she could hear.

She sucked in a breath as I moved around her.

She didn't know that I needed to marry her to get the trust fund.

And the shares.

Because I hadn't told her.

Because I didn't want her to think that's why I was marrying her. Because in the end, it didn't even matter.

Because Julian still wasn't awake.

And if he wasn't awake.

There was no point.

I took a look around the room and realized this was going to be the new normal. CEO to a company I actually liked, working with a father I wanted to strangle ninety percent of the time, and Izzy.

Maybe love did prevail in the end.

I was in too good of a mood to let my father's knowing grin piss me off, so I lifted my champagne to the bastard and counted down the hours until I could be naked with my fiancée.

I smiled.

Mine.

Not his.

Mine.

Chapter Forty-One

ISOBEL

"Wait, start over." We were both lying naked in bed eating ice cream. He handed me a chocolate chip cookie and then grabbed the spoon from me, dipping it back into the rocky road. "You said no to Julian when he asked you out the first time?"

I rolled my eyes. "He was arrogant."

"I would have paid to see that." Bridge laughed. "He had his first girlfriend in kindergarten. The guy wasn't used to rejection from the fairer sex." He licked the spoon; I'd never wanted to be a piece of silverware more in my life.

He licked one side while watching me.

And then that perfect tongue of his slid across the top.

I jerked it out of his hand and dipped it into the ice cream.

"It's cool, I was done." He shook his head at me, his mouth pulling an amused smile.

"You were taking too long eating it." I wagged the spoon at him, mouth full. "I don't know if you're aware of this, but . . ." I crooked my finger and whispered, "Ice cream melts."

"Let's just add 'sarcastic little shit' to your resume, shall we?" he teased, grabbing a pillow and holding it high.

"Noooo . . ." I laughed. "Fine, sorry. Here, have a bite, watch the airplane, brrrrr . . ." I circled it in front of him.

He glared and flipped me off then leaned in. "For the record, I'm only doing this because I really want another bite and because I'm a sucker for naked girls making airplane noises."

He bit down on the spoon.

Warmth spread down my body. "If someone thought I'd be making airplane noises the night before my wedding . . ." My voice trailed off.

His face fell. "I'm sorry, I know this isn't how you pictured—"

"It's better," I interjected. It was like I finally came to grips that Julian wasn't waking up. Bridge said talking about him made it easier, and I think it did, but it still hurt that this part of my life would forever be gone.

That he was gone.

"It's so much more than I could have dreamed, though the whole evil twin thing is a bit farfetched." I scrunched up my nose while he nodded in agreement. "Do you think he was upset, the day he got in the accident? Do you think his last thoughts before the crash were angry ones, toward me?"

I didn't want to ask the question, because I was afraid of the answer.

His face that day had been disappointed.

But there was nothing else there.

Was he upset?

Or was he his usual cool, indifferent self? The face he wore at the office.

"Izzy." Bridge took the ice cream carton from me and set it on the nightstand, then pulled me into his lap. "We'll never know. And you can't blame yourself or beat yourself up over it. It won't give you closure. It won't solve anything."

"When you showed up at the apartment, it reminded me so much of all the reasons I loved him, only to realize later that the reasons I loved him are the reasons I fell for you."

He kissed the top of my head. "Say that last part again."

"I fell for you."

"It seems I can't stop falling," he added. "Every day there's more I learn, every day you sink into my heart deeper and deeper. I can't imagine there will ever be a day where I say, 'Today, today is the day I'm done exploring her, done learning about what makes her so incredible.'"

I clung to him then, as he held me close. It was the dream I'd always had and wanted with Julian. To always have this openness with him, to lie around naked, eating ice cream, talking about life.

And it was the night before my wedding to his twin that I finally saw my dream coming true.

I sighed and looked up at Bridge. "Say the best happens, then say he wakes up a year from now . . ."

"Okay." He was quiet, his eyes searching mine.

"What do we tell Julian?"

Bridge exhaled and closed his eyes then pinched the bridge of his nose. "I guess that depends on what you want to do."

"Me?"

He frowned. "Izzy, I want you, you know I want you, and yes it would destroy me, but you're your own person. I won't make the mistake of leaving you out of any major decision again, so if you want him . . ." He clenched his jaw. "Shit, I can't even believe I'm saying this, but if you still want to try with him, if he goes back to how things were . . ." He looked heartbroken, and his expression grew shuttered as he sucked in another sharp breath. "I want what you want, Izzy. Your happiness. And your freedom, whatever the cost. And that's the truth."

I hugged him tight. "The evil twin isn't supposed to say things like that."

"When did we decide I was all evil?"

"The minute you had sex with me on your brother's couch, evil."

"You were naked, I had no other choice." He laughed against my hair. "And Izzy, it's going to be okay, it has to be."

I stayed in his lap, eating ice cream, talking about his childhood, asking about Julian, trying to put the pieces together as best I could, why he resented him so much, why there was a chasm between them.

The more he told me, the heavier my heart became.

It seems that I wasn't the only one who wasn't chosen.

Julian chose work over me.

Edward chose Julian over Bridge.

Two outcasts, sitting in a bed, eating rocky road. Yes, there was something very poetic and some might say romantic about that.

Chapter Forty-Two

BRIDGE

I was standing in front of the mirror sweating under my designer vest and shoes. We were supposed to do a photo shoot right after the wedding and then change and join everyone at the reception an hour later.

I had six outfits to change into for the photos, each more alarming than the last, and one without a shirt, just suspenders.

I didn't understand it, but maybe I didn't have to. I just had to make it through the rest of the day without anything happening to my mom or to Izzy.

I checked the heavy, gold-plated Rolex on my left wrist and then grabbed my phone to dial my mom.

I was in one of the back rooms waiting for a text from my father, and Izzy was being watched like a hawk by Marla in the next room while all the stylists did her hair and makeup, and pinned things to her that I wanted nothing more than to pull off the minute I poked my head in and got shooed out.

I'd imagined my wedding differently.

Maybe in a small church, or on the beach where everyone could just get drunk afterward and then sleep in and surf the next morning.

I stared at myself in the mirror and saw my skin visibly pale.

Today I looked like him more than I looked like me.

Chest tight, I stared at myself and wondered if Julian would have done this. Would he have gone this far?

Would he have put on this suit, kissed her mouth, fallen in love?

I didn't know the man he was now, all I knew was the boys we had been together, and all I remembered was trying to protect him and then him stealing my shit on a daily basis.

I sighed and looked away.

His Rolex was heavy on my arm.

This was his money.

His wedding day.

I dialed my mom using FaceTime and squeezed my eyes shut. The phone rang, and rang, but finally Mom picked it up. "HONEY!"

"Mom." My voice cracked. "I wish you were here." I needed her there, but it was dangerous traveling in her condition. The feeding tube was doing its job and she looked healthier than I'd seen her in the last two years. She even had color in her cheeks.

I could at least thank my dad for that.

Julian too.

"I wish I was there too, baby." She sniffled. "You look so handsome, so much like your brother and yet so much uniquely you."

Tears welled in my own eyes. "I hate that I miss him in moments like this. I hate that I still resent him too. I don't know how to feel, Mom. I'm marrying—"

"Sweetie." She held the phone close to her face. "Just answer me this. If the situations were reversed, do you have any doubt in your mind he would be doing the exact same thing?"

I was ready to say yes.

And then I really thought about it.

How he sent money and then set up a separate fund for me and Mom, but also how he never visited, never once reached out to me once we were out of college, the emails just dwindled and disappeared.

"Yeah, Mom, I think he probably would, though I highly doubt he would have lost his grip with reality and started believing it was real, that Izzy loved the stand-in rather than the real one."

"Honey . . ." She used her mom voice, the one that had me standing a little straighter, listening a little better. "You can't help who you love, or who you fall for, that's just life. It's not something that you can control. Worry about today, there's only enough energy for today. Stop worrying about tomorrow, live, honey, just live your best life in these next few hours and be the boy I raised into this spectacular man I see in front of me. I'm so proud."

I squeezed my eyes shut and nodded. "You made me who I am."

"Damn right I did," she teased. "You're what makes the Tennyson name worth having, son. Never forget that. And call me when you can. I want an update. I'm feeling . . . restless about all of this. You guys have been on the news every single night I've watched. People keep saying that this is the start of a dynasty for this family, they're comparing you to royalty."

I winced. It wasn't just a lot of pressure.

It was the fact that the world thought I was someone else when I wanted them to know . . . that it was me.

Ten years from now, they'd still think that Julian Tennyson was alive, and nobody would ask about the other brother who changed his name.

I looked in the mirror again and realized.

My father had done it.

He'd actually done it.

He'd killed Bridge.

And resurrected what he saw was a better version of Julian.

Son of a bitch.

I paced in front of the mirror.

"You still there, honey?"

"Yeah," I croaked, feeling more panicked than I had in years. "Same here."

"But . . ." Her smile was back. "You're my Bridge. You'll figure it out, and I will never"—tears streamed down her face—"forget the sacrifice you made so that I could talk to you like this on your wedding day without blacking out."

"Mom."

"Go." Her smile was watery. "Tell that lovely girl to take care of you."

"She has been," I said, and then heat crept up my neck into my face, and I knew I was blushing like an immature kid.

Mom's eyebrows shot up. "Huh, so it's like that?"

"It just happened." I looked away.

"Oh, you fell on each other while naked? What, you slip on a banana peel?"

"Oh hell, I'm hanging up now." I laughed, loving that she could cheer me up when I was ready to have a panic attack over the stark realization that I was him now.

Truly him.

She winked. "Love you."

"Love you too."

I hung up and stared down at the phone in my hands, no texts saying Julian had suddenly woken up.

I had two groomsmen who were friends with Julian, friends I knew shit about. One was named Oz and the other douche was Rhett, who, upon seeing me, handed me a shot of tequila and said, "To getting laid by one chick for the rest of your life."

Then they'd stepped out to give me privacy.

A knock sounded at the door, interrupting my thoughts.

"Come in." I slipped my phone back in my pocket as the door swung open, and my father walked in with both groomsmen. Photographers and paparazzi were already snapping photos in the hall. When I looked out the window, I saw at least a dozen news vans.

"Son!" Father slapped me on the back. "You ready for the old ball and chain?"

God save me, I'm surrounded by idiots. "Hey, as long as it's Izzy."

He winked at me. "She's a beautiful girl."

I simply said, "She's perfect."

"You dog," he muttered approvingly under his breath. "Now, let's make a toast. Oz, the flutes?"

Oz held four flutes while my father opened the champagne with a resounding pop that sounded like a gun going off. It spilled over as he poured us all champagne.

He raised his glass. "To my *true* son." It wasn't lost on me that he emphasized *true*. "I had my doubts, Julian." He shrugged. "But now, seeing you in front of me, I realize that maybe I did pick better than I thought, because this ends with you, doesn't it? I'm proud that you want this, so damn proud."

I felt sick.

Like I was going to hurl all over him.

Because it was wrong.

This was so wrong.

Those words, he was supposed to say those words to Julian, not to me.

I didn't need them.

Julian would have died for them.

Julian was in a coma over them.

I needed air.

Another knock sounded at the door, and the coordinator poked her head in. "It's time!"

I was out of time.

So was Julian.

Why did this feel so final?

Like I was the one doing the killing.

By saying yes to her, I was turning my back on him.

Ultimate betrayal.

By a brother who should love you the most.

By your other half.

Each step felt wooden as I made my way to the main ballroom. A flurry of activity hit me all at once when I looked up and saw Izzy standing at the doors, her expression more nervous than I'd ever seen it.

I stopped and drank her in, not realizing that we had an audience, not relying on all my senses, because she was overwhelming me in every way. "You're breathtaking."

Izzy turned and smiled so bright that I wanted to cry. She was too pretty. I moved toward her then swept her in my arms and swung her around, much to the irritation of the wedding coordinator, who cleared her throat multiple times before I finally set my bride on her feet.

"I'm afraid to hold you too tight." I sighed against her neck. "You're too pretty in this dress, too beautiful to be real."

And she was.

Her dress was formfitting and off both shoulders, it had lace inlay across the top and was hand stitched. It also, *thank God*, wasn't white but a deep champagne that brought out her flawless coloring. She was wearing a veil that went all the way to the floor, it too was lace, and her hair was in loose curls hanging around her shoulders.

"Perfect, you're perfect."

The wedding coordinator moved to the side and spoke into her headset. "Send out Edward Tennyson. We're about to get started."

"I wasn't supposed to see you yet," I whispered, still holding her in my arms.

She touched my forehead with hers. "I know. I just needed to see you, to see your face before everything, before . . ." She choked on a sob. "I just realized how desperately I really want to walk down that aisle . . . toward you."

My heart damn near exploded. "I want that too."

"I know." Her hands were shaking as she rose up on her tiptoes and pressed a kiss to my cheek. "I guess I'll see you at the end of the aisle."

"Possibly sooner." I grinned.

She gave me a look of hope just as Oz and Rhett came up behind me, followed by my father, who looked completely relaxed.

Because he had won.

And I'd let him.

Because it meant Izzy.

"Alright!" Our coordinator clapped her hands. "Men, down the hall and take the second left and make your way to the altar. And Isobel"—she beamed at Izzy—"Edward and you will begin your walk once I see that the men are in their places."

"It's really happening," Izzy said with excitement.

My father gave her a tentative smile. "I'm glad you're so excited about this and not ready to run in the opposite direction."

I gave her one last look and joined my groomsmen down the hall and out the door.

There was no way to describe the feeling that hit me then, like something was going to happen.

Goose bumps erupted down my arms despite the three-piece tux. I was being paranoid.

Right?

I moved to the front of the church and stared down the aisle.

Something inside me said it was wrong.

Some gut instinct told me we wouldn't come back from this.

Not me and Izzy.

Me and Julian.

And then all thoughts of my twin dissipated as the doors opened and the bridal march started.

"Forgive me, Father," I whispered under my breath. "For I have sinned . . ."

Chapter Forty-Three

ISOBEL

I hated that I had to loop my arm in his.

He was so arrogant.

So pleased with himself.

The music started. It was beautiful, hundreds of white candles glowed up front by the altar where Bridge was waiting. The smell of lavender filled the air. My dress was perfect, my shoes even more perfect, and the man I loved was waiting for me.

Looking at me the way every bride wants to be looked at on her wedding day.

With complete adoration.

With love.

His eyes glistened with tears as he mouthed *"I love you."*

Tears slid down my cheeks as I mouthed it back.

His grin was huge.

It was taking forever to make it to the end of the aisle.

But we finally made it.

"Who gives this woman?"

"I do." Edward claimed me loudly and then leaned in and kissed my right cheek, then my left.

Bridge held out his arm.

I looped mine in it and then I leaned my head against him, I just needed to be closer.

Touching him.

He wrapped an arm around me.

And that's how we said our vows.

With me practically in his arms.

And Bridge Tennyson, twin to my real fiancé, refusing to let me go.

It was a happy moment, being claimed by him, followed by sweeping sadness that Julian wasn't here, that we'd never had closure.

That he was lying in bed, with machines beeping around him instead of being surrounded by friends and family.

This would have been his day, ours.

But Bridge and I were stealing that too, weren't we?

You can't help who you love.

I knew that more than most.

Because when I was still grasping at the love I had for Julian, I'd fallen for Bridge.

"I now pronounce you husband and wife. You may kiss the bride!" I was already turning in his arms.

Bridge grinned down at me and then swept in with a kiss that stole my breath as he lifted me into the air amidst cheers from the crowd.

It was perfect.

I was crying.

He swiped his thumb beneath my eyes and winked as we held hands and made our way back down the aisle.

I almost tripped on my dress when Bridge suddenly stopped.

I smiled up at him and then froze.

He was pale. So pale.

Disbelief etched on every part of his face, on his rigid body.

And I knew.

I don't know how I knew.

I just knew.

Slowly, while people still cheered around us, I looked down the aisle where Bridge stared.

And in a three-piece suit, looking every inch the billionaire playboy.

Stood Julian Tennyson.

With rage in his eyes.

And vengeance in his stance.

Chapter Forty-Four

BRIDGE

I couldn't breathe.

Couldn't think beyond what the hell was he doing there and why did he look so damn healthy?

I snapped out of my shock but not quick enough. People around us started pointing and whispering.

Tears poured down Izzy's face by the time we reached the end of the aisle, and with the confidence of a Tennyson, Julian walked right out in front of us toward the ballroom.

Hundreds of people were invited to the reception, though only fifty or so had been invited to the actual ceremony, which meant we had a room full of people waiting for us.

Including the media.

I clung to Izzy. "Julian, wait—"

"So you do remember my name." He didn't turn around. Instead, he shoved open the ballroom doors.

People cheered.

Cameras flashed.

And then they gasped.

Happy music pounded through the sound system as people sat at their tables with shocked expressions.

And then Julian turned to Izzy. "I think I should at least be given the first dance, since this was supposed to be my wedding, since you were supposed to be mine, since this is literally the most fucked-up thing a person can wake up to after fighting for his life. I mean at least give me, your *fiancé*," he said through gritted teeth, "a fucking dance."

Izzy held out a shaking hand to him. He took it without looking at me, without looking at anyone but her.

And I let him.

I let him because I didn't have a leg to stand on.

Because he was right.

Because all the guilt I'd been feeling was suddenly suffocating me to death, so I stood there while he took my dance, the way I had taken his life.

And with each turn around the room, the pain intensified, so much so that I thought I was going to pass out from it.

Because he was touching her.

He was dancing with her.

I burned with jealousy.

I let myself hate because it was easier to hate him than it was to look at him as a victim.

It was easier to hate him than to look in the mirror and realize I was the villain.

Truly the evil twin.

Because I had stolen it all.

And I would do it again.

A thousand more times.

To have her.

It was a slow-motion effect, the way he twirled her around the room, his expression hardened.

My dad came up behind me and clapped me on the back. "Bad publicity is still good publicity, am I right?"

Slowly I turned. "Excuse me?"

"Woke up a few days ago, heard us all talking in the room, and wanted some time to gather his thoughts, and then he wanted his revenge. And I saw something change in Julian, something you put there. Something he was always missing. I don't care that hate fuels him, just like I don't care that you married Izzy when she was meant for Julian. All I care about right now is that the number one thing trending on Twitter is my company and the fact that I have twin sons."

A sinister smile crossed his face when he handed me a newspaper. "Tomorrow's news. Thought you may want to get ahead of it."

Twin brothers reunited in twisted love triangle, Tennyson Financial stocks soar.

My stomach dropped as I reared back and punched my dad in the face and dropped the paper on the ground. "Maybe the next day they'll include a picture of your black eye."

I stomped into the middle of the dance floor, interrupting Julian and Izzy, not that they were talking. He was glaring. She was sobbing.

"We need to talk. Now," I snapped.

Julian gave me a cool stare. "And miss your reception?"

"Cut the bullshit, Julian. Dad set us up."

"I know." His voice was low. "For twelve years I've been waiting for that man's approval." His eyes raged with fury. "Twelve. Years."

"Julian, not here."

He reared back and punched me in the face.

And I let him.

Because I deserved it.

I didn't fall like our father had, but we were giving the press a fantastic show and proving everything in that newspaper to be true.

Dad was standing again, adjusting his tie, while Izzy was holding on to me for dear life.

"For Izzy," I rasped. "We do this in privacy. For Izzy."

Julian's gaze softened a little while his jaw flexed like he'd been clenching his teeth too hard. "Fine."

"Are you okay?" Izzy asked. Her makeup was a mess, her face swollen and tear-streaked.

"No." I shook my head. "I'm not."

We walked hand in hand out of our own reception with Julian stomping ahead of us and my dad smiling from his spot on the floor like it was the best outcome in the world.

Both his sons.

At odds with him, with each other, over a woman.

And over a life stolen.

When we reached one of the empty rooms, Julian turned to face us.

And I finally saw it.

He was livid.

But more than that.

My brother was fucking heartbroken.

Chapter Forty-Five

ISOBEL

I was wrecked.

A huge part of me wanted to run into Bridge's arms and ask him to make it all go away. The other part of me was sick to my stomach over the fact that this was how Julian had found out.

By showing up at what should have been our wedding, his and mine.

I went into it with my eyes wide open.

So did Bridge.

Julian, however, had had his eyes shut throughout the entire thing. He hadn't seen how we fell in love, he hadn't seen the struggle on both sides, and he hadn't heard the conversations between me and Bridge, the worry over what would happen.

And now he was there staring at me like I'd ruined his world.

And me, staring right back at him with guilt in my eyes because I couldn't say otherwise.

"I heard your voice, Iz." He stared me down, like he didn't know me anymore, like I was a stranger to him. "The day you and Bridge came into the hospital discussing—" His voice cracked. "Maybe it was the betrayal that woke me up, for that I guess I can thank you both."

Bridge sighed. "You woke up three days ago?"

"I saw you holding her hand," Julian admitted. "I saw your kiss. I saw you take what was mine, and Dad—" His nostrils flared. "He came back because he forgot his damn sunglasses in the room, and there I was, wide-eyed, ready to tear the world apart."

"Dad knew?" Bridge muttered a curse. "Why didn't you say something to us? Why let him do this?"

"Let him?" Julian exploded. I'd never seen him this angry. I'd never seen him be anything but in complete control. "I don't know, Bridge, how could you take over my life? Huh? Wear my clothes? Spend my money? Take my job!"

"I did it for you." Bridge glared at him. "And for Mom. She's dying."

"Yeah, I know," Julian spat. "Why else would I send money? Why else would I put a separate account together for you guys? Do you really think that all this time I've just been blind?"

"You never visited. You never contacted us." Bridge crossed his arms. "What the hell was I supposed to think?"

"Because I finally had everything!" Julian swore. "I was going to be CEO! I found out about the trust fund Dad left you and put two and two together! I knew we could take back what was ours! And then you go and pull this stunt, marrying her just so you can get it! What the hell is wrong with you?"

I gasped at his outburst and then dread washed over me as I turned to Bridge. "Wait . . . what?"

Bridge stiffened. "I was going to tell you, but I didn't really think it mattered since I married you because I love you."

Julian looked between us and shook his head. "Unbelievable. Dad said Bridge had to marry you in order to get the trust released to him along with the shares. Congratulations, you married a true Tennyson after all. Liars. All of us."

"Cheaters." Bridge glared.

Julian shook his head. "You don't get it, the pressure he puts on you, the constant attention, women throwing themselves at you."

I almost plugged my ears.

"Doesn't excuse cheating." Bridge gritted his teeth.

"Doesn't excuse lying," Julian fired right back.

It was my wedding day.

My perfect day.

I slowly sank into the nearest chair and my dress billowed around me. My chest was tight as I looked up at the two brothers.

Both of them had hurt me.

In different ways.

I squeezed my eyes shut as more hot tears slid down my cheeks.

"I was breaking up with you," I whispered to no one in particular. "Julian, I was leaving you."

"You don't know, then." He looked away. "I'd turned around, Iz, I was in the car, and I asked them to turn around because I knew a text wouldn't do it, not this time. The driver pulled a U-turn, wasn't paying attention, we were hit head-on. I got in an accident, was in a coma, nearly died because I was planning on going back to you, getting down on my hands and knees and begging you to take me back."

"That's not how this works, Julian," I whispered. "You can't just hurt someone over and over again and apologize and make it all better."

He let out a long drawn-out sigh. "Even if that person realizes he's been a jackass?"

"Even then." I reached for Bridge's hand. "Both of you . . . I can't right now . . . Bridge, you should have told me."

"I know." His face was crestfallen as I stood on wobbly legs and exhaled. "First things first, you need to figure out what to do tomorrow."

"What?" they said in unison.

"Sixty percent of the company's shares." I said it slowly. "You want to be free of this hatred, start with the man who planted it."

And just like that, I swallowed my tears, turned around, and started walking out of the room.

"Izzy, wait!" Bridge grabbed my arm. "You can't leave, we have to talk about this. We have to—"

I shook my head. "If you love me, you'll let me walk out of this room, you'll let me go."

"I'm never letting you go."

I believed him.

"Just for today. I need time."

"Okay." He kissed the top of my head like he always did and repeated himself. "Okay."

Chapter Forty-Six

BRIDGE

"I'm sorry." I didn't look at him. In fact, I was still staring at the door that Izzy had walked through, taking my still-beating heart with her when she left that room.

Empty.

I felt so damn empty.

"For everything." I hung my head. "I know you won't believe me, but I tried. I tried to stay away. She thought I was you, and all I kept wondering was, Why does this beautiful woman treat her own fiancé with such hostility? Why am I having to earn her trust when they're supposed to be getting married?"

Julian didn't say anything.

I finally turned around and saw guilt in his expression. "She fell for me because she thought you were coming back to her, that the old Julian was finally paying attention. So yes, I took what was yours, but I also fixed what you broke, and I won't apologize for that."

He locked eyes with me, but said nothing.

"When you got in the accident, Dad showed up. He did what he does best, convinced me that I had to act as CEO so stocks didn't drop, told me people were relying on him, relying on you, said the board would look the other way and know the entire time. He basically said the Tennyson fortune rested in my hands while you slept. And I knew this was everything to you, I knew it was everything you had worked for. I knew you'd been VP for two years and were just waiting for your chance. So I took it, with the understanding that the minute you woke up, you'd have it back. Seamless transition."

"It won't be seamless, though," Julian said with a hard edge to his voice. "Because somehow you're better at my job than I am."

"I'm not better."

"That's not what my own father said to me within minutes of waking up. 'Bridge has a natural gift with business. Maybe if he had worked as hard as you, he would have been something great.'"

The compliment was both offensive and backhanded.

To both of us.

"The job is yours, Julian."

"And the girl?" He just had to ask. "What about her?"

I said nothing.

Julian finally sat, and then his eyes searched the room before landing on an open bottle of champagne.

He walked over to it and took a few swigs. "Not how I imagined my wedding day going."

"You mean your twin marrying the girl you love? Yeah, I figured that wasn't really in the ten-year plan," I said sarcastically. "Should you be drinking so soon after the coma?"

He flipped me off and took another swig. "Should you be marrying someone else's fiancé?"

"I love her."

"I know, damn it." Julian swallowed more champagne. "She's easy to love. Hard to leave."

"Then why cheat, Julian? Why make her feel less important than she is?"

"I woke up."

"What?"

"I woke up," he repeated. "It was a Sunday. She was lying in bed staring at me, and it just clicked, like I'd been sleeping my entire life and was finally awake . . . this family is a poison. It was in my blood, in my makeup. Don't deny it's in yours too. Tennyson, through and through." He hung his head. "She had lost a little of the light that made her special. She looked . . . older, wiser, and bitter, and I knew I'd put the bitterness there by asking her to be the wife that I knew Dad wanted her to be for me. Wear the right clothes, shop at the right places, jump through five million hoops so hopefully in the end, you can get what you deserve. I was a coward. Instead of breaking up with her, I went out and got extremely drunk, and one thing led to another. I remember maybe half the night. I came back smelling like someone else's perfume, apologized profusely, and we set a wedding date. And I hated myself a little bit more each day I kept her, knowing that one day she would wake up too, and she'd realize she wasn't the person she wanted to be, not with me, and she would never be."

"You woke up," I repeated, finally understanding what he was saying. "Julian, you can walk away from all of this, you know that, right?"

"No." His gaze met mine. "I really can't. Dad owes me, he fucking owes me for the hell he put me through, and so do you."

He was right about that.

I did owe him.

"We have sixty percent equity combined," I reminded him. "What do you think about using it? Together?"

"I think we need whiskey." He shook his head. "This doesn't mean I don't hate you. I still want to throw you off the nearest cliff. I don't know how to process the depth of this kind of betrayal, but I'm a Tennyson, so business"—he choked back another swallow of champagne—"comes first."

Chapter Forty-Seven

I was back at the apartment.

Out of my wedding dress.

With a bottle of wine in one hand and my cell in the other.

I wanted to scream at them both.

I wanted Bridge to hold me.

Just like I wanted Julian to forgive me.

It was closing in on midnight, and I was Cinderella with two shoes and no prince.

Neither man had contacted me.

Then again, what was there to say?

I didn't blame Bridge for not telling me. I knew he loved me, the way I loved him.

And I didn't blame Julian for being angry beyond reason.

Because he had every right to hate us.

To hate me.

Because he'd loved me first.

The way I had once loved him.

The knob turned.

I glanced up as Bridge walked in the door, still in his tux, looking like he'd been run over by a car.

His expression darkened when he took in my face, and then in long, determined strides he was in front of me, dropping to his knees, pressing his face against my legs. "I'm so damn sorry, Izzy."

"Bridge." His name fell from my lips like a prayer. "Me too."

"I love you." He clung to my legs. "I love you so much. Know that I love you more than anything in this world, will love you more than you could ever possibly imagine."

Tears slid down my cheeks onto his head. "Why does this feel like goodbye, then? If you love me? If I love you?"

"Because." He finally looked up into my eyes. "I hurt him. We hurt him. We knew we couldn't come back from this. I got my brother back only to lose him for good. I want to think we can survive this, I want to think we can survive anything." He stood and then cupped my face with his hands and pressed a feather-soft kiss to my lips. "I love you enough to let you choose what happens next, alright? I'm going to stay at a hotel."

"Don't." I clung to him, afraid to let him go.

His gaze softened. "Are you sure?"

I nodded. "Is Julian . . . is he stopping by?"

"It's his apartment," Bridge reminded me. "But tonight we decided—together—that walking in here, seeing us together, knowing what we did, would be a bad idea, and since he'd been drinking, I figured it was better to let him sleep it off. He's at the Ritz-Carlton."

"And you're here with me," I whispered. "Forever."

"If you'll have me," he confessed. "I'll be by your side forever."

"He didn't love me, not anymore," I said, more to myself than to him. "The love I feel for you is so different. It steals my breath and makes me want to run in the other direction. The love I have for you, Bridge Tennyson, is terrifying."

"Well, Izzy Tennyson, I think that's going to be our first argument as a married couple. Because the love we have between us, while terrifying, is perfect."

He kissed me hard on the mouth.

And I was lost to him.

I parted my lips as his hands wrapped around me and lifted me to my feet. Fingers pulled at my dress until it was free from my body, and all I felt was cold air from the room and the heat of his mouth on my skin.

My eyes drifted closed, and I released a sigh.

I just wanted to feel him.

My husband.

My forever.

He braced my hips with his hands and I lifted my eyelids, taking in his face as I spread his shirt open, touching his smooth skin while he made promises against my neck.

Ones I knew he would keep.

"I love you so much." The lights from Manhattan glittered outside the tall windows, and I wondered if anyone would believe that the man in this apartment making love to me with his hands, with his mouth, was the self-proclaimed villain in our story.

And that as he pulled the remaining pieces of clothing from my body and bent me over the couch, I thanked the universe that he wasn't the white knight.

"Look at us." He exhaled against my neck, our naked bodies reflected in the living room window.

The lights of Manhattan.

And me and my villain.

He gripped my hips again, pulling me against him as he thrust inside me, as he made me his and said my name.

I didn't want to shut my eyes.

I wanted to see us.

To feel us and see us.

It was all-consuming, wave after torrential wave.

Not all stories end happy.

Some end messy.

Ours would be filled with chaos.

And I would always remember the day I fell for my fiancé's twin and vowed to keep him forever.

Chapter Forty-Eight

BRIDGE

I went to bed Sunday night with the world knowing that the CEO of Tennyson Financial was me.

Bridge Anderson Tennyson.

The news of my identity and the fallout with Julian wasn't just front-page news. It was on every single newspaper, on every single channel.

My picture. His picture.

My phone was blowing up, and all I wanted to do was hide under the covers with Izzy's body.

Instead, I had to get up early Monday morning and meet a brother who hated me, so that we could once and for all fix what we should have fixed when we were kids.

I'd told Izzy what we were planning.

And then I told her I would need her later.

The car stopped at the hotel. I sent a text to Julian.

And out he came, in his perfect suit with his Ray-Bans and stoic expression. Paparazzi were already waiting outside the building, but he took it in stride, not once opening his mouth to deny or confirm.

He got in the car as more cameras flashed, and shouted questions went wild with speculation. Who else was in the car with him, his long-lost brother?

"They make it sound like I'm the prodigal son," I grumbled when the car finally took off.

He shrugged. "The only part of that story I remember is where the dad throws a party for the shitty son while the good one gets jealous."

"Trust me, our father's not going to be throwing a party for either of us today."

"Good." Julian let out an exasperated sigh. "I hope like hell you're right about the board eating out of your hand."

"Yeah, me too."

Julian turned and gave me a murderous look.

"What?" I smiled. "I was trying to make you laugh. Not working? Lose your sense of humor?"

"Yeah, about the same time you slept with my fiancée."

"What about the maid?"

"Excuse me?" Julian frowned. "What the hell would the maid have to do with this?"

"When Izzy returned home the day of the accident she found her very naked in your bed."

"Son of a bitch." Julian wiped his hands down his face. "No wonder Izzy was pissed when you showed up. The maid has been after me for the last year, but I never thought she'd take it that far."

"I think it was more than just that, but good to know the maid didn't stand a chance with you." I made a face. "I also may have fired Amy."

He stared me down. "Anything else I should know about your actions while claiming to be me?"

"Benefits." I shrugged. "Lots and lots of benefits for old IFC employees, parental leave, gym memberships." The more I talked, the more he seemed to listen, until we were finally at the building.

"Shit, Bridge, could you have at least tried to suck a little bit at my job?"

I winced. "Sorry."

And for the first time since waking up, a ghost of a smile spread across his face. "Don't be. This company is my life. You did well."

I didn't realize how much I needed him to say that until that moment.

"And you've done well, Jules. I stepped in for a few weeks, but you've been running this place for years. I know he never said he was proud, but that's because he's a selfish jackass. You've done incredible. This"—I pointed to the skyscraper—"is all you."

He put his hand on my shoulder and then pulled it away.

It was all I was going to get.

And I was okay with that.

"Let's get this over with," he said under his breath.

The car door opened.

We both got out.

And all hell broke loose.

So many cameras I was blinded. We walked tall, right next to each other. We entered that building as equals. We got on that elevator with a charged sense of purpose.

An eerie silence followed us as we walked down the familiar hall to the boardroom. People stared almost in reverence as we moved in sync.

I opened the door for Julian and followed.

It shut quietly behind us.

No board member stood.

Our father, however, did. "Boys, good to see you. Have a seat."

"Actually"—I grinned—"it's feeling a little crowded in here."

Board members exchanged glances while I nodded to Julian, who chose that moment to stare down the man he once would have done everything for.

And lost everything because of it.

"I make a motion to remove Edward Tennyson as corporate president of Tennyson Financial."

"I second." I stood by him.

Dad slammed his hand onto the table. "How dare you think you can walk in here and—"

"Third," Harry interrupted.

"Fourth."

"Fifth."

More voices chimed in. Every man pledged their allegiance to us in front of our father. The men representing the company he'd built.

The company that was ousting him.

He finally got what he deserved.

"All in favor?" Harry asked.

It happened fast.

So fast that my head spun.

Our dad looked at us like we had betrayed him.

And I wondered if he finally understood what it felt like to have your own flesh and blood reject you, the way he had rejected us and our mom.

I pressed the com button. "Can we get security in here to escort Edward Tennyson from the premises? Thank you."

"This is my company!" Edward roared.

"We're not saying it isn't your company, Dad." Julian spat the word *Dad*. "We're just taking the reins. After all, isn't that what you wanted? Both of your sons making their way in the world? I hear Florida's wonderful this time of year."

"It really is," Harry piped up.

Security walked into the boardroom.

A look of absolute fury twisted our father's features, but he didn't put up a fight as they took him out of the room.

Leaving me and Julian with the board.

I cleared my throat and hoped Julian wouldn't be pissed. "I have a proposition for you."

Julian frowned at me.

"The CEO position is Julian's, not mine. But I hope I've proven myself enough to ask that you consider hiring me to take over as CFO."

Julian stared at me like I'd just lost my mind.

"It's yours, Jules, it's always been yours." And I'd taken enough. I left that part out.

He nodded and a look of surprise crossed his face as talking ensued around us, everyone agreeing it was a fantastic idea.

Both Tennysons running the company.

Both Tennyson boys reunited.

And what's more, both Tennyson boys finally side by side, the way we were always supposed to be.

By the time the board voted to legally transfer the CEO position to Julian and papers were signed to that effect, I needed a stiff drink and wanted to go home. Then again, I really had no home, so there was that.

Julian told me to meet him in his office.

The door was slightly ajar, so I knocked and let myself in.

He was standing there with Izzy.

I hated the vision.

I also hated the guilt.

And the need to punch him in the face or throw him out the window. What the hell was wrong with me?

"Iz brought you lunch," he said, slightly amused. "Weird, since she never brought me lunch, and even then it probably would have been poisoned, especially those last few months."

"Did you guys talk?" I crossed my arms.

Izzy nodded. "Yeah, we did." And then she rolled her eyes. "Stop staring at him like that. You look ready to throw him against the wall."

I just shrugged.

Earning a smirk from Julian.

"And I never brought you lunch because you didn't like me coming to the offices, no mixing business and pleasure."

Julian's smile fell. "I'm sorry, Iz."

"I know you are."

You could cut the tension with a knife as Izzy walked over and handed me a brown paper bag.

It was awkward.

All three of us were probably praying for the building to swallow us whole.

"Let's go eat . . ." It was all I had as I reached for Izzy's hand.

"Wait," Julian called.

Almost escaped.

He reached into his pocket and tossed me his keys. "Both cars' titles are in the safe. Think of it as a bonus along with the apartment. My clothes . . . I'm going to want back. I'll come by later and grab all my things. I just can't . . ." He swallowed and looked down at the carpeted floor like he was trying to control his emotions. "Knowing you guys were there, I can't move back in. It's yours, a wedding present along with your bonus."

"Julian." Izzy's shoulders drooped.

"No." His smile was forced. "It's better this way. I don't want to live there alone. It just seems . . . like a really shitty ending after waking up from a coma, you know?"

"Thank you, Jules." I meant it.

One day it would be better.

One day I vowed that we'd be able to sit next to each other without thinking about the woman that was between us, or the almost five weeks spent where he fought for his life and I fought for her heart.

One day it would be okay.

Today was not that day.

"Go eat before I fire you," he finally said like he was annoyed with me, when really I knew he just needed time.

We all did.

I grabbed Izzy's hand and walked her down the hall to my new office.

And when I shut the door, she grinned at me with love in her eyes.

I didn't want her to go, but I knew that Julian needed me, so after having lunch together I kissed her and got to work.

Side by side with my brother.

For the next six hours I went over everything that took place while he was in the hospital. I talked so much my voice went hoarse, and when the sun finally started to set, he leaned back in his chair and stared me down. "I had already lost her."

I looked at the floor. "You only lost her because you stopped seeing her, because you put yourself first, the company . . ."

"Don't make that same mistake," he whispered. "Or I really will kick your ass."

I looked up with a sad smile on my face. "I want to fix this, between us."

"It took you one month to fall in love with my fiancée, and to me, that time was like going to sleep and waking up seconds later, wondering what the hell happened to the world I used to live in. I'm going to need longer than that to come to grips with this . . ."

"That's fair."

He stood. "I'll send Kelsey to the apartment to pack me up tomorrow."

I moved from my seat and held out my hand. "Thank you. For everything."

He stared at it, then at me, slowly pressed his palm to mine, and firmly shook my hand back. "We're still brothers."

I grabbed my things and made my way out of the building, my thoughts a jumbled mess as I took a town car back to the apartment. I could understand him not wanting to live there after everything.

I felt like I'd aged ten years when I finally put my key in the lock and let myself in.

Izzy stood there waiting in a long black coat holding two glasses of champagne. "Welcome home, husband."

My heart slammed against my chest at the sight. "Is that a new coat?"

I took my glass and then she handed me hers too. Curious, I watched as she very slowly unbuttoned the coat and opened it to reveal thigh-highs, a lacy thong, and a corset that shoved her breasts together, creating a creamy crevice I wanted to bury my head in.

"Wow . . ." I rasped, quickly setting the glasses down on the bar. "That's . . ." I shook my head. "The thoughts aren't coming, Izzy, but I guarantee you will be in about two minutes."

"I'll time you." She winked.

And I reached for her.

Today wasn't the day my brother and I would find peace.

But it was the day I would find love again and again in her arms.

"Your underwear is red."

"Someone told me I wasn't allowed to wear anything white anymore. I wanted to surprise you."

"God, I love you." I devoured her lips, moaning her name as she clung to me like she belonged there.

And she did.

She was a part of me.

And I was a part of her.

And in that apartment, I gave everything to her.

She kissed me with tears streaming down her cheeks.

And I kissed her back like my touch would heal her pain.

We made it to the dining room table with my suit half off, my trousers already kicked down as I deepened the kiss. "It's just us, Izzy."

"Just us," she agreed. "There's so much to think about, so much to do—"

"Right now, we make love. Tomorrow we make plans." I silenced her with another kiss and another.

And then I was inside her, exactly where I wanted to be.

Feeling her clench around me.

Skin on skin.

Her hips were smooth as I pressed my palm against them. "I'm never leaving you."

"Not even if it's for my own good?"

"I'm too selfish."

"I like you selfish." She arched toward me.

I sucked in a breath. "I can tell."

And then my beautiful Izzy smiled.

It was all I needed.

We would be okay.

Maybe not today.

Maybe not tomorrow.

But one day, we would be okay.

"Iz?" I whispered, feeling our bodies slide against each other, I would never get enough of her. "Marry me?"

Her lips parted, I could feel her coming apart around me, trying to focus on my words, on our joined bodies. "We are married."

"I want to hear you say my name." I cupped her face. "Please?"

"Anything for you, Bridge Tennyson." Her eyes filled with tears. "Anything."

I swallowed the ball of emotion in my throat and kissed her hard, I made promises to her that I would keep forever, and I prayed that Julian would one day find it in his heart to forgive me.

To forgive us.

Epilogue

JULIAN

"Hey!" a random stranger said as he walked by. "You're that guy? The brother that almost died? Hey, is it true that your twin and your ex-fiancée are expecting a baby?"

I never wanted to punch another human more in my entire life. Well, maybe that was a lie, I still owed Bridge several punches with bloody knuckles.

He knew it.

I knew it.

I planned it with a smile on my face.

And he wouldn't flinch. The bastard was persistent, at least, and he refused to leave me alone.

I almost flew to China to get away from him, but I wouldn't put it past him to follow me there too. It was hard enough that we worked on the same floor, that he reported to me every day.

And also that he was so damn likable I wanted to strangle him and then greedily search for flaws I could expose.

He wanted to give me the family I'd lost.

And I just wanted to forget everything I did lose.

Everything he took.

Mainly Izzy.

I'd lost my fiancée and my best friend to him, and now that my father hated me, it felt like I had nobody.

"Wrong guy," I snapped at the jerk. Then I put on my sunglasses and stomped toward the hospital room.

My mood changed the minute I saw her face. "Mom."

"Julian!" She beamed at me then held out her open arms. How many times had I dreamed of that? Of hugging her? Of holding her? And now I got to do it on a daily basis.

"You look better today, Jules." Mom patted the spot next to her. I went and sat down, my body angry at me for putting it through hell these past few months. I'd stopped running. I had a hard time doing anything that reminded me of my old life with Izzy, of life before Bridge.

I started lifting weights.

And when I woke up thinking about Izzy and the fact that they were already pregnant, planning for a family.

I lifted more weights.

And I imagined a world where I won in the end, where I got the girl, and she thanked me for the mountains I moved and dragons I slayed.

"I feel better." It was a lie.

"Bridge called again."

I snorted. "He always calls, plus I see him every day."

"He worries about you."

"Then he shouldn't have fucked my fiancée," I said rudely. And then I sighed. "Sorry, Mom, that was uncalled for."

"Not really." She shrugged. "He did a lot of things, but he's still your brother and you're still not without some responsibility. I know how you treated her."

I instantly felt defensive.

"My point is, there's hurt on both ends, on all three ends, actually."

"They're expecting a baby." I almost couldn't get the sentence out.

A baby.

My life.

That was my life.

Thief.

Liar.

Betrayer.

"One day, you'll forgive him," Mom said cryptically. "One day you'll have to."

I frowned down at her. "What are you saying?"

She shrugged. "Holding on to the past hurts. You have to let it go, Jules. You have no choice but to release it. You look more like him now, you know."

"Don't remind me."

"It's not a bad thing to look like one another."

It sure as hell was.

"I'm going to go grab a cup of coffee. Want anything?" I asked, ignoring her because I needed an escape so desperately.

"Sure, one more thing, though." Mom pulled a folder from the stand near her hospital bed. "You're family, brothers. He needs you."

They were baby pictures. Low blow, of course she would pull that card, she was relentless and I loved her for it.

"And when I needed him, look what happened." I glanced away from the smiling picture of us at the cabin—my happiest memories took place there.

"Stop feeling sorry for yourself, and be the man I know I raised you to be."

I kissed her on the forehead. "You're lucky you're beautiful and I love you. I've fired people for raising their voice at me."

"Who? You? You're like a tame little kitty cat." She laughed.

I shook my head and smiled. "Let me be in my bad mood."

"No."

"You're so stubborn."

"Son, go look in the mirror then get back to me, mmm?"

"Fine, fine." My phone went off. "It's the office."

"Go." She grinned. "I'm only a phone call away! Plus I'm not going anywhere."

I felt my heart breaking. "Please don't make jokes about that, about being stuck in this godforsaken hospital."

"If you don't laugh, you cry, Julian. I would much rather spend the remaining moments I have laughing."

"Stop making sense," I grumbled. "I love you, Mom."

"I love you too, Julian."

She held open her arms, and I held her tight. I memorized the lavender perfume she put behind her ears, the softness of her skin against my neck.

I memorized every minute detail.

Not realizing.

That it would be the last hug I would ever receive from her.

The last conversation we'd ever have.

I smiled at her one last time.

And I left.

About the Author

Photo © 2014 Lauren Watson Perry, Perrywinkle Photography

Rachel Van Dyken is a *Wall Street Journal, USA Today,* and #1 *New York Times* bestselling author of regency, paranormal, and contemporary romances. Her books include the Red Card novels, *Risky Play* and *Kickin' It,* as well as her Liars, Inc., series and her Wingmen Inc. series, which has been optioned for film. A fan of *The Bachelor,* Starbucks coffee, and Swedish Fish (not necessarily in that order), Rachel lives in Idaho with her husband and her adorable son. For more information about Rachel's books and events, visit www.RachelVanDykenauthor.com.